COUNTERFEIT ROAD

Further Titles from Kirk Russell

The John Marquez series

SHELL GAMES
NIGHT GAMES
DEADGAME
REDBACK *

The Ben Raveneau series

A KILLING IN CHINA BASIN *
COUNTERFEIT ROAD *

* *available from Severn House*

COUNTERFEIT ROAD

A Ben Raveneau Mystery

Kirk Russell

This first world edition published 2012
in Great Britain and in the USA by
SEVERN HOUSE PUBLISHERS LTD of
9–15 High Street, Sutton, Surrey, England, SM1 1DF.

British Library Cataloguing in Publication Data

Russell, Kirk, 1954–
  Counterfeit road.
  1. Police – California – San Francisco – Fiction.
  2. Suspense fiction.
  I. Title
  813.5-dc23

ISBN-13: 978-0-7278-8145-8 (cased)

All Severn House titles are printed on acid-free paper.

Severn House Publishers support The Forest Stewardship Council [FSC],
the leading international forest certification organisation. All our titles that
are printed on Greenpeace-approved FSC-certified paper carry the FSC logo.

Typeset by Palimpsest Book Production Ltd.,
Falkirk, Stirlingshire, Scotland.
Printed and bound in Great Britain by
MPG Books Ltd., Bodmin, Cornwall.

For my mother, who refused to pack up four kids and move after my father died, and grew a business, and kept us in the same house, the same schools, right on through.

ACKNOWLEDGEMENTS

Once again, many thanks to Holly Pera and Joe Toomey of the San Francisco Homicide Detail for much needed help and unflagging generosity. And three books in, I want to say to Severn House publisher, Edwin Buckhalter, my editor, Kate Lyall Grant, Managing Editor, James Nightingale, and Michelle Duff, who keeps the train on the tracks, you are smart, quick, and fun to work with. It's been a delight. Thank you.

ONE

The video ran two minutes twenty-eight seconds, about the length of your average YouTube. When Raveneau hit play the camera panned from left to right, catching winter sunlight reflecting off windows of the Ferry Building. A glittery sliver of bay showed as the victim, Alan Krueger, and the unknown shooter waited for a car to pass before crossing into the shadows of the lot once used by commuters beneath the former Embarcadero Freeway.

They threaded through parked cars, Krueger ahead, shooter trailing, and once again Raveneau got the feeling they were friends, or at least knew each other. He let it run another five seconds then clicked the mouse and froze the frame. He stared at the screen.

The videotape was made with a hand-held Sony camcorder and shipped four days ago in a used Amazon box from a FedEx drop in Los Angeles. It arrived here addressed to him, Inspector Benjamin Raveneau, Cold Case Unit, Homicide Detail, Room 459, Hall of Justice, San Francisco. That was two days ago, Tuesday, January 11, 2011, exactly twenty-two years to the day after the murder of Alan Krueger.

Raveneau had cut the packing tape, opened the box, and emptied out the Styrofoam peanuts. He left the cassette taped to the bottom of the box and walked it down the hallway to the video unit in the Crime Scene Investigation lab. In the lab they eased off the tape holding the videotape cassette and tested the sticky side for fingerprints and DNA. But whoever sent it was very careful.

Whoever sent it stuck a white label on the black plastic videotape cassette that read 1/11/1989. Raveneau took that date to the cold case closet. He pulled the murder log for '89, looked up January eleventh and found the Krueger files. In the Crime Scene Investigation lab they produced ten digitized copies of the videotape. They gave him the ten CDs, emailed him another, and he forwarded that to his

Cold Case partner, Elizabeth la Rosa. He had watched the videotape at least a dozen times since. He started it again now and the shooter and Krueger cleared the cars, the dark hulk of the Embarcadero's decks towering above them as they moved toward two concrete pylons.

They moved diagonally away and as they got smaller the steady-handed filming turned jumpy. In the video unit they said whoever made the tape had started walking, probably following Krueger and the shooter. Raveneau zoomed in now. He froze the video when Krueger had only seconds to live.

Alan Krueger worked for the Secret Service for fourteen years before quitting in 1986 and becoming an independent contractor. At the Secret Service he'd been a counterfeit expert. He was carrying sixty-one new US one hundred dollar bills in the left breast pocket of his coat, the bills folded and held by a silver money clip. The second bullet, the fatal shot, passed through a corner of the bills but missed the clip.

Two homicide inspectors who used to be called the go-go twins, Ed Govich and Henry Goya, caught the case. Goya and Govich showed the bills to the Secret Service and were told they weren't counterfeit. That was well documented. Yet yesterday Raveneau retrieved the bills from storage. He signed them out and handed them off to a Secret Service agent he knew, figuring they were worth another look.

The rest of Krueger's effects were stored out at Hunters Point in Building 606. Krueger was left-handed and wore a hand-tooled leather shoulder holster on his right side. He was licensed to carry a gun but the holster was empty. The holster was out at Hunter's Point. So was a wallet found near his body. The wallet was lying against one of the concrete pylons holding up the freeway. It was covered with newspapers. No driver's license, credit cards, or smaller bills were found. The wallet was empty. Two forged high-quality but fake passports were found in his coat, one Canadian for an Alan McCormick, the other a US passport with the name Allen Jons. In the right front pocket of his pants was a piece of paper with 'Captain Frank' written on it and a phone number that PacBell had identified as a pay phone at San Francisco Airport.

*   *   *

Goya and Govich chased the Captain Frank lead and without any good place to start they worked the wharves and local marinas. They talked to boat captains and harbor masters. They canvassed. They knocked on doors. They didn't get anywhere.

In the video the shooter shortened his step now. He drifted behind Krueger, who turned with a gesture Raveneau read as frustration, as though they had started to argue. When he turned back, his left leg jerked up spasmodically as the first bullet struck. The video barely caught it. If the cameraman intended a clean recording he failed.

Krueger fell and the shooter closed. He read as a dark shape leaning over Krueger. He was fast, efficient, without hesitation, and though in all his previous watching of the video Raveneau had frozen the action at this spot, he didn't now. He let it roll and thought about the two newly-wed Canadians who had found Krueger's body. He was trying to locate them and so far had learned they divorced in 2001. Both claimed not to have heard any gunshots, though an anonymous caller had. The caller didn't leave a name but did leave the time of day he heard the shots, 3:42 p.m.

The Canadians also noted the time they found the body, 3:45, so were probably close enough to have heard the shots. But maybe they were talking or distracted by something else. He remembered how noisy it used to be, the big trucks and busses, the echoes. The old Embarcadero Freeway was gone, demolished after the 1989 Loma Prieta earthquake, and the Ferry Building where the video started, renovated and reborn as a food court and now a popular tourist destination. He was there this morning. He bought a coffee, and carried it outside across the promenade and the tracks of the light rail system and worked his way down and tried to find where the video maker had stood.

Raveneau's cell phone buzzed now as the video went dark. He turned the computer off as he answered, knowing it would be la Rosa.

'They're here. I took them into the kitchen.'

'How many are there?'

'Three. Two that look like regular Secret Service and a third who looks like he's in charge.'

'Then it's about the money. The bills must be counterfeit and they're worried about something. I'll be there in a few minutes.'

TWO

The conference room off the Cold Case Unit office had a few beat-up chairs and no table, so the kitchen was where they usually met. The kitchen had two tables pushed together and covered with a striped tablecloth. The Secret Service agents took up the corner of the table that put the refrigerators behind them.

'Can I get anyone water, a soda, or anything to eat?' Raveneau asked.

'We're not here for lunch.'

The one who answered was Nate Brooks, assistant special agent in charge. The other two agents were Jack Swensen, who Raveneau had turned over sixty of the hundred dollar bills to yesterday, and Michelle Raff, a counterfeiting expert.

The bills were no longer in a San Francisco Police Department money envelope, instead were individually wrapped in clear plastic slips and in bags with the Secret Service stamp. Raff looked like she was guarding them. Swensen looked uncomfortable and Raveneau guessed there was some sort of game plan here that Swensen didn't like. He nodded toward the money.

'Thanks for returning the bills.'

'We're not,' Brooks said, and Raff followed with 'They're counterfeit. We were wrong in 1989.'

She said that as if she owned the mistake but she was probably eleven years old at the time. Brooks wasn't there either, also too young. Raveneau took a closer look at him, trying to get a read, trying to understand why anything about this meeting would make him tense. Watchful eyes stared back at him.

Nowadays, one hundred dollar bills were all big-head Ben Franklins with the colors and squiggly lines, but these notes predated those changes. These were what an advertising company would now market as 'classic' bills, the design used for decades, the design before counterfeiters upped their game following advances in printers.

Brooks reached over. He touched the bag in front of Agent Raff.

'These were printed in the same series as bills used last summer to buy weapons grade explosives. Those bills were laundered through two foreign banks, one in the Cayman Islands, and the other in Mexico City. Both banks took in substantial quantities, as in two million, give or take.'

'Just like these?'

'Exactly like these, same series, same print run, and though you wouldn't see many of this style inside the US, there's a lot of cash floating around the world. The dollar is still the world's reserve currency and sometimes caches pop up. The banks probably didn't want the bills, but they have relation-ships, and their client is a black market weapons dealer who moves a lot of money so they took them in.' He paused before adding, 'We were already tracking this particular weapons dealer.'

'Why?'

'It has to do with a threat I can't talk to you about yet. In fact, I'm here to ask for your complete cooperation. We need your murder files on Alan Lansing Krueger. How these counterfeit bills tie in or why Krueger had them, I don't know the answer to. But as we learn information and as I can, I'll pass it on to you.'

'Is that why there are three of you here?'

'Special Agent Swensen could have come alone, but I don't want any misunderstanding. We want to work with you.'

'OK, well, the murder files are on my desk. I'll go get them and you read through them in here, and then decide what you need.'

'We'd rather take them with us and get more time to go through them.'

'Of course you would, but that's not going to happen.'

'I'm not bullshitting you when I say this is a very significant threat.'

'And I'm not stonewalling you. I'll give you plenty of time to read but I don't think you're going to find there is that much in these files.'

La Rosa was at her desk when Raveneau walked back into

their office. She took off her reading glasses. She watched as he picked up the Krueger files and the murder logbook for 1989.

'I'll be right back.'

In the kitchen he opened the logbook and showed them the entry with Krueger's murder. He explained the columns with date, time, location, victim's name, if known, and the inspectors assigned to the case and their summary.

He slid the murder files out to the middle of the table like a plate of sandwiches.

'Inspectors Goya and Govich didn't have much to go on. They had a piece of paper with a phone number and the name Captain Frank, but that turned out to be a phone booth at SFO. The Secret Service did their own investigation but they didn't share what they found with us, so you probably already know a lot more than I do.'

He looked at each of them. 'I'll give you fifteen minutes or so to read. Then we can talk.'

When he returned to his desk he slid one of the CD copies of the murder videotape into his coat pocket and asked la Rosa, 'Want to go across the street to Roma and get a coffee?'

'Aren't they still in there?'

'They're reading.'

'That won't take long.'

When he shrugged, she stood up.

'All right, I'm ready for coffee anyway.'

Everybody shares the same elevator in the Hall of Justice and you can wait awhile for a ride. When Raveneau and la Rosa returned from across the street there was a wait and the Secret Service agents were a little agitated as they got back upstairs. Also, the kitchen smelled like popcorn, so they probably weren't alone in here and didn't get much of a chance to talk. Brooks avoided eye contact now, focusing on the cuff of his shirt as if something there had suddenly drawn his attention. That changed as Raveneau laid the CD on the tablecloth.

'What do you want me to copy?' Raveneau asked, and sounded like he was at a baseball game getting a head count before he went for hot dogs and beer.

'Everything,' Brooks said. 'And what's that in front of you?'

'A copy of a videotape we received Tuesday.' He turned to

Raff. 'I've never known the Secret Service to look at counterfeit bills and mistake them for real bills. Are you sure it was a mistake?'

'Inspector, it was before my time, but I'm sure it was a mistake.'

'Would you mistake them?'

'No, but now we know what to look for.'

'And you didn't know then?' She looked to Brooks. She wanted his permission and when he didn't say anything, she said, 'The bills are very, very good.'

'What am I starting to remember?'

Raveneau knew la Rosa was starting to remember something as well, something right about that time. He asked Raff, 'North Korea. Help me here, Michelle. When we called out the North Koreans for counterfeiting our money it was around that time wasn't it?'

Raff looked to Brooks and Raveneau said, 'Let her talk.'

She waited until Brooks nodded.

'The bills you're referring to were called supernotes. That was because the quality was so good. Before these here on the table the first known supernotes were spotted by a banker in the Philippines in 1989.'

She touched the bills in front of her.

'That's what these are now. Alan Krueger's murder occurred before those in the Philippines were spotted, so now these are the first known supernotes.'

Raveneau took a moment to absorb that.

'And these are the same as those passed by the weapons dealer to the Cayman Island and Mexican banks?'

Brooks answered. 'That's correct.'

Raveneau pulled Brooks' card from his coat. 'What's the best number to call you at?'

'Hand me that and I'll write it on the back.'

Raveneau watched him write a number and when he got the card back slid the CD across the table. 'Watch this and then give us a call. You'll recognize Krueger. If not, he's the taller one.'

THREE

Retired homicide inspector Henry Goya was in his mid-sixties. Not too long ago he had a quadruple bypass surgery that Raveneau knew about only because Cynthia, the Homicide Detail's secretary, was good friends with Goya's daughter. Goya's daughter also got her dad to join Facebook.

On his Facebook page Goya looked like an ageing, slightly crooked art dealer. A photo showed him in a wicker chair on the porch of his house in Petaluma, gray beard cut short and carefully trimmed, left hand resting on the carved knob of a wooden cane. In his right he held a thin cigar. A whiskey sat on the glass-topped table in front of him, a small terrier expectantly at his feet. The photo was probably meant to communicate the wonderful time Goya was having in retirement, but Raveneau had heard the quiet excitement as Goya connected with the Krueger case again.

'Did you find the Canadians?'

'Not yet.'

'Did my old partner ever call you?'

'No.' Raveneau had left several messages for Ed Govich, but Govich was yet to call back.

'Henry, tell me again what you remember about the Canadians other than there was something off about them.'

'OK, well, they were newly-weds here for a week and staying at the Hyatt, so that put them in the general area where the murder happened. They told us they liked to walk a city when they visited it, and that's what they were doing, out walking when they decided to cross under the Embarcadero Freeway. They happened upon the body and called 911. Ed and I weren't far behind the first uniform officers, so we got to the Canadians right away, and they were helpful, especially her.

'But she was also shaken up or seemed to be. Or she was nervous. Ed thought she was nervous in the way a suspect might be, but I didn't get that from her. Now the husband was different.

He got huffy later when we asked them to come in with us to Homicide, and when they did come in he stopped cooperating. That's part of why Ed flew up to Calgary to re-interview them.'

Goya sighed.

'I'm sorry, Ben. I'm not answering what you asked about. They showed us passports, wedding rings, their itinerary, where they had eaten and visited, all the details of their visit, maybe too many details. So many that we checked on a restaurant they said they ate at and there wasn't any record of them. Ed checked on that. Then a few days later we got an anonymous tip from someone who was farther away than the Canadians said they were and he reported hearing gunshots, but I already told you about that. Are you getting any closer to finding them?'

'Not yet.'

'Maybe I ought to look for you.'

This was the second time Goya had suggested this and the department did occasionally hire retired officers in what got called the 9-60 program. In it a retired officer could work twenty hours a week, but no more than nine hundred sixty hours a year. Goya wasn't particularly coherent in how he framed his memory of the case, but then the murder was twenty-two years ago and what mattered most to Raveneau was that Goya still carried the case with him.

Raveneau had learned the truth in the cliché after he and la Rosa started the Cold Case Unit, that the good inspectors often carried their unsolved cases with them. Anytime a retired inspector phoned he always took the call. He thought of the retired inspectors as a collective consciousness that made the Cold Case Unit larger. They were his network. But Goya was a decade into retirement and getting him into the 9-60 program would be a very, very hard sell.

'Henry, why don't you come in tomorrow and we'll go to lunch and talk the case through.'

'Are you buying?'

'I am.'

'What time?'

'Eleven thirty.'

'I'll see you then.'

Unlike him Goya and Govich didn't have a videotape to

refer to. They had tested different theories including an idea that Krueger was a spy, before settling on robbery because his wallet and the shoulder holster he wore were both empty. They figured Krueger's gun was stolen too. But that the thief didn't want to stick his hand in the bloody breast pocket, so the counterfeit bills got missed.

Before leaving for the night Raveneau made a list of what he wanted to go over with Goya tomorrow. AFIS, the Automated Fingerprint Identification System was in place in '89, but barely. California, Alaska, and Tokyo were the first places to use it. Goya and Govich ran his prints through AFIS and as soon as they got a hit the Secret Service stepped in and ID'ed the body. Something was wrong there too and Raveneau was pretty sure the Secret Service ASAC, Nate Brooks, knew the back story.

Overall, Goya and Govich did a lot of things well. They pushed the Secret Service. Govich dogged the Canadians and traced an appendix scar to the hospital where Krueger was operated on. That led to Krueger's Vietnam War record that the Navy previously couldn't find. They found the London maker of the shoulder holster and the Hong Kong tailor who made Krueger's pants and coat. They chased down the stamps on the false passports and they got feedback on the quality of the passports. The quality was so good one expert said he believed them to be real. Krueger's shoes were handmade in Rome and the shoemaker kept records. The shoemaker had shipped four pairs of shoes to a Hong Kong apartment, but SFPD wouldn't pay for a trip to Hong Kong in 1989, and they drew a blank with the Hong Kong authorities. Raveneau finished with his notes and questions for Goya just as Cynthia put a call through from the front desk.

'You've got a Captain Frank call, a young man who says his name is Ryan Candel.'

'Put him through.'

'OK, and then I'm gone for the day. Hey, when does your girlfriend's place open?'

'A week from Friday.'

'She must be excited?'

'She is.'

'I can't wait to go there.'

Cynthia put the call through. This was the fourth call since they put out the piece last week asking for help from the public. So far the calls were sketchy, but that they got any response at all surprised him. The case was so old he hadn't expected to hear anything from anybody on this one.

'Inspector, I'm calling about Captain Frank.'

'What do you know about him?'

'I know I was the abortion that didn't happen.'

'You were what?'

'Dude, Captain Frank was my dad. He was poppa. He was the man, but he didn't want my mom to have me. I've got these photos she saved. I'll give them all to you. Do you want to meet me tonight?'

FOUR

Raveneau parked on Eleventh Street half a block from Café Agricole. He stepped between people waiting in line to hear music at Slim's, then crossed Agricole's front deck and went inside. The bar was to his left and it was easy to find Ryan Candel at the far end with a drink and a faded green shoebox on the bar top in front of him. He looked mid to late twenties and dressed like he wasn't quite sure who he was yet, constructed hip but about a year or two back, dark pants, a leather coat with a Euro feel, styled hair, narrow, long sideburns dropping to his jawbone. It didn't look comfortable.

Raveneau worked his way through a happy knot of people drinking and blocking the path to the tables and the rest of the bar. As he neared, Candel picked up on him, lifting his drink in a gesture that said you stick out too. Candel was drinking a Tequila Daisy, lemon, grenadine, and hellfire bitters and from the shine in his eyes as they shook hands Raveneau guessed it wasn't his first drink.

Raveneau ordered rum with ginger and lime. He knew the Agricole from drinking here with Celeste as she debated mixology and what direction she was going with her new place, Toasts, whose concept was basically a bar with small plates, mostly appetizers. Not tapas though, she kept saying it was going to be different than that and mostly crostini. Her plans and the building permit said restaurant but a lot had changed since then.

As Raveneau's drink arrived, Candel ordered another Tequila Daisy.

'I've got some friends meeting me here so I don't have a lot of time, but we can pretty much get this done in a few minutes. All the photos are in here.'

He tapped the shoebox with his fingers then rested his drink on top of it and Raveneau watched a dark drink ring form. He had gathered that Candel's mother was dead, but this box supposedly held photos she cared about so it surprised him.

'There are some things you should probably know about me.'

'Did you kill somebody?'

'No, but pretty close. I got busted a couple of years ago for assaulting the doctor who killed my mom and did ninety days in jail then home confinement and months of picking up trash and crap, the community service trip thing.'

'Killed your mom?'

'She died because her doctor blew her off.'

'When was that?'

'It was like June a year and a half ago. She was in a car accident and really badly hurt, in the hospital and just hanging on and he went golfing with his pharmaceutical company buddies.' He glanced at Raveneau and added in a tone that made Raveneau think he'd gone through some court-ordered counseling, 'But that doesn't excuse what I did.'

'And what are you doing now?'

'For work, you mean?'

'Yeah, for work or school or whatever.'

'I'm DJ'ing four nights a week but that's mostly spinning an iPod. It's bullshit, I know, and not really work but I get paid a little and I'm trying to get something going in the music. I know a lot of musicians, and I'm trying to get into producing.'

'How badly was the doctor hurt?'

'Broken wrist, concussion, and some bruises.'

Raveneau would have to check out Candel's record, but it didn't change the photos his mom had saved.

'Let's talk about your dad. Was he a boat captain?'

Candel stared then smiled.

'You really don't know shit about him, do you?'

'No, I really don't.'

'His first name was Jim. He was an airline captain not some fucking crab boat captain. He flew for the Navy in the Vietnam War and then for some airline that went out of business. Pan something.'

'Pan Am?'

'Yeah, Pan Am and then United Airlines between Hawaii and San Francisco. That was his gig, a bus driver in the sky. He did the Honolulu run for a long time. My mom was like the stewardess he got pregnant then ditched. But even when he dumped her she was still in love with him. She never would have made this call. She would never give you this box. She'd be crying right now if she could see me giving up the great Captain Jim Frank, asshole of the skies.'

'Did she call him Captain Frank?'

'She called him Captain. Is that weird or what?'

'How close were you and your mom?'

'Yeah, I know how I sound, but we were tight. My mom and I were close.'

'Do you miss her?'

'I definitely miss her.'

That quieted him for a moment, and then he signaled the bartender, ready for another. After he got the bartender's attention he started sliding the rubber band holding the shoebox top on. It snapped before he could do that. He lifted the lid. He moved his drink to make room and said, 'She was in a van with this friend of hers and this guy ran a red and hit them on Folsom.'

'It must have been very hard.'

'It was really horrible. I dream about it a lot, but the thing was it looked like she was going to pull through. She was talking again. Then she had a bad night and I was there the next morning when Dr Leonard came through. He's the doctor I knocked down. There was another doctor or wannabe, an intern who was worried about her, but Leonard shut her down. I overheard it. Probably none of it would have happened if I hadn't heard Leonard say he had an appointment and he'd be back in at three that afternoon.

'But he didn't come in until like seven o'clock, and basically by the time they figured out she had an infection it was too late. Her internal injuries were so bad she went fast. But, OK, I know you're just here for the photos. Thing is, she's in some of these.'

'I'll get copies made and get this back to you.'

'I just want the ones of her back. I don't care about him or any of the slides or any of the rest.'

'I'm going to make copies and get everything else back to you. Keep going with your story about Dr Leonard.'

'After she died, I blamed him and started following him, like stalking him, weird stuff I would never picture myself doing. At first I was going to kill him. In the end I just kind of tackled him hard and he hit his head on a car bumper and trashed his wrist on the street. I totally lost it.'

He took a sip of the new drink then turned to Raveneau.

'I was like waiting my whole childhood for my dad to show up because my mom made it sound like it was always just about to happen. But he never showed, you know, never once.'

'What was your mom's name?'

'Allyson. Allyson Candel.' He took a significant swallow, halved his drink. 'I hated him from the time I was twelve. I'm hoping you take him down.'

'Is that why you called? I'm wondering because I'm picking up some resentment toward your father.'

Candel smiled at that. He smiled and his face completely changed.

'You've got a sense of humor, dude. Here he is. This is him in the war, the one in Vietnam.'

He handed Raveneau a photo of a young man standing near the nose of a fighter jet on the deck of what was probably an aircraft carrier.

'You look like him.'

'Except I'm a failure and he was flying jets when he was my age. Here's another with his friends from the war. They all stayed friends. That one on the right was his best friend. I don't remember his name. Here's one when he flew for United.'

Raveneau studied a photo of Jim Frank in a United Airlines uniform and then glanced at Candel. Candel didn't need any DNA test. This was father and son, right to the cowlick on

Candel's left side. Good looking guy, Captain Frank. Raveneau didn't doubt he attracted women. Candel handed him another six or seven photos and Frank had his arm around the waist of a woman in a bikini. Frank wore bright red swim trunks. Surf broke behind them.

The next photo and the one after it were landscape shots. 'Where were these taken?'

Candel shook his head. 'Don't know, probably Hawaii. He lived there. He definitely lived there when she was there.'

'Which island?'

'Check out the back of the photo.'

Raveneau flipped it over and read 'The house, Big Island.'

Candel slid the box toward him.

'Got to go, dude, my friends are here.'

'Give me your cell number.'

Candel scratched his number on a bar napkin and waved at two young women and a man working their way through the bar crowd. Before moving on, he said, 'I want one thing in return. You bust him, I want to be there.'

'He's not a suspect.'

'When he becomes one, when you go after him, you call me. Give me your word on that, man.'

'I'm not going to do that, but I'll call you tomorrow and we'll talk more.'

FIVE

C eleste sat under a street light on the curb next to a dumpster, a black plastic garbage can on wheels next to her like a best friend. He tasted dust and sweat as he kissed her, and when he emptied the garbage can Sheetrock dust billowed out and enveloped him. He had a pretty good idea what her answer would be, but asked anyway.

'How did it go?'

'We failed all the inspections. Want to see?'

She showed him where the fire marshal who had reviewed

and stamped the plans months ago now wanted her to add two more fire sprinkler heads. That meant draining the system, cutting into the walls, adding the sprinkler heads, patching, painting, and calling for another re-inspection. The Sheetrock dust that had spread through the almost finished space was from cutting into the finished walls.

'It's like fallout,' she said. 'It's everywhere.'

There was also a code problem with the main flue and she unfolded a Health Department correction notice on the bar top for him to read. This was the day she had hoped to have everything to do with the City of San Francisco signed off and done. She pointed at two employees of the mechanical sub and said softly, 'Double overtime,' then brushed a strand of hair back from her cheek and acknowledged, 'They've got me. I can't do anything about it. Sprinkler sub is back at six in the morning. I have to get it done. I have to pay the overtime. The tables are delivering tomorrow. I don't know where I'm going to put them.'

'What does this do to opening day?'

'I'm opening no matter what.'

Raveneau thought about Captain Frank and Ryan Candel's story as he helped her clean. It was another hour and a half before the mechanical subcontractor finished. After he left they ate sandwiches and split a salad and a bottle of red wine at a place that served until midnight.

Then they went back to his place, an apartment on top of an industrial building at the edge of China Basin. Wind blew off the bay tonight and there was rain coming, but it was just the wind right now and he sat out on the deck as Celeste showered. The night was cold though not too cold and it felt good to sit out here and think. When he turned Celeste was in a T-shirt and otherwise naked.

'What are you doing?' she asked.

'Holding on to the day.'

'How would you like to come in and hold me instead?'

SIX

Before dawn Raveneau was back in the Homicide office. Yesterday he'd borrowed a portable ultraviolet light from the crime scene guys. He plugged it in now and spun la Rosa's lamp around to use as a second light. Two one-hundred dollar bills lay on the desk in front of him. One was a new 2011 bill in the current style and the other taken from the sixty-one counterfeit notes before turning the rest over to the Secret Service.

The Krueger bill was tattered where the bullet had passed through it. La Rosa called them the shot-dead notes, and that wasn't a bad name. He turned on her desk light and adjusted it to the highest brightness, then held up the new one hundred dollar bill first. With light shining through, it was easy to see the tiny print that read *USA one hundred dollars*. Using a magnifying glass he read *United States of America* and saw the embedded American flag. When he turned on the ultraviolet light and held the bill under it the threads turned red in the light.

He turned off the ultraviolet light and moved the new one hundred dollar bill back under the desk lamp, studying the watermark, a shadow of Ben Franklin alongside his face on the bill. The Treasury started making these changes in 1990 and steadily improved on them. The shot-dead bill had none of them. He picked up a counterfeit-detector felt pen and marked the tattered bill. This was stuff store clerks did daily, either holding the bill up to light or using the pen. The pen reacted with starch binders and acid. Genuine US notes were starchless and acid free, and he waited for the counterfeit bill to turn brown, but it stayed yellow.

He made another mark on it then marked the new bill to test the pen. It stayed yellow as it should. Raveneau wasn't sure what to make of the counterfeit bill not reacting. Either the pen was defective or the counterfeit bill was printed on starch-free paper back in 1989. But that wouldn't have been easy to do. He held it up again and it was still yellow.

He had learned that all the embedding was in response to counterfeiting, in particular to the supernotes. The supernotes scared Treasury and ever since US bills kept evolving. The latest had a textured surface, but given the way things had gone, the way printing also evolved, that wasn't going to be enough either. Neither was his trying to learn about counterfeiting. He unplugged the lights and slid the ultraviolet under his desk. He put la Rosa's light back where she liked it to sit, then adjusted it. He put the shot-dead bill back in an evidence bag and sent la Rosa a text before riding the elevator down.

It was still early when he walked out but he guessed Lim would be there by now. He walked to his car. Someone once likened the end of the peninsula where San Francisco was built to a thumb pushed out into the bay. Raveneau drove to the south-eastern side past the desolate poverty of the Bayview and beyond the old power plant out to the crime lab in Hunter's Point with Allyson Candel's shoebox in a plastic bag on the passenger seat next to him.

At the crime lab Howard Lim who headed the lab slid it out of the bag and with gloves on opened the top.

'You've handled these already. Why didn't you bring them here when you first got them?'

'I just got them last night. I won them in a card game.'

'You see, you're getting old. When you were younger you would have driven them straight out.' He looked over at Raveneau and shook his head. 'You should see yourself. I hear the medical examiner comes up every afternoon to just make sure you're alive and not a cold case. If you've already handled everything why did you come out here to bother me?'

'I want to know what you can tell me about the photos.'

Banter aside, Lim got it. He understood. He was an avid photographer, had been for decades. He sifted through. There were seventeen photos and a handful of Kodachrome slides. Six of the photos he set aside, glancing at Raveneau, saying 'Polaroid. You remember Polaroid. Seems so long, long ago now, like when you were fifty.'

In one of the six Polaroids a dark-haired woman swam beneath a waterfall. Raveneau thumbed through the shots and left the waterfall picture on top. Lim adjusted his glasses, looked at

Raveneau, started to say something and didn't. He picked up a small black and white of Jim Frank in his Navy uniform.

'In Honolulu there used to be these photo booths for sailors. This is from one of them.'

'Taken when?'

'I guess early 1970s.'

'Is your family still in Hawaii?'

'Some are. My father is. He's old but he still drives. In Hawaii it is OK to drive when you are older. Everyone drives slower, not like some old crazy detective in San Francisco trying to catch a killer who is already dead.' Lim turned. 'What connects now to this killing?'

'I don't know yet but it ties to counterfeiting and a victim who once worked for the Secret Service and later possibly other US agencies.'

'A spy?'

'I haven't learned much yet about what he was doing, but I think he was trying to penetrate counterfeiting rings.'

Raveneau and Lim came in the same year. Then, Lim was black-haired and smooth-faced, and ever-so-serious about crime lab techniques and cross contamination. He was much more easy-going now. He set the photo booth shot of Jim Frank trying to look like Robert Mitchum or James Dean in uniform off to the side. He picked up another black and white. He kept the banter going because it helped him think.

'You need to sit down, rest your back?' Lim asked. 'You want to get your walker out of your car?'

'No, I rode a bike out here. I exercise every couple of hours. I've got two marathons next weekend, both are on Saturday.'

'That's probably the only way to get blood to your brain now. Other agencies you say, maybe the CIA?'

'The original inspectors actually thought it was possible, but I don't have any reason to believe that.'

'You don't have any reason yet.'

'That's right.'

'Very careful slow inspector and . . .' Lim seemed to forget where he was going with that. He picked up one of the 4 x 6 photos and said, 'Hapuna Beach.'

'Where is that?'

'On the Big Island and a very nice beach, a famous beach. Who is the woman with the man in the uniform?'

'Allyson Candel. His name is or was Jim Frank. He was a pilot for United. I'm trying to locate him and hoping he's still alive.'

'You are, so maybe he is too.'

Raveneau smiled and let it be.

'She was a stewardess and her son told me that photo was taken in the mid 1980s.'

'Mid eighties is about right, I think.'

'How do you tell?'

'The type of paper.'

Lim turned the photo on edge and ticked his thumb along it. He flipped it over and showed Raveneau spots where the paper was yellowing. He flipped it back over, laid it down gently. In this shot Jim Frank had his arm around her. It looked as if they both had just gotten out of the water. Frank was dripping wet but wearing dry sunglasses and Allyson Candel was quietly beautiful.

'What about the one you set aside?' Raveneau asked, but you couldn't rush Lim. No one could rush Lim. The chief of police wouldn't get anywhere pushing him. Lim took the photo with him and came back a few minutes later.

'Ben, come back here,' he said, and then picked up the shot of Frank and Allyson Candel on the beach. A different photo was under a lens and magnified. Lim slid it out, replaced it with the beach shot. Now the beads of water on Frank's face were more visible as was the unevenness of how he'd shaved that day. But the photo also became grainy. The look Raveneau caught in Allyson Candel's eye was less resolved, became blotchy.

'OK, now look here.'

Lim slipped the other photo, the landscape shot back under the lens. His voice was quieter as he asked, 'What differences do you see?'

On the back of the photo written in pencil were the words, 'the house.' But the photo caught much more than a house built in a notch on a steep grassy slope. The day was quite clear and the line of the Kohala coast swept south with a white line of breakers.

The corrugated roof of the house and the stand of trees below and the two-lane highway well below stood out sharply.

'It's nowhere near as grainy. The quality of detail is at a whole other level.'

'Many levels up,' Lim said. 'This kind of resolution at that time was uncommon. This is very high quality. It could be a professional photographer who shoots this, someone who photographs landscapes for art or books. This is better than you would use then for magazines. Some military and government agencies were at this level, so maybe this Frank is a spy. Maybe he worked for the CIA.' He smiled at Raveneau and added, 'If I took your picture with this camera, even you would look good.'

'Thanks, Howard.'

'No problem, I'm here for you.'

He was chuckling as Raveneau shut the door.

SEVEN

Raveneau met with the captain and lieutenant before Goya showed up. He made his pitch for bringing Goya on for this case and the captain's only response was to clear his throat. When Goya arrived Raveneau walked him around the office and showed him some of the changes, and then took him back to the Cold Case office and his desk. Goya lowered himself into the chair and Raveneau slid the CD in.

'This is the digitized version. They do this down the hall now.'

And just like that Goya shifted from lunch to the case. He went quiet. He asked how it got here and what Raveneau had learned about it as Raveneau showed him how to freeze the action if he wanted. He hoped the video would trigger some memory in Goya. He played it four times before Goya was satisfied, Goya murmuring quietly to himself each time the shooting started. On the fourth run he figured out the freeze function and stopped the action.

'This is not how the body was lying.'

'What's different?'

'He was on his back and his left leg wasn't crossed over.'

In the video he was on his side. In the video there was also an editing gap where whoever filmed it stopped some distance back and started again close to the body. He knew Goya was thinking about that as well, but they'd get to it later. It surprised Raveneau that Goya still remembered the body position, but he was correct. In the crime scene photos Krueger lay on his back, legs apart. Someone moved the body between the filming of the video and the crime scene photos.

'Did you move him before you photographed him?'

'No, but we checked his pockets. Remember, we didn't have DNA in those days.'

He turned in the darkness toward Raveneau and asked for the files. As Goya compared the crime scene photos to the screen Raveneau said, 'Maybe the Canadians moved him. Maybe they rolled him back to get at his wallet. You said they were honeymooning on the cheap. Could be they called the police but also stole money from his wallet?'

'Could be,' Goya said, and then asked, 'Where was the person who made the video if the Canadians got there so fast?'

'I've been wondering.'

'With a mob hit no one hangs around to make a movie. They take a photo if they need proof.'

'I don't have an answer for you, Henry. I want answers from you. I want to know what you see and remember, though I do have one other piece of information you didn't have. The one hundred dollar bills in his coat were counterfeit. I found that out yesterday.'

'They weren't counterfeit in 1989, but now they are?'

'That's right, and that's kind of how I read it too. So what changed with the Secret Service between now and then and why do you think the bills in his coat were left behind and the wallet cleaned out?'

Goya had found the wallet with ALK in tiny red letters stitched into it. Goya picked it up and handled it and no fingerprints were recovered as a result, an unanswered mistake.

'Are you wondering if the wallet had money in it when I picked it up?'

'No, I'm asking about the Secret Service. Could Krueger have been at a meet, a buy of some sort with this shooter and the Secret Service was filming from a distance? Then someone pulled his wallet to make it look like a robbery so whatever operation was underway kept going. Let's say the undercover operation was deemed so important there was a cover-up.'

'The Secret Service agents I knew never would have taken part in something like that. They were all good people, some of the best, and, Jesus, he was one of theirs for years. They were Feds so they were stiff, but they were still good people.'

'Who did you deal with?'

'I can't remember his name. It started with a P; you can find it out easily enough.'

'Tell me about finding the wallet.'

'Did you bring me in to interview me or have lunch?'

'I need your help, Henry.'

'Well, we didn't find one on him and we figured if robbery was the motive then the shooter might have stripped the money out and tossed the wallet. And sure enough, there it was and trash around it, you know, paper and crap that had blown up against the concrete pylon.'

'Was the afternoon that windy that it could get covered that fast?'

'Are you asking now if we were stupid? Sure it was windy and I wasn't even sure it was a wallet.'

Goya frowned and stroked his beard then let his hand drop. He slowly stood up and as Raveneau popped the CD out he moved to the door and then out into the hallway ahead of Raveneau.

When Raveneau caught up to him at the elevator, Goya said, 'You think Ed and I made mistakes.'

'Not at all, you're misreading me, Henry.'

'No, you're wondering things.'

'I'm doing what I have to. Let's get some lunch.'

But Goya had withdrawn. He seemed disappointed and saddened as if his integrity had been questioned. When they got down to the street he said, 'I'm going to pass on lunch.'

'Henry, I wasn't questioning you.'

'Yeah, I know, but I remembered something I've got to do.'

Raveneau watched him limp across the street to his car, his

pride hurt. He laid his cane across the passenger seat as he got in, and nearly got hit as he pulled away. He kept his head straight and never looked over as he drove away. Raveneau felt lousy as he climbed back up the steps to the Hall.

EIGHT

Later that afternoon the arrest report on Ryan Candel was faxed to Raveneau. He visualized as he read, Dr Leonard walking up California, Candel coming down, and according to a witness 'running as if being chased' when he slammed into the doctor.

Leonard's head struck the bumper of a parked car. He broke his right wrist landing on the street and suffered a concussion that kept him under observation for forty-eight hours. According to responding officers, Candel was disoriented and confused. He was standing over the injured Leonard when they arrived. When he refused to follow commands, Officer Sanchez drew his gun. They believed him to be under the influence of drugs, though no evidence of that was found.

Raveneau called a friend in the District Attorney's office who said, 'I don't have to look it up, Ben. I remember Candel. If you're about to tell me he killed somebody, I'm not surprised. He got an ankle bracelet and picked up trash for six months, but should be in prison. He could have killed him. What's he done now?'

'Called us with a tip on a cold case.'

'Then he's probably fucking with you. He's a self-serving manipulator.'

'Sounds like this was your case, Gerald.'

'It was and the doctor quit on us after Candel filed a malpractice suit. The doctor wouldn't testify so the charges got downgraded. Then one of these blogger geniuses who specialize in shit disturbing got a story out about how Dr Leonard was out on a golf course with pharmaceutical reps as Candel's mother was succumbing to an infection. Meanwhile Leonard determined he had already suffered enough and the collateral damage to his practice wasn't worth it, so he friggin' bailed. That's how Candel ended up with trash patrol.'

'He regrets it now.'

'Oh, I bet he does. After all, he was inconvenienced briefly. This is a very emotionally immature young man who by the way doesn't like police.'

'A lot of people don't.'

'He was loud about it. I'd be very careful with him, but you're defending him so obviously he's got something you want.'

'Ease down, Gerald, he responded to one of our ads and brought me some photos we're using.'

When Gerald didn't respond, Raveneau said, 'Let's get together for a drink soon. My girlfriend is opening a bar at the edge of the Mission. Or it's mostly a bar. It'll have some food. We can meet there after she has it up and running.'

'OK, so drinks on you, she owns it? I'll look forward to it. What's the name going to be?'

'Toasts.'

'Cute.'

'I've got another call coming in. I'll talk to you later.'

Raveneau checked the number on his cell screen before answering, 'This is Inspector Raveneau.'

'Oh, hello, I'm Barbara Haney's brother. The police here called me. What's your interest in my sister?'

'We have new evidence in a cold case and I'd like to re-interview her.'

'You would.'

That was a statement not a question and Raveneau left it alone. He waited.

'I'm going to be frank, Inspector. Barbara was quite put off by your department. She and Larry spent a lot of hours in San Francisco talking to police rather than honeymooning. They didn't have any problem with any of that, eh, but one of the inspectors came to Calgary and threatened them. But that's America, getting treated like criminals for trying to help.'

It went on another several minutes this way, the brother as gatekeeper, the brother venting about American arrogance abroad, Raveneau listening to how the world was turning away from the

United States, and then repeating quietly that he had new evidence and was trying to solve the murder of a man who was gunned down. Finally, the brother gave him a phone for Barbara Haney's daughter. The daughter, Cheryl, answered on the second ring.

'Everyone in the family knows what happened when your inspector came to Calgary and that worries me because my mother has mental health issues. She suffers from depression but refuses to take anything for it. She's fragile and I feel like I should be there when you question her, but I can't travel right now. So I don't think now is the right time.'

For the next twenty minutes Raveneau worked to convince her that this was the right time.

'I'd also like to talk to your dad. Do you have a way I can get in touch with him?'

'I don't have much contact with my father.'

'Do you know where he lives now?'

'He's in China.'

OK, that's easy, Raveneau thought. I'll just look for him in China. But in the end she gave him an email for her dad, and then gave him her mom's phone number after he promised not to ask Barbara Haney to come to San Francisco.

'I don't want you to upset my mother.'

'I'm sorry for whatever happened when our inspector interviewed her last, but your mother and father may be the only ones who can say whether our new lead is worth anything or not.'

'First, I don't really believe you.'

'You can believe me, Cheryl.'

'And secondly, it's not my mother's responsibility to evaluate something like that. I don't want you to put pressure on her.'

'The pressure is on me, not on your mom. I'll make sure it stays that way.'

That got silence, then, 'She lives in Truckee. Her husband is an American.' She said that last in a way that suggested that was a life mistake her mother had made. 'He's an executive for a ski corporation based in Colorado so they live half the year in Colorado. Do you know where Truckee is?'

'I do.'

He called Barbara Haney as soon as he got off the phone with the daughter. She must have known the call was coming because almost immediately she asked, 'Can you bring Inspector Govich with you?'

'I'm sure he'd like to come with me, but he's retired.'

She laughed and Raveneau chuckled and guessed he was going to like her. He said, 'I could drive to Truckee Monday morning.'

'It's that urgent?'

'It's the case I'm working.'

She was quiet before saying, 'I knew this wasn't over.'

NINE

S even floors up at the FBI Field Office on Golden Gate Street Special Agent Mark Coe picked up the phone and called Ben Raveneau's cell phone. He assumed Raveneau's work day heading the Cold Case Unit was more orderly than when he was on-call and in the rotation. San Francisco was staring at a three hundred eighty million dollar deficit this year and he knew the police department was keeping close tabs on overtime. Raveneau was probably about done for the day. But then you couldn't know with him. Raveneau would work with or without pay.

When Raveneau answered Coe said, 'Raveneau, I'm back in your life and I've got information to share. It's important enough to show you as soon as possible. Is there any chance of getting you to stop here early tomorrow morning?'

'Not tomorrow.'

'What about now?'

Raveneau took a right at the next light and called Celeste. This would disappoint her. She was ready to hire a cook with the title of chef, a New Orleans transplant named Bo Rutan, and had asked a week ago if he'd make the time to meet Rutan. That was supposed to be now. Rutan was there for a final interview.

Raveneau liked Mark Coe. He liked it that Coe never seemed serious about appearing serious, which was a pretty good trick when you worked for the Feds. Coe sounded serious now though. He looked it too. He stood patiently as Raveneau dug coins from his pockets to quiet the FBI metal detector. Coe was physically fit in a wiry way, four or five inches shorter than Raveneau, but probably one of those guys who could run up a mountain without panting. He carried the same sort of confidence at work without seeming full of himself.

'Did Brooks tell you the counterfeit bills you're chasing with your cold case may have a connection to a threat against the President?'

'He didn't tell me that part, but our victim was killed in 1989.'

'Did he tell you Krueger was carrying the same series of counterfeit bills as were used to buy explosives last July?'

Raveneau nodded.

'We're coming at this from a different direction and I'm going to give you more than Nate did. I can do that because we got there a different way. We were working a fraud case. I've got wiretap transcripts from that investigation I'd like to play for you. I can put them on audio or if you'd rather hear and read I can give you both.'

'Give me both.'

Raveneau followed Coe into a conference room. There was a long oval table with an American flag in a stand, a big-screen TV to the side of it with a computer set-up. The screen came to life and Coe said, 'These transcripts are from a wire worn by one of our agents out of Salt Lake.'

Raveneau pulled a chair over in front of the TV.

'This conversation is between a former Utah banker named Jamison Garner and our agent who's making a contribution using the alias Robert Jenner. Garner used to work for Zion Bank but now works for a very private and political group. Within that group we think may be people who belong to yet another more exclusive group. There's twenty minutes of talking before they really get to it, and I could fast forward but I think it's worth hearing all of it. Coffee?'

'Sure, double espresso, refined sugar, not brown.'

'You bet, and would you like some fresh pastry?'

'I would. Bring the cart out and I'll pick something.'

Coe left as the audio started and Raveneau leaned back and listened to Jamison Garner, deep voiced, easy going, sounding like a big guy who life had treated well. They were talking politics and Garner, like many on either side in these times, was confident he was right. He quietly trash-talked Obama and Congress before launching into the gold bugs' rap about the Federal Reserve destroying the US dollar. It was talk you could hear a lot of places nowadays. You could turn on the TV and hear experts like Garner on any number of channels. Garner and the man he was talking with were brushing around the edges of 'something needing doing' when Coe walked back in.

'I didn't look for any milk. Hope you like your coffee black. Sorry it's in a paper cup.'

Raveneau took a sip. He was watching the transcript and listening to Garner as he asked, 'Does the Bureau have a file on Alan Krueger?'

'I knew if I invited you here you'd start asking questions. To get hired on to the Homicide Detail do you have to prove you can ask two hundred questions in an hour? We do have a file. Yes, you can read it. No, it hasn't been updated since he was killed.'

'Was it started before or after he left the Secret Service?'

'After.'

'Good guy or bad guy?'

'Good guy doing business with bad guys as near as I can tell.'

'Who set him up with the bad guys?'

'That's a big open question.'

'Was he an embarrassment to the Secret Service?'

'No, but they were worried about it at the time and something happened there they're fuzzy about.'

'They shut out our inspectors.'

'They had their own investigation going and they were working hard to figure out who Krueger was dealing with. They had supernotes starting to spread around the world.'

'Did they begin to question Krueger?'

'Maybe, probably, and it's possible more than one party was making supernotes.'

'Could that party have set-up the North Koreans?'

'They may have, yes.'

'What was the Bureau's theory of who killed Krueger?'

'We never concluded anything. You'll read it.'

Raveneau quit talking as the conversation between Garner and

Jenner changed abruptly, Jenner getting a little whiny when Garner asked, 'Can I deposit this today?'

'You can, but when is anyone going to talk to me? A hundred thousand dollars is still worth something. I just want some sign things are progressing.'

'We're doing fine and I'm talking to you, and you knew when you got in that your contributions would be directed to making the changes we know need to happen.'

'Give me something concrete. You know damn well it's not going any farther than me.'

'I don't know the things you want to know. My job is to gather and pass the money on to those overseeing the work.'

Raveneau heard exasperation creep into Garner's voice. Exasperation as if he'd had this same conversation before.

'Jamie, you're treating me like an outsider.'

A chair shifted, probably Garner.

'We can return your money.'

'Don't be so hardnosed. I'm not asking for much. Three contributions downstream I'm owed something, so just give me a time frame. Am I going to turn on the TV in three months, six months, and see things have started and there's news?'

'You're making me think I misread you initially, and I don't like making that kind of mistake. I rarely make a mistake about character but you're starting to disappoint me. You're asking something you have no business asking and I'm advising you to stop now. I strongly suggest you don't make me question you any more than you already have today. I don't want to think I've made a mistake that needs to be rectified.'

'Are you threatening me?'

'I'm being honest with you.'

Something got whispered that Raveneau couldn't make out and no text appeared on the screen.

'The agent didn't hear it either,' Coe said. 'Whatever Garner said, he said under his breath.'

'I'm as certain we need change as anybody,' Jenner said. 'I'm as solid as anybody and you shouldn't talk to me the way you are. Three hundred thousand dollars is what I'm in so far.'

'Three hundred thousand dollars is nothing compared to what

others are contributing. All you need to know is it's in motion now.'

'Just tell me it begins with him.'

'I'm tearing this check in half. The rest of your contributions will be returned to you. Good day, sir.'

Garner hung up.

'How long did it take your agent to get that close?'

'Over a year and a half and it wasn't easy. We were asked by the Secret Service to push harder, so we did and as you heard it was a mistake. There are other pieces. There are two former Army snipers we're also watching. We believe there are military links but that's not confirmed. This next clip is an individual talking about a military supply depot in Kentucky. In this passage the individual working with us is X4. He's not an FBI agent. He came to us and the man he's talking to he's never met or seen. X4 is trying to sell him black market current grade US military hardware.'

> *X4:* 'I'm calling about the parts order. I can get what you need in time.'
> *Unsub:* 'Then we're probably doing business.'
> *X4:* 'There is a glitch though. My supplier won't disassemble and ship.'
> *Unsub:* 'Disassembly and separate shipping is the only way we'll do this.'
> *X4:* 'I know. He's not set-up to disassemble.'
> *Unsub:* 'That's a problem.'
> *X-4:* 'It's my problem.'
> *Unsub:* 'You're right about that and you've got a week before I go somewhere else.'
> *X4:* 'Understood.'

Coe changed the screen now. 'Here's another Garner and sorry to do this with scraps, but I'll sketch it together for you. This is an older Garner tape from last July. We don't know who he was talking to. The party on the other end had a throwaway phone.'

Raveneau listened and read the text as it passed by. It was all Garner, a monologue, a diatribe on social values that morphed into protecting the Constitution from enemies foreign and domestic as if somehow there was a natural connection. He segued into corruption in Washington and said they were using someone in Washington to gain access, but that those getting paid for that would not 'make the long trip with us.' 'Their purpose will have been fulfilled,' he said. He spoke about sacrifice and necessary shock to the country, corruption trials, and public executions 'after the mobilization.'

'What do you think the mobilization is?' Raveneau asked. 'And what are you calling this guy?'

'We call him Jericho.' He paused. 'You'll think we've gone nuts in here.'

'I already think that.'

'Let me say first we have no real theory yet, but there is a link to weapon purchases and this counterfeit series you're caught up in. We've recorded references to a first event. The Secret Service believes that's an assassination plan and we gather that's just the initial step. These are planners. The mobilization, and this is where you're going to shake your head and laugh, is later and involves some aspect of our military and a temporary occupation of Washington. It's possible the planning began a decade or more ago.'

'Oh, come on—'

'Ben, I'm with you, it's another wacko conspiracy hunt, but something is going on. Garner is well-connected and the group he's with is well-funded. A year ago you could never have convinced me that anything like they're talking was even remotely possible. But now I'm not as sure. Maybe I've been drinking the Kool-Aid. Maybe I've listened and read too much into these conversations.'

'They're living a fantasy.'

'I know and I agree with you, but I think they're going to try.'

TEN

S now was alongside the road in the foothills but the road was dry as Raveneau drove over Donner Pass. The high mountain rock caught early sunlight though the snow-covered slopes lower were still shaded, the snow smooth and hard looking. He lowered his window and let the cold air reach him as he exited in Truckee and found a gas station, then called Barbara Haney from there, his breath clouding in front as he told her he was close.

'Do you need directions?'

'It's been awhile but I can still find my way around.'

The big Cottonwood sign was still up there on the hill and it was easy to remember sitting out on the deck. He drove toward the Tahoe Basin and turned off into the shadowed snowy Martis Valley. He found her house among the big new houses built in the last decade.

When she opened the door he saw a tall woman nearing fifty, big-boned but not heavy. She had a fluid walk, an athletic ease to her. Her cheekbones were sharp, eyes dark, iron-colored streaks running in her black hair. She led him to a large, high-ceilinged, open room that could have been the lobby of a boutique mountain hotel. Heavy fir beams held up the roof. The stone fireplace was big enough to set up a card table inside. Tall windows looked up toward the backside of the Northstar ski resort up above in the near distance. Skiers were on the slopes, not too many but some, dark and small as they skied the runs. He watched a fast skier and asked her, 'Do you get out there?'

'I usually ski once or twice a week, but not lately. We need a storm. It's hardly snowed in January. The snow is hard and I've become softer, and I don't really like to ski alone. But when I'm here I'm usually alone.'

'Where's your husband?'

'Working. We have a house in Colorado and the corporate headquarters my husband works out of are there. He's there most of the time.'

Raveneau could ask why they didn't move from house to house together, but instead said, 'I used to ski but I haven't in awhile. It's one of those things I don't seem to do any more.'

'That's how it works, one day you just don't do what you used to and you wonder why not.'

She smiled and Raveneau saw sadness. He looked from the mountain slopes and the skiers to her. 'Some new evidence came in on the Alan Krueger murder and I'm actively working the case.'

'Well, where do you want to start?'

'With your ex-husband, how do I get in touch with him? Your daughter, Cheryl, gave me an email address. Do you have a phone number?'

'Not any more. I email him. He always responds. Just don't tell him you're a San Francisco homicide inspector. Did my daughter tell you I'm fragile?'

'She said you suffer from depression.'

'I suffer from her theories but there's nothing unusual about me and I'm certainly not fragile. I won't burst into tears after you leave, but I would like to think I can put what happened in 1989 behind me at some point. We were tourists on our honeymoon.'

'I understand.'

'Good, and I understand we brought suspicion on ourselves. I have to admit we did avoid Inspector Govich when he came to Calgary. My husband simply couldn't stand him.'

'You can tell your ex that Govich retired.'

'I don't think retired would be quite enough to satisfy Larry. He'd want a little more than that.' She smiled a wry smile now, brushed a strand of hair from her face and said, 'Bit of an irony that all you had to do was call me yesterday to set up an interview this morning. Don't tell Govich how easy I've become. What about Govich's partner? I've forgotten his name.'

'Henry Goya.'

'What does he say about us?'

'He's circumspect.'

'Wonderful, we're making progress. It's been how many years?'

'Twenty-two.'

She smiled again, but less brightly.

'Let's move into the kitchen. It's warmer there.'

She got out a plate and put scones on it that she said came from a bakery in town. She made coffee as she talked and Raveneau ate a scone and drank a mug of coffee while Barbara offered pieces of what she remembered of the day Alan Krueger was murdered. She was nervous. It showed in her hands and voice and Raveneau wanted to put her at ease.

'I brought the murder files with me. I didn't bring them to

show you crime scene photos but because I thought you might want to see what was written about you then.'

'Why would I want to do that?'

'So we start from the same place. They're in the car. They can stay there or I can bring them in.'

His tactic was to show her everything written about herself and her ex-husband, Larry Benhaime. He wanted to get her off the defensive and break the pattern. Her family members could only be echoing what she had told them.

'You can leave them in the car.'

'OK.'

'And I should say I understand much more than you may realize. I know Inspector Govich discovered we lied about the dinner and that made him suspicious. I would be too. The truth about that particular thing is rather bizarre but simple. Larry, my ex, is a contrarian. If you say yes, he'll say no, and maybe not right away but sooner or later. He didn't like your Inspector Govich and I think he told him that we ate dinner at that restaurant that I can't even remember the name of just to be perverse. When you finally track him down in some bar in Hong Kong I think he'll tell you he didn't believe it was any of the inspector's business where we ate dinner or when we came back to the hotel, or anything else about our honeymoon.'

'I think they realized that, and from talking with Henry Goya the lie over where you ate dinner didn't mean anything.'

'We actually had a reservation and we had looked forward to eating there that night. But we got asked to come to the police station and then we were kept waiting for hours. That's what made Larry angry.' She shrugged. 'We were young and it was a murder and we were tourists. If it happened now I'd have told you everything we know and we'll talk to you again tomorrow if you want, but we're leaving now.'

'It was never about the dinner, Barbara. There were other things.'

'Why did you go back to this case?'

'We received a videotape that someone made of Krueger's murder.'

'You mean of the actual murder?'

'Yes, and it's been looked at and we believe it's authentic.'

'That's quite astonishing. You couldn't have seen that one coming.'

'Definitely not, and now I'm going back through Inspectors Goya and Govich's investigation. I'm retracing their steps. I have to first understand where they were coming from.'

'Why would you do that if they didn't solve it?'

'Because they had leads and questions.'

'Like Larry and me.'

'I don't know that either you or Larry were ever suspects.'

'Of course you do, it's why you're here. If you hadn't received the videotape when would this have finally been tucked away in a file cabinet?'

'We never close an unsolved case.'

'There's a TV show where they say dramatic things like that. It's not a very good one though and I'm more interested in real life. I'm going to put forward my theory of why you're here. You're here because you think the original inspectors were on to something about us, or you think it's possible they were. You aren't sure, of course, but you're curious or you are entertaining the idea or maybe they've convinced you that they should have arrested us.'

'They didn't suspect you and Larry of killing Alan Krueger.'

'As I said, I don't believe that.'

'And I brought the video – which you don't have to watch because it is graphic – but I'm here with it because I'm hoping when you do watch it, if you do, that it'll trigger a memory that will help me. It's the killing with the shooter and you're not the shooter and I'd say your husband is too tall.'

'He is six foot three.'

'So I hear.'

'OK, Inspector, if it proves once and for all it wasn't us, let's watch it. Bring your coffee. I'll bring the scones. It'll be like a date. We'll play it in the den. Do you watch things like this often at your police station?'

'We don't get many like this.' As they walked into the den, Raveneau asked, 'How long were you married?'

'Too long. I've learned that I tend to recognize things long before I act. My daughter thinks medication could help that. What do you think?'

'I try to avoid medication.'

'Do you ever feel like your life is a series of connected failures?'

'I know what that feels like.'

'What Larry discovered during our marriage was that he liked being out of town and a long way away in a hotel in Asia where he would have a clean uncomplicated room to come back to and a time zone reason for not being able to call me, not to mention an expense account for dinner and drinking. It was perfect for him.'

'Who was he working for then?'

'He was a kind of accountant for our Revenue Service, looking for corporate fraud, that sort of thing. That's probably in your files.'

Oddly, it wasn't. She handed him the plate of scones and he handed her the CD.

'What were you doing for work?'

'Something very similar but more numbers oriented, and trust me working for Canada's Revenue Service can't be any more fun than working for the IRS.'

Raveneau broke off a piece of scone. He took another drink of coffee. She hadn't asked the question he wondered about so much, why whoever sent this video held on to it for so many years. But she was going to say something more about Govich and Goya. He could feel that coming. Then it did.

'Your Inspector Govich had a hunch about us that was free-floating. Like the man who is always suspicious of his wife. Now maybe that makes a good investigator, allowing that amorphous feeling to exist without a fact to attach to. When all he could find was the restaurant discrepancy, he let it attach there and Goya went along.'

'When you found Alan Krueger's body did you touch it?'

'Larry did. He wanted to make sure he was dead.'

'How close did you get?'

'I had to turn away it was so awful.'

'Do you remember the position of the body?'

'No.'

'Did you see what Larry was doing?'

'Only when he first leaned over.'

'Did he remove anything from the body?'

'Such as?'

'A wallet to see who the victim was.'

'Don't you think we would have said?'

'Did he remove the wallet?'

'Goodness.'

'I'm thinking it would be natural to make sure the man was dead, and possibly look for ID.'

'Most people would wait for the police, don't you think?'

'Most would, but perhaps your ex-husband didn't and there wasn't a wallet found on the body.'

'I don't remember anyone asking us about a wallet.'

'Inspector Goya told me they asked you. There are notes in the file saying they did.'

'Oh, well, I don't remember.' She added, 'How well would you remember twenty-two years later?'

'It would depend on how much of a mark it made on me.' He gave her a moment. 'I think the murder affected you.'

'Oh, absolutely, it made a wonderful honeymoon. Almost as good as the marriage.'

Raveneau studied her. 'I can't picture you forgetting the position of the body?'

'Does it really make a whit of difference now?'

'It could. A man called in a few days after the murder and left a message saying he heard shots and that he'd looked at his watch afterward to remember what time he heard them. He called us after you and Larry flew home and left a message saying he put it together after reading about the shooting in the newspaper. He didn't leave a phone number or contact us again, but he did leave the time he heard the shots. He sounded credible to the inspectors. The time was very close to when you said you found the body, so close that Inspector Govich thought you either saw or heard the shooting.'

'Do you suppose he believes his wife when she tells him things or is she always a suspect?'

'That's one of the reasons Inspector Govich flew to Canada.'

'He flew to Canada because he got an anonymous call? That's great.'

'The time he gave was 3:42. Larry told the inspectors you found the body at 3:45.'

'I can walk a long way in four minutes, Inspector, and watches didn't always match. I'm sure you remember that. Nothing like the precious cell phones we have now that let us all keep exactly the same time together. Are you going to ask if he was dead when we got there?'

'I know he was dead, but I'm still wondering about his body position.'

'You're back to that.'

'I haven't left it.'

'I've tried to block all of it out. It was a horrible thing to see.'

'I'm sure it was.'

'His brains . . .'

Raveneau nodded and she looked down at the floor. She moved her right hand over on top of her left.

'He was lying on his back with his legs apart.'

'When you found him?'

Her voice rose slightly. 'You have photos. I don't know what you call them, crime scene photos. We saw the photos taken. Look in your files. Haven't you seen them?'

'Let's watch the video.'

She pushed it in and the monitor lit up.

ELEVEN

After the homicide inspector left, Barbara Haney felt light-headed and anxious. She picked up the cordless phone in the kitchen and called her house manager from the den, pulse pounding, fingers drumming as she waited for the house manager to answer. The house manager, a thirty-two year old lawyer named Gail Hawkins, ran the house here and the one in Vail, as well as their New York apartment and the island property. She was well-educated, skilled, and discreet. She worked for them with the rationalization the salary of one hundred eighty thousand dollars a year was about the same as she would earn as a lawyer right now. It was also more than they needed to pay, but Barbara's husband, Doug, was generous that way. He had a hard start at a career himself.

Gail worked for them but it was understood that the house managing was temporary and even though she might never practice law again, she wasn't anybody's servant. She certainly wasn't. She was much more than an employee. She was her husband's lover, something she had yet to confront Doug with but was never far from her thoughts and a big contributor to the depression her daughter insisted needed pharmaceuticals. Of course, Cheryl didn't know anything about the affair.

Barbara called Gail rather than Doug because one side effect of the guilt from the affair was Gail always took her calls and was extremely solicitous and attentive. Ironically, that over-the-top caring courteousness is what made her suspicious in the first place.

'Gail, I haven't spoken with Doug yet today and I thought I would check with you first. How's he feeling?'

'He's better. He's much better. I saw him this morning. He said the fever broke in the night. He wants to go ahead with the dinner. I was just working with the cook. Are you going to be here?'

'No, things have changed; it doesn't look like I will be.'

Yesterday Doug had a fever or said he did. It was impossible to tell any more, though he did sound sick.

'Was he coughing this morning?'

'Bit of hacking.'

'Did he take anything for it?'

'No, you know him.'

Maybe she did once, but not any more. Barbara was quiet and then said, 'I'll let you get back to the menu.'

'No hurry, I'm fine.'

New York investment banker types liked to ski in January, so this is when Doug usually entertained the ones he needed. No doubt the two bankers coming to dinner tonight were both wealthy and incredibly boring. No doubt they would talk their cars and their houses. That they even got called bankers was a joke to Barbara. They were more like hustlers in expensive clothes. They worked where the money was. That was their whole secret. All their smug certainty came from that and trained as she was in finance she had learned that few of them really understood numbers.

Barbara had paused too long and Gail was a little curt asking, 'Shall I give him a message?'

'No, don't worry about it. I'll call him later. When is he due home?'

'At six thirty. Dinner is at seven thirty.'

'Tell him I'm out this afternoon but will call him later tonight.'

'Should I tell him a time?'

Barbara hesitated. She wanted to leave her guessing. It was her way of making her presence felt, her scream.

'I don't know what time yet, but it'll be after his dinner.'

'We'll miss you here tonight.'

'Are you eating with them?'

'No, of course not, and I didn't mean to sound as if I was. I may be in the kitchen helping though. Doug said tonight is very important.'

They are all very important until they don't matter any more, Barbara thought. She hung up without another word and now felt like she might faint. She didn't know why she bothered to make the call. She couldn't believe her marriage had come to this and sat for an hour without moving, without knowing what she should do next.

Then her thoughts returned to the homicide inspector's questions. She scrolled through her cell directory to the name Lisa Chou and called it as she rose and walked unsteadily back down the hallway to the great room. It rang four times before he picked up.

When Larry answered she said, 'It's me. A San Francisco homicide inspector visited me this morning. They're working the case again. He wanted to know if you moved the body or removed a wallet.'

'What did you tell him?'

'That I wasn't watching you.'

'Barbara, what's wrong?'

What's wrong, everything is wrong, she thought, you, Doug, almost everything I've done with my life is wrong.

'He and his partner run the Cold Case Unit for San Francisco. He said they have new information.'

'Good for them.'

'They have a videotape of the killing.'

'They what?'

'They were sent a videotape.'

There was a very long quiet now and Larry's voice was the low flat one that used to sometimes scare her when he asked, 'Well, how could that be?'

'I saw it. He brought a CD with him.'

'When did they get it?'

'Recently, and he wanted to surprise me with it.'

'Are you all right?'

'I'm fine.'

Larry wouldn't ask any more than that about her. He didn't care at all about her. He probably never had. If she said she was considering killing herself he'd insist she get help, but he wouldn't feel anything.

'They'll do a little bit of investigation and then give up,' he said. 'It'll go back to being a dormant file.'

'You figure it out. It's yours to deal with.'

'I'll take care of it, but there's nothing to worry about. There never was. You built all this in your head. I'll find out what's going on and the homicide inspector isn't going to get anywhere. He's going through the motions. The bottom line is everyone has bigger problems to worry about in 2011 than a dead ex-Secret Service agent killed in 1989.'

Barbara thought about Raveneau. She thought about his eyes. She saw the video in her head. She saw Krueger fall. She couldn't stop the next words from coming out.

'In all the time we were married you were never once truthful with me. You were always controlling, but you aren't as good at it as you imagine you are. You say there's nothing to worry about but this inspector is smarter than you. Do you know why Inspector Govich came to Canada?'

'There was never anything you ever had to worry about. You didn't do anything wrong. You've obsessed on this way too long and it's not going to go anywhere now. The homicide inspector is just going through the motions.'

'You already said that.'

'I'm saying it again to make sure you hear me.'

'Inspector Govich flew to Calgary because a witness phoned them after we went home. They couldn't get the witness to come in. He wanted to remain anonymous but said he heard shots. He left them a message with the time of day he heard the shots. He checked his watch. Inspector Govich came to Canada because the time was very close to when we said we found the body. That was the real reason he wanted to re-interview us.'

'What's this current murder cop's name?'

She reached over to the coffee table and picked up his card. 'Benjamin Raveneau.'

'Spell the last name.'

She did and her head was floating, Doug lying to her, Doug sleeping with that bitch who had wormed her way into their lives. Doug was happy to get her calls because it told him where she was and meant she wouldn't bother him for several more hours. He probably got a text from Gail as soon as she hung up. And Larry had always lied to her. Nothing was real. She couldn't believe anything, not even herself. Her whole life was false. She was just a form of property stored in the house here.

'I could answer some of his questions,' she said. 'I could end that part.'

Larry was quiet for several seconds before answering, 'It all ended quite awhile ago and it's very troubling to hear you talk like this. Do you really want to risk the life you have?'

Yes, she thought, I want to risk it all.

'Don't take any more calls from the inspector and I'll look into it. Don't say anything to anyone until we talk again. Can you do that? I think it's important that nothing more get said and I'll ask for help. You don't need to worry. How's the skiing?'

She looked out the window at the skiers in the far distance. She pressed End and cut the call off. She had lived and slept with him. That seemed impossible now.

TWELVE

La Rosa was in her car on her way to Santa Rosa to sit next to an elderly woman and take her cold arthritic hand with its misshapen and swollen knuckles into her warm hands.

Then she would tell her bones found during a construction excavation seven months ago were a positive DNA match for her daughter who had disappeared forty-two years ago. The daughter was a fifteen year old runaway in 1969 and though the rest of the world forgot about the girl long ago, her mother couldn't.

The last time la Rosa saw her she revealed the fantasy world she had constructed. Her daughter had fallen in love with an Australian and lived in an unnamed remote area of the Outback without a phone. Marsha Fairchild had an answer for all the reasons why her daughter had never contacted her.

From a distance it was an inability to face the probable truth, but for all her toughness, la Rosa dreaded this meeting. She was in her car north of the Bay Area driving through hills south of Santa Rosa where the cell reception was poor. Her focus was on what she was going to say to convince the woman when Raveneau called.

'Govich was right. There's something there.'

'Did you get anything we can use?'

'Not yet. Hold on, I've got a call coming in from the lieutenant.'

Raveneau knew immediately from the lieutenant's tone that something had happened.

'Inspector, where are you?'

'Vallejo.'

'I need you here.'

Traffic was lightening. He was moving at fifty miles per hour and it was picking up.

'There's been a shooting at a cabinet shop on Sixteenth Street, three dead and one dying. I need you and la Rosa to help secure the scene.'

'Where's the one who is still alive?'

'With paramedics on his way to the hospital, but you go straight to Sixteenth. Where's your partner?'

'On her way to Santa Rosa.'

'Oh, that's right.'

'Tell her to come to Sixteenth when she's done there. I'm going to tell Inspector Ortega you're on your way.'

Ortega and Hagen were on-call, so caught the case. Raveneau still checked the board. He kept track of who was on-call and who was backup, but he and la Rosa no longer were. Unless something like this happened, they stayed on the cold cases.

Becker hung up. Raveneau told la Rosa.

'Disgruntled employee?' she asked.

'Becker doesn't know.'

A few minutes later he was talking to Bruce Ortega.

'The saws were still running when we got here. The owner of the shop returned from measuring a kitchen cabinet job, found one of his employees lying in a pool of blood and called 911. That call came in at 1:47. He had left to go to his appointment for the kitchen project at 12:15 and according to him all four employees were here and working when he left. The employees agreed to come in early today and not break for lunch until two, and then work until seven tonight because they were late on a delivery. He says measuring for a new project was his only appointment today. Otherwise he was there to help finish this one. Are you with me so far?'

'Sure. He left at 12:15 and called 911 at 1:47.'

'That's right, and the window is even narrower because there was a plywood delivery signed for by one of the victims at 1:07. The delivery time is on the receipt. We haven't verified anything yet, but it appears the victims were shot between 1:07 and when the owner got back, so call it a twenty-five minute window.'

'What's the owner's name?'

'David Khan. Khan's Cabinets. We've got him here.'

'What about the one that went to the hospital?'

'He was dead when he left here. It looks as if the shooter walked through from one end of the building to the other. It's a mess. How far away are you?'

'Half an hour.'

'See you here.'

When Raveneau arrived he was the fifth homicide inspector on the scene and Ortega didn't need him. He walked the building. It was long, rectangular, an old wood frame resting on a concrete slab foundation. Two rolling doors opened on to trucking bays on Sixteenth Street. The truck that delivered the plywood backed into one of these bays just after one o'clock this afternoon. They needed to find the driver of the delivery truck.

One victim, possibly the first, was a young man who looked

like he was shot while cutting a piece of plywood on a table saw. Two CSI teams were here but they hadn't gotten to him yet. Raveneau saw the spray of blood along the length of plywood. His body lay on the gray concrete near the metal table legs of the saw. A pool of blood darkened near his head. The pool had spread and mixed with sawdust. He wore a black long-sleeved T-shirt with the sleeves slid up to the elbows. On his inside left forearm was a tattoo of a martini glass. His black hair was on the long side and tied. He wore jeans as did the next victim.

That victim was older, forty to forty-five, short hair, thick neck, thick shoulders, and looked like he'd worked with his hands all his life. The entry wounds at the back of his skull were close together. Raveneau guessed the shooter came right up behind him, and like the previous victim he was shot in the chest, then in the head, and probably in the chest first, Raveneau thought, one in the heart, one in the head. He had pitched forward on to the cabinet he was working on then slid down. A cordless drill lay nearby.

Raveneau checked out the space again, a long rectangle with rooms divided according to the work being done. At one end was the owner's office. In the bay nearest it finished cabinets were stacked ready to deliver. Adjacent to that was the bay where this victim was. His name was Dan Oliver. He was the one who had signed for delivery of the finish-grade plywood. That meant he used the forklift to unload the plywood and then drove it down to the far end of the building where materials were stored and where the forklift was parked now. After parking the forklift he made it back to here and started work on the cabinet. All that must have taken several minutes and Raveneau turned to Ortega.

'Where's the delivery truck driver? Where are we at on him?'

'We're trying to locate him. He did his last delivery before we called his boss.'

'He would know whether Oliver signed first.'

Ortega didn't respond, instead asked, 'What else do you see?'

The third victim was a woman in her early thirties named Amber Diaz. She was about five foot four, one hundred thirty pounds, a masculine look to her, and a bloody trail. After being shot she tried to escape and the shooter had stepped on blood droplets as he moved in. She was also chest shot and Raveneau wondered if she had then ducked her head. She made it halfway across the room and by then was bleeding badly from the trough a bullet plowed through her scalp. When the shooter caught up to her he put one through her skull, and yet it appeared from blood smears that after that she convulsed on the floor. Hers was the most affecting for Raveneau because though wounded she fought to live.

'He shot all four but didn't wait for the owner,' Ortega said. 'What do you make of that?'

'I don't know.'

What struck Raveneau most was the narrow window of time the shooter was operating with and the improbability of the coincidental timing. He talked with Ortega about that as they moved to where the last victim fell and the paramedics worked on him before taking him to the hospital. Pieces of alder trim were scattered. Ortega pointed at the bloody concrete where they worked on him.

'He was sixteen, a boy. Wrong place, wrong time, should have listened to his mother and stayed in school. She arrived as they were loading him. They don't live far from here.'

'Where's the owner?'

'In his office down there at the end and his wife and lawyer are on the way.'

'Let's get him out of here. Let's see if we can get him to go in with us right now.'

Raveneau knew Ortega didn't really want his help. It was Ortega's to solve with Hagen, Gibbs, and Montoya. With the new way of doing things they would all work as one team, and Raveneau had a reputation of liking to work alone. No one really believed that he and la Rosa got on as well as they did.

'Why don't I go find the plywood delivery guy and bring him in,' Raveneau offered.

'We've already talked to his employer. We're working on that.'

'But we should have heard something more by now.'

Ortega stopped on that. He wanted to say no, but knew it was true, and in the end Ortega probably liked the idea of getting him out of the building.

'OK, Raveneau, go find him.'

THIRTEEN

Raveneau called the trucking company owner from his car while still parked down the street from the cabinet shop. He heard an edge of exasperation and pictured a man used to giving orders, not answering questions.

'You are Inspector who?'

'Raveneau.'

'Look, Raveneau, I understand it's a terrible situation, but I talked to another homicide inspector an hour ago. Don't you people talk to each other? I gave him the name of the driver and his cell number. The driver's name is John Drury. Tomorrow is his day off, so I'm not sure where he is.'

'I've called the number you gave Inspector Ortega and I get voicemail. Will Drury answer if you call him?'

'It depends.'

'Put me on hold and try.'

Drury didn't answer the call from his boss either, but Raveneau had a home address from the Department of Motor Vehicles. He was still talking to the owner as he started driving toward the Bay Bridge. The owner was explaining his system.

'I have them report in when they reach a delivery site and as they leave. That way if there are any problems I know about it immediately.'

'Do you record the time?'

'It gets recorded automatically.'

'Will you check and tell me what time he got to the cabinet shop and what time he left? Also, the deliveries that came after, you said he made two more and then he was off. Is that correct?'

'It is. Hold on, while I get that for you.'

A few minutes later he gave Raveneau 1:19 p.m. as the time the driver left the cabinet shop.

'So when he makes that call he's on the road.'

'Yes, or just starting to the next stop. My rule is don't call me when you're about to leave. Call me after you've made the delivery and are rolling toward your next one. I don't care if you're going one mile per hour, I just want to know you are done with the one behind you, you've got a signature for the delivery, and what the problems were, if any.'

'Where does he usually go when his shift ends?'

'Their personal lives are their own. Drury has a girlfriend. I'm not sure where she lives. He goes there nowadays, I think. Or he goes home. But when he gets off work it's his life. I expect them to relax.'

'Not today.'

'No, I understand, Inspector, and I'll keep trying him.'

'He's a critical link in our timeline. It's important that we get to sit and talk with him while the day is still fresh in his memory.'

Raveneau gave the trucking company owner his cell number and thanked him several times before hanging up. By the time he reached the bridge and crawled up the onramp in traffic it was dusk. The bridge was slow and traffic heavier still as he worked his way south on 880. Drury's address was in San Leandro. It was well after dark when Raveneau stopped down the street from a small stucco house with an asphalt roof and a bare front yard. Six or seven years ago it would have sold for half a million dollars. That seemed unbelievable now.

A window at the front threw yellow light from around the corners of the curtains. The delivery truck sat at the curb tilting slightly toward the gutter, its bed empty, the truck a large presence in the neighborhood. Raveneau watched the front curtains as he called Drury's cell again. This time a man answered and sounded both suspicious and cautious. After Raveneau identified himself, Drury's tone changed. He apologized.

'Sorry, I didn't have my phone with me. My boss just called and said you're trying to get a hold of me, but all I did was drop a load of plywood and leave.'

'Yeah, but we need to sit with you and go through the timeline.'

'I'm with my girlfriend and on our way to her house in Santa Cruz so it's going to have to be tomorrow, guy.'

'It can't wait.'

'It's going to have to. It's like my one day off and I don't know anything anyway. I'm not going to be able to tell you anything. I was there and gone, man. It was like one unit of plywood and the older dude there unloaded it. You got the delivery time from my boss, right? He said he gave it to you.'

'I need to sit and talk with you tonight.'

'Not going to happen, and besides, whoever wasted them did it after I left.'

'Where's the truck you delivered the plywood with?'

'Parked in front of my house.'

'Where are the keys to it?'

'With me, and what's with the truck? What do you need the truck for?'

'Where are you in Santa Cruz? I'll come to you and we can talk and I'll get the keys to the truck from you then.'

'This is getting weird. It's like you're suspicious of me or something.'

'Four people were murdered and other than the killer you may have been the last person to see them alive, but you don't think it's important for you to let us interview you today. It's more important that you spend time with your girlfriend.'

'I didn't say that.'

'You're avoiding us, and yeah, that makes me wonder about you.'

'You've got everything already.'

'You keep saying that.'

Now the lights went off in the front room of the house and Raveneau watched the front door open. He couldn't read the face of the man coming out of the house until he passed under a street light. Then he knew it was Drury. Raveneau watched him climb into an old green Honda Accord parked in front of the delivery truck and pull away with his lights off. He didn't turn his headlights on until he reached the end of the block. But before that he told Raveneau he would come to the Homicide office at noon tomorrow and hung up.

Raveneau followed him to a rundown strip mall across the freeway and north where Drury parked his car away from the light poles and walked across a broken asphalt lot to a bar called Pete's Corner. He went through the door beneath the red neon sign and Raveneau waited five minutes before following. Inside, he moved to the long dark bar and ordered a beer. It smelled like beer and the cleaner they used to wash the linoleum floor. John Drury was in the back near a pool table talking with two other men. A moment later Raveneau's phone buzzed.

'Where are you?' la Rosa asked.

'At a place called Pete's Corner. I'm watching the driver who delivered plywood to the cabinet shop this afternoon. I drove to his house looking for him and he took off while he was on the phone to me.'

'Should I come there?'

'No.'

'Then so what are you going to do?'

'Not sure yet.'

'But you're sure it's him?'

'It's him.'

'If he's trying to avoid us, you need me with you.'

'I'll call you back. He's watching me now.'

The bartender was at the far end of the bar talking with a couple of women and Raveneau had taken a table so he could talk to la Rosa. But now he moved back up to the bar. He sipped the beer and texted Ortega as Drury moved in on the two women and the bartender navigated very full cocktails to a safe landing in front of the women. Before turning to his next order the bartender asked Drury, 'Do you want another?'

'Only if they buy,' Drury said, meaning the women and the one nearest him laughed and said she would. They all laughed and Drury said, 'I'll be right back. I'm going out for a quick smoke.'

A couple of minutes passed and Raveneau felt like a fool when he saw the headlights come on. By the time he came out the door Drury was already pulling on to the road, and he hustled toward his car keeping an eye on Drury's tail lights, watching him pass through one light then another, growing smaller as he accelerated away.

FOURTEEN

Ortega listened to Raveneau's account of getting burned by John Drury and then asked, 'Where are you now?'

'I've gone back to his house. I've got a tow truck on the way and the police here are going to help. The tow driver will get the delivery truck open.'

The San Leandro police sent two units and with Raveneau's urging kept their lights off and the residue test and subsequent search went down with a low profile and fairly fast. When the steering wheel didn't have any gunpowder residue Raveneau doubted they would find residue anywhere. He pulled an old coat out of his trunk and put that on before crawling under the delivery truck with a Maglite.

Despite the trucking business owner's rap about running a tight ship, the truck didn't look well maintained mechanically. In several places the asphalt and curb were dark with oil. That said Drury parked here regularly. Raveneau couldn't avoid getting oil on the back of his coat and pants as he worked his way along with the flashlight beam. He snagged and tore the coat as he crawled back out, and there was Ortega standing above him in a suit and long raincoat.

'You're getting a full day in, Raveneau.'

'I'm trying to figure out if there's another reason he's avoiding us.'

'Anything in the cab?'

'Nothing.'

If anything, the truck was suspiciously clean, the rubber mats scoured, carpet shampooed and vacuumed, as groomed as Drury who at the bar wore a neatly ironed black hoodie. Raveneau carried an image of the lanky pushback from the bar, the casual pulling of his cigarettes from the pocket of the hoodie, wagging them at the women without once glancing at him. Drury worked at it.

But now it was 3:00 a.m. Raveneau and Ortega were in Raveneau's car, and Ortega was tapping away on his laptop writing a search warrant.

'Give me some help here, Raveneau.'

'We're not going to get in his house.'

'Sure, we are.'

Ortega was intent on trying the on-call judge.

'It's one thing to get into a truck that was at the crime scene in or around the time of the murders, but a judge isn't going to give you the house. All we can say is that he delivered plywood.'

'Four dead and Drury was the last guy to see them alive. He's evading us.'

'That's legal.'

But Ortega was juiced. He wanted to try. He finished the search warrant app, emailed it back to the Southern precinct station, and it got faxed to the on-call judge at 4:30 as Raveneau stood outside in the cold wind. He listened to Ortega talk to the judge now. Ortega's voice got louder when he got nervous and judges made him nervous. Raveneau listened and then his mind drifted to the country and something he had read about birthers going after the President today. What was that really about? It wasn't about a birth certificate. More like they needed to make Obama an outsider. But why did they need to do that? Why was that so important to them? What scared him about the birthers was the quiet encouragement they got from people who carefully avoided acknowledging the birth issue was false.

Dark thoughts. He had to shake them off. He heard Ortega still talking too loudly, repeating a phone number back to the judge. He listened and then walked away from the car. He was stiff from crawling under the truck. He was cold and tired and the late night wore on him in a way it didn't when he was younger.

When he walked back Ortega was on a call from a *New York Times* reporter. His door was open and his face had relaxed. Raveneau looked from Ortega to Drury's house aware that they might be completely spinning their wheels here. He'd known truckers who moved drugs and in truth that's what he was looking for underneath the vehicle, the storage compartment, the welded-on container. Drury getting out of his house fast after a call from a cop could have as easily been that as anything to do with the murders.

He was close to telling Ortega to take his interview outside or to his own car, and pictured driving from here to Celeste's and having breakfast with her. He was hungry. He was tired and agitated to the point of anger. He had disliked listening to Ortega laugh at the reporter's jokes.

He could reheat Celeste's bread soup for breakfast, chicken broth, vegetables, and chunks of bread, olive oil, and good coffee. Good coffee was what he wanted now, and to focus on Krueger or have the room to run with this aspect of the cabinet shop shootings. He didn't need Ortega's help. He still didn't get why Ortega drove down here.

From behind him, Ortega said, 'You were right, the judge said no.'

'Well, you tried.'

'Yeah, it was worth it.'

Was it? Raveneau glanced at Ortega but saw bodies on the cold concrete of the cabinet shop floor. The shooter came up from behind. The shooter liked the feeling of getting close. Raveneau could sense that.

'I'll ask the locals to drive by every hour or so,' Raveneau said. 'Drury will come home. He's supposed to drop the truck back at the yard tomorrow afternoon.'

Ortega said nothing and Raveneau knew he'd head back to the Homicide office. It was without question the biggest investigation he'd ever run. Raveneau drove slowly back up a quiet freeway and across the bridge to San Francisco. He didn't wake until after nine that morning and stood at the roof parapet with his coffee and his phone, looking at the city and the bay, a habit. A cool wind blew this morning and the sky was a pale blue when he drove to the Hall.

He knew the captain and Lieutenant Becker would sit with Ortega this morning and decide who stayed on the Khan Cabinets murders and who didn't. And that's what happened. Ortega came to him and said they would work the Drury angle together, but that the rest of the investigation was covered and he could focus on his cold cases.

He was on the phone later in the morning with the storage company in Arizona that held United Airlines' long term corporate records when the San Leandro police called. Drury was home but hadn't gone into the house. He'd gotten out of his car and was in the truck and the engine was on. Raveneau asked if they could have an officer follow him and call if he got on the freeway and let him know what direction he was headed.

He had to apologize to the woman at the storage company for the interruption, but she was fine with it and he asked, 'When was Jim Frank employed?'

'1978 to 1995. He retired in 1995.'

'I'm looking for contact information. Do your records show any supervisors or people he worked with?'

'I don't have any of that but there might be a way I could get it for you. To do that you'll need to fill out a form we use with law enforcement and the IRS. I can fax it to you. You want to mark it urgent. There's a box on the form that you need to check.'

'If there's a box, doesn't everybody mark urgent?'

'You'd be surprised.'

She laughed and he filled out the form, sent it back to her. He was still in the office when the call came to verify he worked as a homicide inspector for SFPD. That she was able to find a Jim Frank made him hopeful. He was on the phone when Cynthia buzzed from the front desk to tell him a San Leandro police officer was holding.

Raveneau picked up and the officer said, 'He just got on the freeway headed north in the truck.'

FIFTEEN

L a Rosa rode with him to the Branson Trucking Company yard in Martinez. She was rested and relaxed and looked a lot better than she sounded after the meeting with the elderly woman in Santa Rosa. Marsha Fairchild had rocked back and forth with her eyes closed and arms wrapped around her chest as sobs racked her. When it was over, La Rosa left feeling that she had done nothing for the woman other than to destroy her hope.

But now, la Rosa seemed to be rebounding, taking it on herself to determine whether he was helping Celeste enough.

'What are you doing to help her get it open?'

'The floor out in the bar is reclaimed wood that got refinished. That's done and we're moving chairs and tables around tonight. She finally passed inspection with the Health Department. That's the one she's been sweating.'

'What about the thing with the flue? Weren't you going to do something?'

'No, with the flue she was forced to use the landlord's contractor. He ripped her off but it got done.'

'So she's going to make it.'

'There's still a lot to happen, but it's looking better.'

'I'm sure she needs your help.' When Raveneau didn't answer that, she moved on. 'So what about this Drury? Tell me again what he delivered.'

'Forty-two pieces of finish-grade larch plywood.'

'Larch?'

'Type of tree.'

The delivery time was on the receipt. The receipt was in the second drawer down on the left side of Khan's desk, though now it was in the Homicide office.

'We know when he got there,' Raveneau said. 'We know when he left. Today we want details about the rest of his day. We want to know about his other deliveries. We want everything about what he did yesterday.'

They dropped off the freeway, the offramp dipping down to Highway 4. They were probably fifteen minutes from Branson's yard. Raveneau turned to her.

'He's going to recognize me. He's going to realize he was right last night in the bar. That's going to unsettle him.'

'OK, but let's do the time frame once more. He delivered the plywood at 1:07 and the delivery receipt is signed at 1:15. He called his boss at 1:19 as he was leaving.'

'That's right, and we want to know about the rest of his day.'

'And David Khan left the meeting where he was measuring kitchen cabinets at 1:21, give or take a few minutes, and that's been verified by both the owner and the designer.'

'Yeah, that's what Ortega's team says.'

'We're not part of the team?'

'Other than with Drury he doesn't want any help, and Drury only because I've already stuck my nose in.'

'Did you and Ortega have a problem last night?'

'No.'

'OK, who checked out the route the cabinet shop owner says he took to come back to the shop?'

'Hagen did. He drove it three times and thinks Khan would have gotten back right around 1:40, which fits with Khan's story. He called 911 at 1:47, so that fits too. But if he got back sooner, say, 1:30 to 1:35, and he didn't call for another twenty minutes or so, then that's a little odd.'

'Could Khan be the shooter?'

'The medical examiner doesn't think so. The paramedics got there within five minutes of the call and blood was already drying.' Raveneau pointed at the sign ahead as he slowed. 'Here we are.' Then turning into the trucking yard he added, 'This is probably our one interview and then Ortega will take over.'

'Bruce Ortega is a good inspector.'

'And a wonderful father and husband.'

'You're in a bad mood today.'

'I'm fine.'

Branson's yard was on Industrial Parkway, an asphalt road with oil refineries as a backdrop. A fourteen foot high chain-link fence topped with razor wire marked the borders. Raveneau studied the razor wire a moment as they got out of the car. It was as serious as a prison fence.

The owner, Hap Branson, turned out to be one of those guys whose face looks older than the rest of him by twenty years. He was in his early forties, a former trucker and probably tough on the guys that worked for him. Within ten minutes of meeting he told them his story, the trucking business that went under in the recession, not the Great Recession but the one before it.

'It took me years to get back on my feet. I lost everything, but now I've got sixteen drivers.'

'How long has John Drury driven for you?'

'Four years and with no accidents or major incidents, though he's got a temper. Once or twice he's got into it with someone we've delivered to.' He pointed out the window. 'He's here. Why don't you come in here and sit down and I'll talk to John and let him know what's going to happen.'

Branson led them into his meeting room. It held an aged oak

table with folding chairs and a floor with a chocolate brown carpet that smelled heavily of dogs. The ceiling was acoustic tile, several of which were yellow from leaks, but everything about Branson said he was serious about his business and it didn't surprise Raveneau that the room was without frills.

When Drury walked in he was already fuming, no doubt feeling his boss set him up. He directed his anger at Raveneau.

'I don't care if you're a homicide inspector or the fucking mayor of San Francisco. Back off. Why were you following me last night? What have I done wrong?'

'I've got two questions for you before I answer the rest of that. The first is, why did you lie to me last night, and why do you have a problem helping us figure out why four people were murdered?'

'You can't put it on me. All I did was deliver fucking plywood. What were you doing following me?'

'You were on the phone lying to me and I wondered where you were going. Right now, your credibility is suspect. You need to change that.'

Drury snorted and turned to Branson, saying, 'This is total bullshit and I don't have to do this.'

'You're right,' Raveneau said. 'You don't have to say a word to us. You can completely blow us off and after you do that we'll focus harder on you.'

Drury looked past Raveneau at the window and rubbed the back of his neck.

'I might be dead too, right. I might be fucking dead if I got there later. That freaked me out last night. I couldn't deal with a lone cop coming to talk to me. I didn't even know if you were real.'

'You weren't sure I was a homicide inspector?'

La Rosa entered the conversation, her voice soft and without any combativeness.

'We've seen homicides where people just missed being in the wrong spot. It can cause a lot of anxiety.'

Drury ignored her. He pointed a finger at Raveneau.

'Last night I knew you had me in mind and I thought you were going to try to kill me. I had all these kind of weird ideas. You said you were a homicide inspector but I talked to a different inspector earlier, and I was picturing you as the killer coming back to get me. You know, like you just missed me when you killed everyone. That's what weirded me out in the bar. That's why I took off.'

'Makes a kind of sense,' Raveneau said and didn't believe a word of it. 'Let's talk through the time frame of your delivery. We know when you phoned in. We know when the foreman there logged your arrival and signed the delivery receipt. We know when you called in and said you were done and on the road to the next delivery. Did you call anyone else as you drove away?'

'What do you mean?'

'What I just asked, did you make any other phone calls between your delivery in San Francisco and your next one in San Jose?'

'No, I hauled ass to San Jose. I was late.'

'Do you have more than one phone?'

'No.'

'What do you mean you were late?'

'I was late all day.' He nodded toward his boss. 'We can't go more than forty hours a week. Yesterday was the end of my week.'

'How late were you running?'

'Twenty minutes.' He gestured toward his boss again. 'When you call in a delivery he tells you how you're running.' After a beat he showed his anger toward Branson, adding, 'He's on our ass all the time.'

'So you must have checked the time when you left to see how you were doing.'

'No, man, there's nothing I can do about traffic. I tried to make up some here and there but I don't sweat the shit I can't control. Like that book, don't sweat the small shit.'

'Let's start with your first delivery yesterday. Take us through your whole day.'

He did it but in a sketchy way and Raveneau returned to details of the plywood delivery to Khan's Cabinets. How long for the forklift to move the plywood? Did he do anything else while he was there? Did he see anybody else in the neighborhood that caught his eye? Did he stop anywhere else as he left for food or coffee or a soda? When he heard about it on the radio what station was he listening to?

'Do you own any guns?'

'Excuse me?'

'Do you own a gun?'

'I have two and they're registered.'

'Do you own a nine millimeter?'

'No.'

'How are you as a marksman?'

'Decent.'

'Do you have a shooting range you go to?'

'Bailey Gun Range.'

'How often do you practice?'

'Maybe twice a year, but I don't think that's any of your business. Do you know what a sovereign citizen is?'

'That's about all the time we get at the range too,' la Rosa said, and eased it all down again. She explained that four people were murdered and they had to ask every question of everyone.

'It's not just you.' She paused. 'But other than the killer you're the last person to see them alive so we'll have to keep working with you. You're our nearest link to what happened.'

She showed a worried look. She turned empathetic.

'I know it's not fun to be questioned like this.'

'It sucks.'

'We understand, but we have to talk to everybody and we really need your help.'

'You need more than my help. You people suck. Four people got wasted and you're following me around. If you're following me you're incompetent. You know, you should be doing something else, being a meter maid.'

Raveneau watched his face change.

'I'm the taxpayer. I drive all day. I hustle and what do you do? You get to retire early with your fat pensions. Fuck this.' He turned to Branson. 'And fuck you for setting me up. I'm going to do the lawyer thing. I'm not talking any more. I'm out of here.'

Raveneau knew they were done but la Rosa tried again.

'We need your help. I can't say that enough. I can understand you being angry, but four people were murdered and we need your help. The questions might feel accusatory but they actually clear you of suspicion.'

'Why would there be suspicion of me?'

'It's what I said before, you were the last person to see them and you have to understand that we work from the last known thing. We know you were there. We're trying to get from when you left there to the killer.'

'You're just looking for someone to arrest, but it's not going to be me.' His face reddened as he said, 'Have I ever fired a nine millimeter? Go ask old man Bailey who's a killer shot.'

'I'll ask him,' Raveneau said.

'Oh, I know you will.' He focused on Branson again. 'I'm giving you notice. I quit as of right now. I'm done with this crap.'

He reached in his jacket and pulled out a key ring, then dropped it on the table, his focus on his boss now.

'You set me up and I quit and I want my last check right now. Get your fat ass up and get your checkbook.'

Branson got to his feet but he didn't look like he was going for his checkbook. He dropped his arms to his sides and balled his fists.

'You'll get your check when I'm ready and not before.'

'I'll go to the Labor Board.'

'Then get going. Get off my property before I teach you a lesson.'

SIXTEEN

I t escalated rapidly and Raveneau knocked his chair over as he stepped away from the table. Branson and Drury were yelling and already out in the front office, Drury trying to get to Branson's desk.

'Ben, wait.'

La Rosa reached for his arm and was too late, and if Raveneau heard her, he didn't give any sign. He followed them out and now Branson was in Drury's face yelling, spittle flying on to Drury. Drury was the longer bigger man, but he didn't have Branson's low thick leverage and she watched as Branson took a boxing stance like someone out of an old black and white movie. His face was solid, fists up, shoulders thick as a bear. He threw a hard punch catching Drury under the right side of his chin with a loud smacking that staggered Drury. He stuttered, stepped back, and almost went down.

'Get the fuck off my property you sonofabitch!'

Drury wobbled to the wall behind him and then stared at Branson with a look that was eerie. Raveneau picked up on that and stepped between them as Drury moved sideways. La Rosa watched him grab a trophy displayed on a shelf on the wall, some sort of industry thing, an insurance company sponsored award for the firm with the most miles without an accident. She read the inscription when she and Raveneau first arrived. Drury grabbed it off the shelf with his right and punched out the window nearest him with the trophy's heavy base. Glass shattered and fell on the concrete outside.

He swung the trophy first at Raveneau, then at Branson, and Raveneau moved. He moved like nothing she'd ever seen in him before. Raveneau was maybe six foot one, and you didn't know it looking at him, but he was very quick when he needed to be. She learned that playing one-on-one basketball against him, and she'd played point guard at Santa Clara College. But Raveneau wasn't young. He was in his fifties. Drury caught Branson on the left bicep with a corner of the trophy, and then he was on the ground, the trophy across the room and Raveneau leaning over him, repeating, 'You don't want to take this any farther.'

'I'm going to call the local police,' la Rosa pulled her cell as Branson begged her not to.

'Please don't, I just want him out of here.'

'He was swinging at your head. I'm going to call it in.'

'I just want him out of the yard.'

She glanced at Raveneau. She read his eyes. She called it in.

'I'm not pressing charges,' Branson said. 'I don't work that way. We settle things like men. Get out of here,' he told Drury, and Raveneau answered.

'He waits.'

A police report got written and Drury didn't say anything, not a single word. He was handcuffed and led to the back of a Martinez police cruiser. She watched him try to stare down Raveneau before the cop holding him pushed him into the back seat.

'You OK?' Raveneau asked Branson.

'I'm fine.'

'Is he going to come back here?'

'I'll get his check cut, that'll end it. He got into it with another driver at a fuel stop a few years ago and I believed his version, but I don't think I should have. He's got a thing about him. On some mornings he's angry at the whole world. He doesn't think he should be driving. He said something to me once and I thought he was joking and laughed and it made him angry for three weeks.'

'Yeah, what was that?'

'Oh, he said Elvis Presley was a truck driver before he was a successful singer and he was better than Elvis and that he was going to become an actor. There's some movie star he thinks he looks like. He had photos taken of himself. He showed them to me and other drivers here and sent them to a talent agency. When they didn't contact him and weren't taking his calls he got angry. I had to sit down and talk with him about it.'

'When was this?' la Rosa asked.

'Last spring, April, right around tax time, and he had a two thousand dollar charge on a credit card for the photos. He was very angry about that.'

She wanted to know more about them.

'What were they? What kind of photos? Were they head shots, poses, what were they?'

'Some were head shots but one was in swim trunks that tied together in the front and it was kind of loosened like they were ready to come off. That's the photo they laughed at around here. But he got himself in great shape. What's the word used now? Ripped, he's ripped. He's strong.'

Branson turned to Raveneau. 'How did you take him down like that?' La Rosa didn't think Raveneau heard him. Raveneau was somewhere else. He was staring at the truck Drury delivered the plywood in. She pushed Branson to keep talking.

'He was looking at modeling also. He talked about getting his foot in the door.'

'Not happy as a driver.'

'That's not really true either. On and off, he was happy or

seemed to be and then he'd get blue and then angry. I've seen
this in other drivers. There's a point where life isn't quite working
out the way they expected and they get angry. I lost everything
and I picked myself back up off the floor. That's what you have
to do.'

'Has he ever threatened anybody here?'

Branson shook his head and la Rosa glanced at Raveneau who
was outside now at the truck.

'I think he really believed that talent agency was going to
call him. In the first week when he was waiting for their call
he was very upbeat, unnaturally so. Then he was just as down.'

Raveneau came back in and they left a few minutes later. That
afternoon he and la Rosa sat down with Ortega and Hagen. Ortega
asked if they heard his press conference this morning. Raveneau
nodded.

'We heard you on the radio on the way out.'

'How did I sound?'

'Like you're doing your best and you're handling the media
but that we have no idea who killed four cabinet makers or why
they did it.'

That quieted the room. It sent a signal from Raveneau to Ortega
and she wondered why he was as hard as he was sometimes. Or
maybe it wasn't being hard. Maybe it was the truth. Either way,
Ortega's feelings were hurt and Ortega wasn't a bad guy. He was
a good inspector and it was just a style thing with him and
Raveneau.

Raveneau didn't care whether everybody liked him or not. He
had no problem telling Ortega now, 'I didn't hear you ask for
the public's help. We don't need to be talking to the media telling
them what we don't know. We need someone who saw something
unusual on Sixteenth Street to come forward.'

'All right, Ben, but I've still got to talk to the press. How did
the Drury interview get so screwed up?'

'I pushed him when I didn't need to. He wants to be appreci-
ated before anything else and I wasn't sending that signal. I was
asking for details of the day of the delivery and I should have
asked him first how he felt and apologized for following him.
He's that kind of guy.'

'That fits with something the owner said about his acting

aspirations,' said la Rosa, and then recounted what the trucking firm owner had told her.

'He may not be getting from society what he feels he's owed.'

Now Cynthia stuck her head in and said, 'Your friend Ryan Candel is holding for you.'

Raveneau stood. 'I've got to take this.'

As he left and shut the door, Ortega asked, 'So did Raveneau blow it today?'

Her first reaction was to defend her partner but she caught herself and tried to be objective. Everything mattered. The San Francisco Homicide Detail was basically nowhere on this case with a lot of pressure to solve it.

'He pushed him,' she said, 'but Drury didn't quit his job today because of Raveneau. He felt betrayed by his boss and said so. He said he was tricked into coming to the yard.'

'But Raveneau just said he blew it, that he was too aggressive?'

Now she did find herself defending her partner. He had a completely different style than her, and sure, he pushed Drury. But then as he did they saw a part of Drury they wouldn't have otherwise seen. Where it would go she didn't know and neither did anyone else in this room, but Raveneau had a way of getting people to reveal themselves and Ortega knew that the same as her. She figured Ortega was still smarting over the press conference comments.

'You and Ben are done on this one,' he said. 'We'll take over with Drury.'

'Sure.'

'After what happened, it makes sense, doesn't it.'

'I don't have any problem with it, it's your investigation.'

'Will Raveneau?'

She shook her head. He wouldn't. Before they walked in here Raveneau told her Ortega will take over Drury today.

'OK, so we're in agreement,' he said, and they were, but that's not how it worked out.

SEVENTEEN

'Hungry?' Raveneau asked Candel as they sat down at a table on the small deck above the sidewalk.

'I'm always hungry.'

'OK, order whatever you want and order me a beer and a burger. I'm buying. I've got to return a call but it won't take long. What made you call me? I didn't know if I'd hear from you again.'

'I remembered some other things.'

'Good. I want to hear about them. I'll be right back.'

Raveneau called the crime lab and asked for Lim but it was several minutes before Lim picked up. When he did, he said, 'Some information for you. The first is we got a good fingerprint from one of the photos.'

'It's probably mine.'

'It's not, I checked. Second is I scanned in that landscape photo and ran an app that compares a photo to a database of hundreds of thousands of photos. It comes up with a percentage probability of a location. The app recognized the terrain. It is the north-west shore of the Kohala coast on the Big Island. Check a map and you'll see there's one road that cuts through from above. That's where the photo was taken from. The last thing is I did more research and I'm sure these photos were taken between 1981 and 1990. I know you want it closer but that's the best I can do.'

'Thanks for what you've done.'

'What about the fingerprint? What do you want to do with it?'

'Put it somewhere safe. I hope to send you prints to compare it to very soon.'

When Raveneau came back out on to the deck he saw Candel had zipped his coat and turned up the collar. The sky was white with winter fog this afternoon and it was chill on the deck, but they could talk easily out here.

'Sorry I was drunk last time we met,' Candel said. 'I rip through cocktails way too fast.'

'I used to have that problem.'

'How did you get rid of it?'

'I started making sure my first drink lasted at least twenty minutes.'

'Like you just changed overnight?'

'Took about fifteen years.'

'Great.'

'You've got to want it.'

'I'm getting there.'

'You'll know when you're there.'

'Were you a cop then?'

'I've been one so long I don't remember what it's like not to be one. But cops are people, Ryan. Listen, I've got a question for you. If your dad turns out to be a good guy, how will you deal with that?'

'He won't be.'

'What if he is?'

'He and my mom had other problems. He dumped her but she was leaving anyway. He was big-time into political stuff, like seriously over-the-top right wing action, which was a major problem for her. His friends too, same deal with them. They had meetings and planned shit. That's what I didn't tell you that night.'

'In laid back Hawaii?'

'Yeah, it tripped her out. You should have talked to her about how laid back Dad and his ex-Nam buddies were.'

'Give me a story she told you?'

The waitress came out before Candel could answer. She brought the beers. When the deck door closed he said, 'The word they used was interdiction. They liked that word. They did interdictions and there was like a small group of them. She thought they killed two draft dodgers, American dudes who went to Canada. She thinks they killed them after the war was over, as in went up there and found them. She was pretty sure that happened.'

'This doesn't sound like your mom the way you've described her up until now. She doesn't sound as in love with Captain Frank.'

'She was. It's all true. What I told you was true. She mentioned this other stuff more as I got older.'

'Your mom loved him, so how bad could he be?'

'She also said he smuggled things for people in his luggage. I guess they didn't use to check a pilot's luggage. A pilot could like walk on a plane carrying his bag.'

'Any idea what he smuggled?'

'No clue.'

'OK, well, thanks for this and I'll do what I can to check out that Canada story.'

Truth was Raveneau was disappointed. After their earlier phone conversation he thought Candel had something more substantial. He pointed down the street toward the Ferry Building. 'There used to be a freeway here.'

'I kind of remember it.'

'Commuters would park in a lot underneath it. Alan Krueger was shot and killed not far from that lot and between two support pylons for the freeway. Very recently someone sent a videotape addressed to me, probably because I'm in the Cold Case Unit. It's a videotape of the shooting of Krueger.'

'Like a snuff film?'

'In a way I guess you could say that. But I think it was proof that Krueger had been dealt with, though I wonder if the shooter knew the video was being made. In the video is a partial profile of the shooter, not a very good one, but enhancement techniques are much better now and I've had photos of your dad compared.'

'I knew it.'

'It's not your dad. Your dad didn't shoot Alan Krueger. He may have known him but he didn't kill him. When your mom talked about his friends did you ever hear the name Alan Krueger, or any nickname that might sound something like his name? If your dad was called Captain Frank it's possible his friends had nicknames too.'

'I don't remember any.' He was quiet now then said, 'So he didn't kill this Krueger, but it's still weird stuff and he was around. I don't think he's going to turn out to be a good guy. I'm friggin' afraid of what I might find out about him.'

'Do you want to see this video to know what this case is about?'

'Why do you want to show it to me?'

'You were five years old in 1989 and that's old enough to have memories. Alan Krueger may have been a friend of your dad's. He may have known your mom, so seeing him might jar your memory. It's a longshot, but it's possible.'

But it was more than that. Raveneau was hoping Candel would feel something for the man gunned down and it would stay with him.

'OK, I'll do it, but when?'

'How about tomorrow?'

'I've got a music gig tonight. I'll be up all night.'

'Then call me in the late afternoon.'

'OK. All right, I'll call you. I want to know more about this. I want to know who this Krueger guy was.'

EIGHTEEN

As Celeste washed new bar glasses her face was lit and happy. She had passed the inspections. Bo, the new cook was there and with the lights down low, the space looked all but complete. And she was no longer looking for a big crowd on opening night. Raveneau wasn't sure why the shift in expectations had come, but it sounded right. She spoke of a soft opening and word of mouth to get people here. He worked alongside them setting up the back bar until late in the night.

Early the next morning he drove to the Hall. Ortega called as he got upstairs to Homicide. It gave Raveneau a chance to apologize.

'Sorry about yesterday afternoon. I know you've worked this thing non-stop.'

'No, I'm the asshole letting the press thing go to my head. This is the biggest investigation I've ever worked and I'm still trying to get my head around that. Despite what I said yesterday, I'm calling this morning to ask for your help. We're going to have to give Khan back the building in a couple of days. His lawyer is on us and now the judge is too. Khan is going to lose his business if he can't get in there and make cabinets, but I want to go through it again.'

'Search the building again?'

'Yes, and I'm wondering if you could come down and help us.'

'When?'

'Eight o'clock.'

'See you then.'

It was the last thing he wanted to do this morning and he'd come in early to get a clean start on the day. But at eight o'clock Raveneau stood behind the other inspectors and listened as Ortega explained what he wanted to accomplish. When he finished Hagen started in on Khan.

'Khan is a naturalized citizen, but his wife doesn't look like she's got all of her papers in order. I'm getting this from Immigration and Customs Enforcement. I've got a friend who works for ICE. We can use this with Khan and I think we should. He needs to tell us why he's still alive.'

Raveneau disliked the immigration angle. He disliked the way it had grown after 9/11 and again as the recession put the heat on illegal Hispanics. It was an excuse not to do police work, but he did agree that the owner, David Khan, was the one with the opportunity to kill the four employees. If any motive arose everything would focus on him. He listened briefly, then walked over to Ortega.

'Where do you want me?'

'I want you to go through Khan's office again.'

'Hasn't it already been searched twice?'

'Even more than that, but let's do it again. We're not going to get another chance.'

'You got it.'

It wasn't hard. The computer wasn't here and neither were most of the files. Raveneau sat at Khan's desk and looked through his pencils and rubber bands. He looked through the window at what Khan saw every day and tried to imagine a believable motive for Khan to kill his four employees, including one who had been with him since the start of the business twelve years ago. Drugs, smuggling, something illicit, but Ortega's team was coming up with nothing. Interviews with the contractors and architects on Khan's contact lists painted a picture of a hardworking man who strove to please his clients.

Raveneau went through a file cabinet that still held older

records of past jobs and invoices. Khan's small careful hand-writing was easily identifiable. The records for 2008 and forward were missing and he confirmed with Ortega they were at Homicide and would also have to be returned soon. The employee records were at the Hall as well. There wasn't much of anything in the office. Even the trash can was empty. The carpet that once sat under the desk was at the crime lab where blood was matched to one of the employees, but it was old blood and he doubted it was anything more than the employees cutting themselves while working.

He looked through the window again at the kitchen clean space where Khan stored completed cabinets. Two jobs were complete and waiting to ship. The newly built cabinets were wrapped individually in thin plastic to protect them, but that plastic was in tatters, cut loose when the cabinet interiors were searched. Khan was a meticulous man. Raveneau glanced at his handwriting again. He ran a small factory from this office and had earned a reputation for accuracy among those whose businesses rested on accuracy.

What was that Ortega said an architect told him? That Khan worked with wood yet worried over dimensions as if he was working with metal. Raveneau was turning that in his head when Ortega walked in.

'Gibbs is back with coffee and something to eat. Come take a break.'

Raveneau checked his messages. He thanked Gibbs for the coffee and then walked down to the steel racks at the far end of the building that held Khan's stored inventory. Different types of wood were on different racks. The larch ply Drury delivered was on stickers on the floor.

From behind him, Ortega said, 'We confirmed he needed this plywood for a cabinet project here in the city. It's on the plans he was working from and I talked to the architect and the contractor.'

Raveneau turned to him. 'Where are you going to go with Drury?'

'We'll interview him again this week. I went back over his delivery sheet yesterday.'

'What do you think about him quitting his job?'

'I talked to Branson, his boss again. He told me Drury was probably going to quit anyway.'

'Who quits a job nowadays?'

'I will if I can't find who killed these people. What happened here, Raveneau? What do you think and what are you doing down at this end of the building? You picked up your coffee and walked straight down here. If you see something I need to know what it is.'

Raveneau reached out. He put a hand on Ortega's shoulder.

'I am sorry about yesterday and I know what pressure you're under. I didn't walk down here because I had any new ideas, but I keep thinking about the delivery, the tight window and that the employees were all at their stations working against a deadline. I keep thinking they were shot by someone who knew where they would be.'

'Khan knew where they would be.'

'But why would he kill his employees? More to the point, you've got to have a very, very good reason to want to draw all the attention a homicide like this will bring.'

Ortega got called away and Raveneau lingered in the material storage area. He smelled fir. He touched smooth pieces of finish lumber and then looked over at the forklift. Dan Oliver, the employee who accepted the delivery set the plywood down on four inch by four inch stickers to keep the unit off the ground so a forklift could pick it up later. Then he parked the lift. The key was still in it.

Raveneau walked back to the unit of plywood and sat down on it. He ran his fingers along one of the steel bands holding it together and took another sip of coffee. Then, he thought, why not, but finished the coffee before laying down three pieces of wood he could slide the sheets of plywood on to. Then he went looking for a band cutter. He crossed the room to where he had seen tools stored and found one.

After cutting the two metal bands he slid the first sheet off and positioned it neatly on the wood stickers. He did the same with the next fifteen sheets, keeping the new pile exact and precise. A light sweat started on his forehead as well as the sense this was a little bit foolish. He felt the weight of each sheet now and each was four feet wide by eight feet long and three quarters of an inch thick. He rested a moment after getting through the next six sheets. That left twenty to go and he hoped Ortega didn't walk back just yet. He didn't really have a good explanation for why he was doing this.

He slid two more sheets off, then slowed and stood up as he slid off the next. At first he wasn't sure what he was looking at. He had a pretty good idea, but he wasn't there yet. All of the remaining sheets appeared to be joined together by long screws, and the oblong metal objects sat in pockets routed into the wood, each looking shiny and deadly, each resting in a wood pocket with packing around it to keep it from moving. There were four of them and routed into pockets alongside them, four end pieces nestled in the way a wedding ring might rest in velvet.

Raveneau touched the end of one and felt where the cap piece would screw in. Pack them with explosives and then screw on the cap piece, four casings about eighteen inches long, fat in the middle, narrowing at the nose, clean curved metal. He stared. He studied them before walking back to the saw cutting room and waving Ortega over.

'Bruce, come take a look.'

And then Ortega was standing next to him saying, 'Khan's a bomb maker.'

Raveneau didn't go there yet. He was still taking it in. Each was well machined, similar if not identical. This was production manufacturing. He turned to Ortega and asked, 'Who's the bomb guy we hired that was with the Army in Iraq and Afghanistan?'

'Yeah, I know who you mean. They call him Hurt Locker but I can't think of his real name. Hagen knows him.'

'Let's get Hagen to call the bomb squad. Let's see if we can get him here without the rest of the squad and before we call the Feds or anybody else.'

NINETEEN

The captain who oversaw the bomb squad told Hagen, 'No way, it's not going to happen.' Raveneau was close enough to overhear. He refused to send Juan Garcia, the ex-Army technician alone.

Raveneau mouthed, 'Let me talk to him,' and Hagen stared hard at him before saying, 'I'm going to put Inspector Raveneau on the line.'

When Raveneau brought the phone to his ear Captain Dixon asked, 'Raveneau, are you ever going to fucking retire?'

'I'm waiting you out. You go, and then I'll go.'

'What would I do every day?'

'You'd do the same thing you do now, you'd sit around.'

Dixon laughed. Raveneau didn't know him well but they liked each other.

'Here's the problem we've got,' Raveneau said. 'We've discovered what look like bomb casings and we don't want to alert the owner yet. We need to keep this very quiet. We need a discreet look at them.'

'Are you staying well away from them?'

'We are.'

'You need to get everyone out of the building. What's the address again?'

Raveneau gave it to him and kept talking.

'We can't risk our suspect finding out we've discovered this.'

'We have a very clear protocol, Ben, and I think everyone in the department knows it, you included.'

'I understand, but we can't risk the word getting out. If you can't send him and give us a look and an opinion, we'll go at it a different way.'

'No, don't call the Feds, we'll get down there. Don't touch anything and we'll come in as quietly as we can.'

'It's plywood that's been moved around with a forklift. It rode here on a lumber delivery truck. It can't be that sensitive.

Look, I'll email you a photo of what we've got. I'll do that right now.'

Ten minutes later Dixon called back, saying he was sending Garcia, the Hurt Locker guy.

While they waited Raveneau made a call to a friend who worked for a company called Shelter Products up in Portland. He figured if there was anyone who could trace where the plywood came from it was Ridge Taylor. He got through to Taylor and after the hellos said, 'I can't tell you why but I need to know. I've got an order and a delivery tag number. We can fax to you and I can tell you what's stamped on the wood.'

No one told a joke better than Taylor, but he was quiet and serious as Raveneau went back and forth with him. Shelter Products sold point-to-point. They sold lumber as it was still rolling on a train. They sold into any number of states and after they were clear on the forty-two pieces of finish grade larch he asked Taylor about Branson Trucking, thinking they might know who to call if they didn't know anything directly.

'Why don't I put you through to Hutton and let him tell you. Your plywood came out of a plant in British Columbia. Here's the address and phone number.'

Taylor gave him that and a website, then put him through to Kurt Hutton. Hutton asked, 'Are you building a wooden jail?'

'No, and I can't talk but I need to know anything you can tell me about Branson.'

'I can tell you they appeared out of nowhere about four years ago with lower prices than anybody. The CEO, if you want to call him that, was somebody we did business with and he ran into hard times and went under. I don't know when he connected with the investor money behind Branson. He's not really the type to go out and find money like that, but obviously he did.'

'If they're less expensive why don't you use them?'

'They did do some hauling for us, but they couldn't possibly have made money at the prices they charged us and it was hurting others we work with. They've got a good idea with their website though. On the website is a truck and you click and drag and as you load the truck it gives you the weight and you punch in the destination and it gives the hauling price.'

'I've been to it.'

'With their prices they had to be cutting corners other ways, so we backed away.'

He thanked Hutton as Hurt Locker showed up. He was probably no more than twenty-five but with a quiet walk and manner that made Raveneau remember his son. He watched how Garcia approached the casings and studied them. Ten minutes later he straightened, turned, and looked at them.

'You've got yourself some pretty slick IED casings, except that they don't look very much like improvised explosive devices. You've got four Cadillacs, depending on who puts them together from here. Anyone of these would make one hell of a bomb. See how the nose is shaped, directs the blast.'

He fixed on Raveneau.

'These are some seriously bad dudes and they aren't one-off deals. They're producing them. This is one scary thought.'

'What would one of these do to a cable car?'

'Oh, I think you'd be looking for pieces and parts four blocks away.' He paused. 'You want to find the bomb maker like right now, pronto.'

TWENTY

Raveneau moved his car so the bomb sniffing dogs and the X-ray robot could enter through a loading bay. Still, you couldn't fool the street. The neighbors quickly noticed the vehicles and a couple of people walked up to ask what was going on.

But nothing more was discovered and the X-ray was negative on anything else hidden in the plywood. Hurt Locker Garcia operated the X-ray robot. He determined the casings weren't booby-trapped and removed them slowly. After that, the only metal the robot picked up were the screws sandwiching the plywood together. Garcia nodded at Raveneau's guess the end pieces threaded on after the explosive was inside.

Other than Garcia no one touched them and Garcia wore gloves.

A CSI team was on its way here and the hope was they'd pull something off them that would help.

Raveneau asked Garcia, 'They looked heavy when you picked them up.'

'They are. They're some sort of alloy.'

Raveneau took photos and then stepped back as the CSI crew arrived and tried to figure out how to approach this. Meanwhile, Raveneau, Ortega, and the canine crew helped load the X-ray robot back into the van. When the bomb squad left Ortega called a meeting in Khan's office. He wanted to caucus on how to proceed. One idea was to restack the plywood, reband the unit, and set up surveillance cameras before turning the building over to Khan. Raveneau favored that idea but disagreed with Ortega over bringing in the FBI.

'You've got to bring them,' Raveneau argued. 'There's really no choice.'

'Raveneau, you know as well as I do what's going to happen. They'll trample our murder investigation. By noon they'll have a press release out saying they're working a significant terrorism investigation in San Francisco. The murders here will become a sidebar. They'll tuck Khan away somewhere. We can wait a few days.'

'I know who to call.'

'Who?'

'Mark Coe.'

'I don't even know him.'

'You'll meet him today. You'll be able to work with him.'

Hagen jumped in. 'Couldn't disagree more,' he said, and they continued on like this, but knew the call was going to get made. Ortega would have cut this debate off awhile ago if it wasn't. Half an hour later, Ortega asked for Coe's cell number.

Thirty-five minutes later Coe and two other agents were in the building looking at bomb casings. More calls got made and a bomb expert an hour and a half down the coast at Fort Ord got in his car. Another boarded a plane in LA. With Coe there Raveneau stepped back. He listened to Ortega sketch out his video surveillance idea.

'We're going to pull the crime tape anyway. We can put the bomb casings back in their nests, reband the plywood, give him the building back and watch what he does. His attorney keeps telling us his client will lose his business and they'll sue if we don't let him back in here soon.'

Raveneau knew Coe couldn't decide on his own. He'd have to call his ASAC at a minimum. That call got made now and late in the afternoon Raveneau left the building to buy a banding tool and steel tape at a lumberyard. A clerk showed him how to use it. When he got back to Sixteenth Street he called Celeste to let her know he was going to be late.

'Let me guess,' she said as she picked up, 'you aren't going to make it tonight.'

'I'll be late. We found something very disturbing.'

'That sounds scary.'

'It is.'

Coe got a wiretap warrant and the FBI tested and retested their video system trying to get at a bug in it as Raveneau stacked plywood with Ortega. Every three or four sheets they stopped to make sure everything was lining up correctly. Lining up the creases the former banding tape made on the edge of the last sheet was hard. It needed to align perfectly and Raveneau struggled with the banding tool. But finally he figured it out and when he finished the stack looked pretty much like it had. One by one, they backed out of the building and as Raveneau stood with Ortega down the block and outside his car, Coe called from back in the Fed field office.

'Everything is working, you're good to go.'

Ortega turned to Raveneau and said, 'Here goes.' He called Khan's lawyer. 'This is Inspector Ortega. Mr Khan can have his building back. If he needs someone we can give you the names of several firms who do crime scene cleanup.'

'Does that mean he is no longer a suspect?'

'We've never called him as a suspect.'

Raveneau smiled as Ortega said that.

'You've treated him as one. You prevented him from reopening his business and cost him a great deal of money. Who is going to compensate him for that?'

'You tell me. I have no idea. Good night.'

TWENTY-ONE

Eight months ago near the end of spring last year, Celeste told him, 'I'm forty-eight. If I don't do this now, I'll never do it.'

She had two hundred seventy-one thousand dollars saved over seventeen years for the sole purpose of opening a restaurant. But the tipping point was when her mother died about a year ago and Celeste inherited $185,000, and with that felt sure she had enough money. Her mother's death also made life much more finite for Celeste. That started the summer of eating and looking at other restaurants and places for lease.

They had fun with it right up to the point where she signed a lease and the clock started. The second thoughts arrived then and the fear she was in over her head in a competitive city woke her at night. She planned to serve food at the bar but had last cooked professionally twenty-five years ago when she imagined a career as a chef before becoming a bartender and later a wine broker.

During the heatwave last September when city temperatures broke one hundred degrees for the fourth day in a row, she had an anxiety attack that almost derailed the project.

She wept and shook as she told him, 'I'm wasting everything I inherited and all the money my mom saved on a vain idea. I'll get panned in the first reviews and will never be able to compete.'

But by then she was committed to the lease and had already spent fifteen thousand on architectural drawings. She broke out in hives. She fought panic with manic focus on restaurant design and construction and by testing drink recipes at home. But the low point was yet to come. It arrived a month later as she got the first construction bids from two general contractors, both of whom had come highly recommended.

The bids were nearly double what her architect had estimated. She found a third contractor and got another bid, then two more before realizing that she needed to scale back her plans radically. She kept the idea that you could still eat at the bar or a bar table.

Not a restaurant style meal, and very casual eating, with the idea there would be six to eight small plates and always pizzettas. You'd get paper napkins not cloth but food would be part of the draw. She focused on the mixology, on bartending, on a culture that would treat customers like friends.

She didn't have to but she also focused on sustainable. She found recycled materials. She bought used bar equipment and chairs and tables. She refinished the tables with Raveneau's help. She found a used pizza oven and the architect came up with a way to capture waste heat from the bar dishwasher, running plastic Pex lines embedded in the concrete bar top so if you rested your elbows on the bar top concrete they would stay warm.

She fought. She negotiated. The flue rebuild became yesterday's problem. The Health and Building Departments signed off. A local advocate for handicap rights came by and measured the bathrooms. Then Bo Rutan pulled up in his old El Camino with Louisiana plates saying he had in fact trained in Rome not New Orleans. He was in chef whites making pizzas when Raveneau walked in tonight.

'It's really up to the bar,' Celeste had kept saying. 'The bar will make or break the place.'

There were twenty-five small tables and rattan chairs, a floor of reclaimed bamboo. The old beams of the ceiling were exposed, the walls white-painted and softly lit. He caught her eye now and she waved for him to come around the back. Her forehead was moist with heat from the oven, face flush, eyes lit with excitement and happiness. People looked happy and it felt right to Raveneau. She pulled him around the corner out of sight of the bar.

'What do you think?'

'It's going to work.'

'You like the bar.'

'Yeah, it's got a good feel.'

'I'll come out in a few minutes. It's been crowded like this since we opened the doors at five thirty. Kiss me and tell me some of these people will come back.'

'They will.'

Raveneau saw la Rosa walk in. She spotted him immediately, looked at his clothes and asked, 'Did you even go home?'

'Never got a chance.'

'How did it go?'

'It's all set up. It's working.'

'How long before the media gets it?'

'My guess is a week at the most.'

'I'll bet it's out in less than three days.'

'Let's get you a drink and then let me introduce you to someone.'

When Raveneau touched his shoulder Ryan Candel turned from his friends. He looked drunk. He looked puzzled. He asked, 'What are you doing here?'

'This is my partner, Inspector Elizabeth la Rosa.'

Candel waved one of the smooth rounded glasses Celeste had searched for months to find. It held a dark rum drink.

'Hello, Inspector Elizabeth.'

The drink slipped through his fingers, almost fell, and one of his friends said, 'That would have sucked.'

Candel gestured with his glass toward his friends. 'These are my drinking friends.' He turned and pointed with the glass at Raveneau. 'This detective here is looking for my dad. Together we're going to prove he was a murderer. Isn't that right, Inspector? We're hunting the fucker down.' He raised his glass. 'Here's to you, Dad. We're coming for you.'

On his left la Rosa said, 'The place is beautiful. Introduce me to Celeste. Let's get away from these guys. I don't need this tonight.'

TWENTY-TWO

R aveneau was groggy as he answered the phone. He recognized Secret Service Brooks' voice and looked at the time, 5:30 on a dark cold morning.

'Hope I didn't wake you up,' Brooks said. 'Special Agent Coe called me.'

'Good.'

'But why didn't I hear from you?'

'Why would you?'

'Those weapons are for targeting vehicles. They were sent here for the President's visit.'

'You're good at big leaps, Nate.'

'I wish I was. It's just a different business, Inspector. In yours you like to have a body to work with. Then you can sit around and try to figure out who killed the victim even if it takes twenty-two years. In ours the game is keeping everybody alive so that means we have to work a little harder.'

'Sure, that's why you brought two other agents to the meeting with me.'

'Are you talking about the meeting where you went out for coffee in the middle of it?'

'It was either that or watch you read. I'm still waiting by the way for a copy of your file on Alan Krueger. Remember, you were going to messenger it over the next day'

'I want to meet with you this morning.'

'So you'll bring the personnel file with you. Is that what you're saying? In that case, let's meet. What's convenient for you?'

He met a different Nate Brooks at ten that morning and by then he had also cooled down. Brooks alluded to the pressure on him and Raveneau wasn't sure about himself. He was surprised he'd gotten into it with Brooks earlier this morning. Could be that the bomb casings troubled him on a lot of levels. He knew the investigation would go full-throated at Khan's roots. Ortega told him this morning the FBI was forming a task force and sending two teams to Pakistan.

Brooks held his hands out in front of him, palms down, fingers spread wide.

'I can feel it coming,' he said. 'I can feel something is going to happen. It's getting closer and closer and I'm not getting anywhere. The only thing I'm getting is more worried. Let's take a drive and I'll show you what I worry about. Come on, let's go. We'll get coffee and I'll show you.'

In the car Brooks wanted to hear about yesterday. 'What did you think when you slid the piece of plywood off and saw them?'

'I thought about San Francisco and how small it is and how powerful they looked. I figured no one would ship something like those casings without planning to assemble and use them here.'

'Welcome to my world.'

'Is that your world, Nate? Have you seen a lot of bombs go off?'

'They are what I worry about most and look at all the people who hate us. I grew up in Baltimore. I learned to watch everything and everybody. That's how I ended up in the Secret Service. But you've been in homicide a long time and I want your opinion. Why kill the employees and bring the TV vans and everything that comes with it? Did they know too much?'

'Someone saw it as a lesser risk to take them out.'

'That's how you see it?'

'It's one possibility.'

'Was it Khan's decision?'

'I don't know but the plywood delivery was to him and the window of time he was gone and the employees murdered was so narrow it's hard to believe it was coincidence.'

'That he just happened to be gone?'

'Yeah.'

'So, Raveneau, you think Khan is in on it.'

'That's not quite what I said.'

'But you're just dancing around it, and if he's involved, he's just one of others. Conspiracy, an organization that knows what it's doing is my nightmare. Weapons like these can take out a motorcade without having to be perfectly placed, and they don't have to get the President to change the country. Kill enough others and a motorcade will never be the same again. You hear that, right?'

'If you're about to start selling me on how you're saving the country then drop me off at the next corner.'

'I'm not.'

'Why did you want to talk this morning?'

'I want to talk because I'm scared of the kind of violence those weapons represent. I'm afraid we're on the edge of this being the new normal. I want to talk because these cabinet shop murders are ground zero right now and you're a homicide inspector and I want to know what you think.'

Brooks pointed in the distance at the Golden Gate Bridge.

'We can close a bridge as the President's motorcade crosses, but we can't clear every corridor, particularly in a smaller city like this one. The Presidential limo is a battering ram but there's a nightmare scenario where the motorcade enters a street without many side escape routes. Let's say a vehicle rigged with an IED like these detonates ahead and pieces of motorcycle cops and fragments of vehicles go flying. At that point we're just trying to get the President out any way we can with as much speed as possible.

'Of course, the other side has thought about side streets too. They have a secondary plan. They've designed for overkill. I'm talking about something planned like a military operation.'

'But you vary your routes. You take precautions.'

'There's only so much you can do in a smaller city.'

'Where are you going with this?'

'Once we have coffee I'm going to take you on one of the routes that could get used when the President is out on this next trip. He's going to give a speech about the subway system San Francisco has started work on. I read they're going to work eight years, twelve hours a day, seven days a week. But you're from here so how many years will it really take?'

'Twelve.'

They picked up coffee and drove toward Union Square, Brooks at the wheel of a new government car.

'Presidents are fatalists. They know the risks can be overwhelming, but it's the tradeoff for an open society. The President is going to give a speech here in Union Square and then go down to Embarcadero and ride the light rail with the mayor and at least one senator.'

He pointed out tall buildings, alleys, bottlenecks the construction was going to cause, the places that worried him most. He doubled back and picked up Grant Street and started through Chinatown where the streets were narrow.

'Bad street but many voters and it'll make people feel good.' He pointed at a car. 'Say there is a bomb in that car but it doesn't go off until the last car in the motorcade is through. It detonates simultaneously with one ahead of the motorcade.'

'How many times are you going to blow us up out here today?'

'As it goes off, we're going to get him the hell away from here, right? What are we going to do? We turn down one of these steep narrow streets and now we're really vulnerable.'

They followed it to the end, to where the President, the mayor, and the senator got on the light rail system built after the Embarcadero Freeway came down. Brooks pulled over and they watched the rail cars slowly go by and Raveneau knew in Brooks' head the President was riding on it. He waited for what he guessed would come next.

But Brooks surprised him, pointing toward the Ferry Building and saying, 'That's where Krueger was shot, a little bit back from the near corner of the Ferry Building.'

'That's right.'

'I'm going to tell you more about him. I'm going to tell you some things you don't know that I'm now authorized to tell you.'

'Why are you going to do that?'

'Because your friend Coe at the FBI has convinced me that the problem is even worse than we thought.'

TWENTY-THREE

'First off, we don't know who killed Alan Krueger, and when he was killed he was working with us, but not for us. I know you probably still don't believe that, but it's the truth.'

'Why wouldn't I believe that?'

'I don't know why, but you seem to want to believe the Secret Service hid information from Inspectors Goya and Govich. Look, Krueger left us in 1985. He'd been outside for four years. In those four years he worked for other agencies as well. He had a pipeline in Hong Kong. He spoke Mandarin, Vietnamese, and Korean. He had an ear for language and a talent for making connections.'

'What's a pipeline in what he was doing?'

'Good sources for the flow of people, money, and information about counterfeiting, what's out there in the way of bills for sale, he was in that, he was a buyer.'

'Were you bullshitting me when you said the supernotes he was carrying are now the first known?'

Brooks tugged on the cuffs of his shirt, a habit he seemed to have, that and pursing his lips.

'You are the worst cynic I've ever met.'

'No, I know you guys would never lie to me.'

'We worked with Inspectors Govich and Goya. We tried hard to find who killed Krueger, in part because he was one of us for a dozen years, but also because he was chasing rumors for us and believed he was on to something. He had heard rumors of printing presses sold to North Korea and another of presses set up in a warehouse in Hong Kong. He was working on that.'

'Do you have names, people I can talk to?'

'Time's gone by on those, but there's someone here in San Francisco you should talk to. He still won't talk to us but he might talk to you. I'm going to give you his phone number.'

'Why won't he talk to you?'

'I can tell you but he'll do a better job of it.'

'Did the Secret Service know about him in 1989?'

'Yes.'

'Did they give Goya and Govich his name?'

'No, and I'm passing it on, but I'm not taking responsibility for what happened before me. I was in college. I wasn't working for the Secret Service. They don't hire kids who are in school.'

It took Raveneau a moment to get it.

'So you've talked to this individual recently about Krueger.'

'I have.'

'Was that because of the supernotes and the current investigation with the Cayman and Mexican banks?'

'Yes. I met with him and as soon as I sat down with him I knew he was going to fuck with me. He was completely uncooperative.'

'I'm ready for a name.'

'Well, try this one. Marlin Thames, Marlin like the fish, and Thames like the river. Before that he was Howard Wright. He reinvented himself out here. He's how Krueger got caught in a lie and outed. The lie involved his residence and where he was staying at night. Mr Thames also had a criminal record that included fraud. That weighed in. If Krueger had stayed on he would have been transferred to someplace very cold and faraway. Someplace where you drive fifty miles to get to the dentist. Krueger chose to resign. Here's the phone number.'

'Are you saying Thames and Krueger were a couple?'

'That is what I'm saying.'

Raveneau called Thames from his car after Brooks dropped him off, and Thames was willing but wanted to meet somewhere neutral. He named a café on Market Street. Raveneau met him in the early afternoon, sat across from him and ate a sandwich as he listened to Thames' story.

'My hair was gold-colored in those days.'

'You've still got some gold.'

'I'm sixty-seven and 1989 was a long time ago. He was killed three years after we broke up and we were still friends, but both of us had moved on. I didn't see him much.'

'But you were together when he quit the Secret Service?'

'Oh, yes, and I was thrilled, but for Alan it was very hard to leave them. I didn't realize how important it was to him. He was never the same after that.'

Marlin Thames wore jeans and a black leather jacket over a T-shirt. He gave off an aura of spry good-nature. Raveneau tried to picture what he looked like in 1985. He watched Thames stir sugar into a double cappuccino and lay the small spoon down.

'How close were you to Alan?'

'We were very close for several years. But those times were very different and our life was even more complicated because Alan had to hide everything from the Secret Service. There was an agent he worked with that suspected Alan was gay. That agent was jealous and suspicious and trailed Alan to my house several times. Then they trapped him in a lie about where he lived and where he'd been the night before, but it was very obvious he lost his job because he was gay. He was outed by Agent Gary Stone. I hated Stone for what he did.'

'Where were you when he was killed?'

'I was at a friend's house near the Russian River when a friend called me and read the newspaper article to me. "Former Secret Service Agent Slain." That was the headline.' He stared at Raveneau and added, 'He was gorgeous. I still think about his smile.' He took a sip of his cappuccino. 'You said you have new evidence. How does that happen after so many years?'

'We have a videotape of the shooting.'

Thames frowned. He put his cup down awkwardly.

'What?'

'It was sent to us last week.'

'Is it real?'

'A film expert thinks so.'

'Does it show him getting shot?'

'Yes.'

'Oh, my God.'

Raveneau went through the details of the cold case with this genial and seemingly gentle man sitting across from him. He studied Thames as he talked. Thames' build was similar to that of the shooter and he looked at Thames knowing he was going to get a photo of him to the FBI. The anger of a former lover could explain the counterfeit bills left behind.

'After he was murdered did you contact the homicide inspectors working the case?'

'No, I was too scared. I wondered if Agent Stone had killed him. It was all so mysterious.'

'Do you know where he stayed in San Francisco?'

'Hotels.'

'The inspectors couldn't figure out where he was staying when he was killed.'

'Well, it was usually hotels. He had more money for whatever he was doing in Asia, but maybe he had met somebody new that I didn't know about.'

'Do you have any photos of Alan?'

'I do.'

'Can I borrow them and get them back to you?'

'If you promise I'll get them back.'

'I promise. Now I'd like to run some names by you. Did he ever mention a Captain Frank?'

'Oh, yes, the airline pilot. He lived in Hawaii. They were good friends and there were other friends he had there. I don't remember any names though.'

'Did you ever meet Frank?'

'Yes, I met him and he was here often, and we went to Hawaii once. We were there a week and it was terrible.' Thames smiled but there was some bitterness in it. 'His other friends didn't like me much.'

'Can you try to remember their names and then call me?'

'I'll try but I wouldn't wait for me to call.'

'You wouldn't?'

'No, I really wouldn't.'

His smile was warm again but the message was clear. Thames owned a well-maintained two-story Victorian. He found the photos quickly and Raveneau didn't ask the next question here. He was afraid Thames might see where it was going and ask for the photo back. In the Homicide office he scanned the photo of Thames and Krueger and sent a copy of the file to Mark Coe. He followed with an email.

Then he called Thames' cell. 'Hey, it's Inspector Raveneau again, and I'm calling to ask if you're willing to watch the videotape and see if you recognize the man who killed Alan. In the videotape you can tell they knew each other.'

'I'd rather not.'

'The way the man walks and moves, you might see something we would never otherwise know, but I appreciate how emotionally hard it might be.'

Thames didn't answer.

'Can I give you my cell phone number and will you think about it?'

After a pause Thames said, 'Let me get a pen.'

Raveneau heard him put the phone down. It took a long time and when Thames fumbled with the phone and picked it up again, Raveneau thought he'd say sorry it took so long. Instead, he hung up.

TWENTY-FOUR

Yesterday, Raveneau submitted to Lieutenant Becker a 'scratch,' the memorandum required outlining the travel Raveneau saw necessary as part of the case investigation. Becker read and passed it on to the captain who moved it to the commander's desk this morning. Commander Saguaro rarely rubber-stamped his approvals, so it was no surprise to Raveneau to get called into his office this afternoon.

Saguaro was on the phone and pointed at a chair. So Raveneau sat listening to Saguaro talk and soon realized the conversation was about the bomb casings. The story was leaking its way through the department.

Saguaro put the phone down and asked, 'Inspector Raveneau, are you a golfer?'

'Not a very good one.'

'Are you planning to take clubs on this trip?'

'No, sir.'

The commander let a beat pass. He stared before asking, 'Are you certain this trip is worthwhile?'

'Well, it was either Hawaii or Rome and I thought this time of year Rome would be too cold, or the sky that endless white. You know how it gets in the winter.'

Raveneau wasn't even sure Commander Saguaro registered the joke. He was studying what Raveneau wrote, reading bits of it aloud, 'memorabilia, swizzle sticks with hula girls, handwritten love notes, photos connecting to one link with victim, Captain Frank's son interviewed.

'Who is Captain Frank?'

'He was an airline captain for United at the time of the murder. I received a lot more information on him today from a third-party storage company holding records for United Airlines. Frank lived in Hawaii. I need to talk to people who knew him. I may even find him.'

'Is he a suspect?'

'He could become one.'

'Is that right? He could become one. I love talking to you inspectors, especially when you're ready to travel. You've got an answer for everything and no information.'

He smiled to show he was joking. Raveneau had printed off what the storage company emailed him today on Jim Frank. He lifted it to show Commander Saguaro, though he knew Saguaro didn't have the slightest interest in seeing it.

'How many days?'

'I'm hoping for two but if I find enough it could turn into three. With everything else going on here I'd like it to be two. Flying first class will make the travel easier. I'll be able to rest on the plane and get right to work.'

The absurdity of that idea got a real smile from Saguaro and his eyes lit briefly. But they changed just as quickly as he moved on.

'When you say with what's going on here, are you talking about the cabinet shop?'

'Yes and no, I'm not on Ortega's team and the Feds are taking the lead on the bomb casings. As you probably know, it's become a terrorism investigation. Inspector Ortega's team is working the murders, but I know Special Agent Mark Coe who's heading the Fed end and Inspector Ortega wants me to keep talking with him. There may be other overlaps we don't understand yet, and I'm part of looking for those.'

'What overlaps?'

'The Secret Service is also involved. There's a cross with counterfeit money the cold case victim Alan Krueger was carrying. It's in the same series as money passed at two banks last summer to buy explosives from a black market weapons dealer. That may tie to a threat to the President.'

Raveneau didn't have to answer any of these questions, but he was comfortable with the commander. Saguaro wasn't going to get on the phone and gossip. He might collect gossip, but he wouldn't trade. Saguaro was a black hole.

'And you're sure this trip to Hawaii won't get in the way?'

'I've got to—'

'I know, I know, you've got to follow the investigation. What you inspectors need is a pack of cards that you carry and that have all your answers on them, so when you come in here you can just hand me the card with the answer you want to give. It would save everybody time.'

'Like the brass at a press conference.'

Saguaro smiled. 'Yeah, like that.' He signed his last signature with a flourish. 'OK, you're approved. Take your clubs, Ben. You've earned a couple of swings.'

'There won't be time.'

'Hold it to two days if you can. We need you here. And keep every receipt. They're all over me nowadays.' As Raveneau reached the door he added, 'Nice work finding those bombs. You're the only one who would have gone through that plywood.'

Raveneau called Jack at Clement Street Travel, gave him the

approval number voucher and said, 'If I can I'd like to go out tomorrow afternoon, be there for two nights and return in the morning. Can you make that work?'

'Give me one second.' Raveneau heard him on the keyboard and then Jack's, 'Yes.'

Jack would book airline, rental car, and hotel. Anything else Raveneau would need to submit to the fiscal department for reimbursement, but in his career he rarely submitted for food or anything else and knew he wouldn't on this one. So in his head the trip was booked and now it was a matter of accomplishing what he needed to there.

When he got back to his desk la Rosa was there.

'You busy?' he asked.

'What's up?'

'I'm going to Hawaii tomorrow afternoon to see what I can learn about Captain Frank. I want to talk with you about some things first.'

'How about if I just come to Hawaii with you and we can talk on the plane? I've never been and I've always wanted to go.'

'I don't think Saguaro will go for it.'

'OK, do you want to talk now?'

'Yeah, let's take a walk and get some air. I learned some things this morning.'

TWENTY-FIVE

Raveneau told her about the drive with Nate Brooks but was having trouble communicating what was bothering him. It was the way he was wired. If you asked him he would tell you he was about facts, motive, and opportunity, but la Rosa knew that just wasn't so. Raveneau stressed the rational gathering of information, but often was very intuitive in how he solved cases.

'Brooks took me down to the Ferry Building to watch the light rail pass by with the President, the mayor, and a US senator riding along. With him narrating I could almost see their faces.

It ended with Brooks holding his coffee cup from the bottom with his right hand, kind of balancing it there as he leaned back against the door of his car and said the Secret Service had more records on Krueger than the personnel file he was authorized to show me. He said I wouldn't get anything out of the file but advised me to keep digging.'

'What does he want in return?'

'Not clear, but he wants to be kept in the loop with Ortega's team and any contact I have with Mark Coe.'

'He knows you aren't going to agree to that.'

'Sure, he knows.'

'So why is he asking?'

'He's saying he wants to communicate. He's worried. He can tell I'm bothered by what we found and he wants information anywhere he can get it. He's casting a wider net than he would otherwise.'

'He sounds to me like a guy unraveling. How much pressure is he under?'

'Plenty.'

'Is he angry?'

'Maybe, but more frustrated than angry. I think he feels somewhat powerless. I understand that. You look at those bomb casings and your imagination just runs.'

'Why don't you stay here and figure out what Brooks is after and I'll go to Hawaii.'

Raveneau smiled and was usually quick with a comeback but not today. La Rosa read that as him being focused on the Krueger investigation and this Hawaii trip, yet at the same time still very disturbed by the discovery of the bomb casings. She thought this whole walk was really about the bomb casings. She didn't really believe he was concerned about Brooks.

'Talk to me about Hawaii,' she said.

'I'll be looking for anything I can learn about Jim Frank or anyone who knew him. He may even be there just waiting to talk. I'm going to find where Frank lived and I hope to find people who knew Krueger.'

They reached the corner of Seventh and waited for the light to change. Raveneau looked out at the traffic going by as he spoke.

'The Secret Service ruled out Marlin Thames as a suspect back in '89, but I borrowed a photo from him today and have asked for the FBI's help getting it enhanced. I don't think it's him. It's almost certainly not, but it needs to get looked at. That's something I won't tell Brooks, yet I couldn't tell you why.'

'You don't trust him.'

'It's not that, it's more that I don't want to have to trust him.' He turned to her. 'I don't think there's anything wrong with him.'

'Then what is it you're picking up?'

'He's telegraphing that he's not happy with the Secret Service. He's telling me things he says he's not authorized to tell me, but it feels like he's trying to steer the Krueger investigation. I feel like I'm being led down a path.'

'What's he asked for?'

'He asked about transcripts I read at the FBI. Coe showed me transcripts on the condition I not talk to anyone, though I told him I would share what I learned with you.'

Raveneau told her now about a Utah banker named Garner and the man code named Jericho who in a wiretap transcript was negotiating to buy weapons from an officer at a US military base.

'A base here in the US?'

'Kentucky and the Feds think it's a small group selling, maybe as small as two officers. But that makes me think of something I heard on the radio a few days ago. Someone did a study or a little fact checking as a reality test; it might have been a professor in Boston. What he did was look at brigadier generals and the number of people in their families who were in the military and compared that to Congress. He did the same with Congress. The generals had one hundred eighty family members who were in the military. All of Congress had a total of ten. One can say, so what, but I think it says a lot about the drift the country has taken. We're already politically polarized. What if we run into a crisis with the national debt and that's coupled with a confrontation somewhere in the world? We could get to a point where our military steps in to stabilize the country. But what if there's a group out there that wants that to happen?'

'This is so unlike you.'

'I know.'

'Do you think there's a larger plot already in motion?'

'They're only showing me bits and pieces and no I don't believe there's some grand plot. But there is something happening and it has something to do with the right conditions being in place.'

'Is that what's bothering you?'

'I'm fine.'

So now he was going to close up on her. Sometimes she wished she had a simpler partner, but never for long. Raveneau had a way of making things happen. If he got stuck he went sideways. He did what you expected and did it again, and then something completely different.

'You wanted to walk and talk and tell me what's bothering you.'

'It's not that something in particular is bothering me. It's more like the way you know it's going to rain in the minute just before it does. I've never seen anything like these bomb casings before. But there they were and I don't know if we stopped a plot or if we just got a glimpse of part of one. That's what Brooks is wigging out about.'

'And you're afraid he's right.'

'He could be and I'm not sure what we can do. Yeah, that's part of what's bothering me. I'm not sure what we can do. We can make contingency plans, form task forces, have meetings and plan, but we're better off being lucky. Finding those bomb casings was luck.'

'I think it's something more.'

'It was luck.'

'Then stay lucky.'

TWENTY-SIX

Two hours later, Drury exited 880 northbound at Grand Avenue in Oakland, dropped off the freeway at an estimated fifty-five to sixty miles per hour and swerved around the cars lined up at the base of the offramp. His tires screamed as he ran the red light. He drove the retail section of Grand Avenue on the wrong side of the road, accelerating and crossing back over the line as the road started to climb.

The Criminal Investigation Unit team following did not attempt to stay with him. They fell back. They notified Oakland Police as Drury's car climbed east toward the hills and the intersection of Highway 13. Close to the onramp for 13 an Oakland police cruiser swung in behind Drury and went to lights and siren, but by then Drury was down the ramp and accelerating again. The officer followed and asked for help from the California Highway Patrol as he closed in on Drury's vehicle.

Now Drury braked hard and pulled over. He forced the officer following to stand on his brakes and the close call sliding to a stop behind Drury angered Officer Hernandez. He used his bullhorn to order Drury to turn his vehicle off, put his hands on his steering wheel and not move. The officer unsnapped his holster as he got out. He kept close watch of Drury's hands as he walked up alongside the car and then ordered him out of the vehicle.

Drury said, 'I'm sorry, officer. I know I was speeding but my girlfriend just told me she's been cheating on me for a year.'

Hernandez glanced at the approaching traffic. He expected the highway patrol any moment and was aware of what the suspect did along Grand Avenue, but didn't want Drury to know that yet. He was unaware that San Francisco Police had a surveillance team watching this individual. For some reason that wasn't communicated to him, and what he saw was a white male, clearly agitated and struggling with his emotions. He could easily be high on something as well as angry and Hernandez wanted backup before handcuffing him. When Drury started to turn, started to explain more, Hernandez barked at him.

'Keep your back to me.'

'I'm going to do exactly what you say, officer, but I'm OK now. I made some driving mistakes but we were supposed to get married in June. I'm sorry for what I did driving back there, but I'm not a danger now.'

Behind the officer traffic was slowing to rubberneck and though Hernandez knew better than to listen to what the man said, it resonated with him. His own wife dumped him just before the holidays, telling him she was filing for divorce and was in love with another man. He pushed that aside, glanced again down the highway looking for the CHP and not seeing any lights.

He positioned himself carefully. There wasn't a lot of room and ten feet behind him the traffic was still doing forty-five or fifty. Drury put his hands on the roof of the car. Drury spread his legs and Hernandez took one more glance down the highway before pulling Drury's left arm down and clicked cuffs on his wrist.

But then as he reached for the other arm Drury launched himself backwards. He drove Hernandez hard enough, fast enough to make him stumble. He slammed into him a second time and Hernandez was across the painted white stripe marking the edge of the right lane. That was where he fell backwards.

Drury heard tires squealing. He heard the cop's yell just before he was hit but he didn't turn to look. He jumped in his car as traffic came to a stop and veered on to the highway. When Drury overtook the traffic ahead he started weaving through. If the car ahead didn't get out of the way, he leaned on his horn. When some aggressive fucker tried to stop him from passing he moved toward him until their mirrors clicked together, which was enough to scare the guy off and open another gap as the highway fed into the larger 580.

He didn't think about the officer he pushed. He didn't really even have a place he was headed. He had picked up on surveillance this morning and knew he'd been used and knew he was fucked no matter where he went, and his mind kaleidoscoped through images of the homicide cop who followed him to the bar and was on to him. He pushed the Honda up as fast as it would go now but debated getting off the freeway before it split again.

Traffic way ahead was slowing anyway. What he couldn't see yet were the black and white CHP cars weaving back and forth across all lanes, bringing the speed of the traffic down from an average of sixty-five miles per hour to thirty down to ten and now almost to a stop. But he saw two coming now from behind. He didn't know the officer he pushed died on the scene but the officers approaching knew that. They were coming very fast and he took his last chance to get off the freeway, exiting too fast and brushing against the side of a passing car as he turned right at the base of the offramp.

Now he was on a tree-lined residential street. He nearly hit a girl walking a dog and went left at the next corner with a helicopter swinging in overhead. He couldn't believe they had a helicopter already and knew he had to get out of the car. He rounded another corner and a police car appeared in the intersection ahead. But to his right a woman was just getting out in her driveway with a bag of groceries.

Drury braked hard with a hand already under the seat finding the gun. He was out very quickly, but she was smart. She dropped the bags and ran. She got inside her front door and tried to lock it before he slammed into it. The door split the skin of her forehead right down the middle and still she tried to get up. She called to her kid to run and a little girl cried as he tied up the mom with electrical cord.

He tied her up and then grabbed the girl and dragged her out the front door on to the lawn, leaving her there, as he retrieved the woman's purse and got back inside. Then he went through the house locking the doors and looking for anyone else and found a babysitter or nanny hiding in an upstairs bedroom closet.

'Downstairs now,' he said as he took a phone from her. 'I'm not going to hurt you. You're going to take a message to the police car at the corner. There's a San Francisco cop named Raveneau. I want him here in less than two hours or Mom here dies. Anyone tries to come in, she dies, anything other than the inspector named Raveneau knocking on the door alone and she dies. Do you understand me?'

She couldn't speak.

'Get a fucking grip and repeat what I said to you.'

She quavered and teared-up. He almost hit her when she couldn't get the name right, though what she said sounded more like the fucker. 'Rabidno.'

'He's in Homicide. You watch TV. You know what that is.'

She did and he shoved her out a back door. Then he went looking for tape to tie up the mom better. After he did, he closed all the curtains and found her cell phone. His was in the car and there were more of them out there now. He could hear the radios. He lit up her cell and checked the time as the house landline began to ring.

TWENTY-SEVEN

Raveneau listened as la Rosa said, 'Drury killed an Oakland Police officer and then took a woman hostage. They're in a house in San Leandro and he's saying if you don't get there within two hours he'll kill her.'

'Wants me in exchange?'

'He's not saying exchange. He's saying he'll kill her if you don't knock on the front door in time. But you're not going to do that.'

'When did the two hours start?'

'Ten to fifteen minutes ago.'

'Is anyone talking to him?'

'They're trying.'

'Do you want to ride with me?'

'I'm driving you and you're going to get a CHP escort, but you aren't going inside. I'll shoot him through the head first.'

Raveneau scooped up his cell phone. He ejected the CD and turned the computer and the lights off.

'I'll meet you out front.'

Outside the Hall of Justice two CHP cruisers waited. The eastbound onramp was just up the street on Seventh, and within a few minutes they were on the Bay Bridge, la Rosa sitting tight on the lead cruiser, both CHP running with lights flashing. When they hit traffic dropping south in Oakland the officers went to siren. As they left the bridge Raveneau talked with the head of the CIU team who advised, 'Don't go in there. When he made us he went nuts. We stayed with him until he drove up the other side of Grand into oncoming traffic. He's flipped out and could take you with him.'

'Does he know he killed a police officer?'

'It's not clear.'

'What do you think?'

'He knows the officer got hit by a car.'

Raveneau talked with a hostage negotiator on scene as they

got closer. Local police and highway patrol were positioned at an intersection three quarters of a block from the house with Drury and the hostage. Fifty-one minutes remained before Drury's deadline ran out and Raveneau moved away from the impromptu command post as he called Coe.

Coe's cell went to voice mail. Eleven more minutes passed before he called back. Coe was unaware of the hostage situation.

'What can you tell me about Drury?' Raveneau asked.

'We've got text messages, emails, a lot of it cryptic but it's probable he got used, and none of this is certain yet, but it's sounding like he got paid an undisclosed amount of cash to swap out the plywood he was supposed to deliver for what he did deliver. The plant where they make the plywood has cameras that run 24/7 and tape all of their production. The plywood is identified by lots and units. They were able to call up this order and look at it. When it was banded and shipped out there weren't any bomb casings in it. That's what we have so far.'

Raveneau had a heart to heart with the local police chief after hanging up with Coe. She was a solidly built woman, no nonsense, blonde hair cut short, uniform crisply ironed. He didn't doubt that at civic functions she saw San Leandro as up and coming.

'This is a unique situation for me,' she said, 'and I don't send police officers into danger without a very good reason. What does he want from you?'

'He wants us to leave him alone. We're working a joint investigation with the FBI and he's scared.'

'I know about the four homicides at the cabinet shop. Tell me what I don't know.'

'I can't tell you much so I'm not going to tell you anything, but the FBI is on the way here. Ask them or listen in as they're talking to me when I'm in there.'

'We have a SWAT team here. It'll be dark in less than an hour and we're prepared to go in behind you.'

'Does the SWAT team know where he is in the house?'

'We know where the phone he's using is.' She tugged at his arm. She wanted to talk privately and they walked ten yards away. 'You're taking a very big risk. He just killed an officer. You don't have to do this. You could lose your life.'

Raveneau looked from her to his cell. The screen lit again and it was the captain calling. But he didn't see any real choice. He didn't see another way. He looked at the police chief.

'No matter what happens, don't let him get killed. He needs to stay alive. He is the link to people who have to be found. Tell your SWAT team they can incapacitate him but under no conditions kill him. The FBI will tell you the same thing.'

'Are you married?'

'What?'

'Are you married?'

'Not any more.'

'Do you have children?'

'I had a son who was killed in Iraq.'

From the way he recited that she knew it still hurt. He saw that in her eyes and said, 'Let's do this.'

TWENTY-EIGHT

When Raveneau walked down the street to the house his pulse was loud in his ears. He wanted to be calm, but that was impossible. He stepped on to a flagstone path and followed that to a concrete stoop and a green-painted front door. He knocked. He listened and waited. He knocked again and the door opened but Drury didn't show himself.

'Get in here!'

The door closed fast, deadbolt snicking into place as the gun pushed into his neck.

'On the floor now! Down! Get down on your knees! Lay down!'

Drury made a clumsy search then kicked at Raveneau's head before ordering him to get up. He walked Raveneau at gunpoint down a hallway. The hostage negotiator had advised talking as soon as he was in the door. So far, Raveneau hadn't said anything and the gun barrel jabbed at his back again.

'In there, go in there,' and Raveneau walked into a bedroom.

'We're not doing a trade any more,' Drury said.

'Where is she?'

'Shut the fuck up.'

'Show me her.'

Raveneau looked up at him both hands gripping a Glock, the veins on the side of his neck bulging.

'How about I shoot you instead?'

'Shoot me and a SWAT team will be in the door in seconds after hearing the discharge. They're out there getting ready right now. You've got about thirty seconds to get her outside, so maybe forty-five seconds to live.'

'You've got less.'

Raveneau took a step toward him. 'OK, you can do that or I can free her, get her out the front door and we can talk. The Feds know you got used. You got set-up. You were framed and you can trade what you know. You can make a deal with the FBI but let me get the hostage out the door. We're running out of time. Where is she?'

'Shut up.'

'You've got me, you don't need her.'

'Shut the fuck up.'

'They want to deal. They're worried. They're scared. They'll listen.'

For a moment he thought Drury was going to pull the trigger, and maybe he was. But he didn't and motioned with the gun barrel for Raveneau to get up and walk down the hallway.

She was in a tub in the bathroom with duct tape wrapped around her head holding a crushed roll of toilet paper to her forehead. He saw the blood and figured the toilet paper was about a wound. She was light, maybe a hundred and thirty pounds. Raveneau carried her down the hall. He tore the tape off her ankles and led her to the front door. Drury was two-handing the gun behind him as he opened the door just enough for her to go through. He didn't doubt Drury would pull the trigger if anything happened, and he didn't know if the door was going to knock him backwards as a SWAT team charged in, or whether glass was going to shatter somewhere else in the house.

As soon as the opening was big enough she was gone. He heard her running as he locked the door again and Drury stepped back.

'Down the hall and up the stairs.'

They climbed carpeted stairs to the master bedroom. With the lights off and dusk falling it was nearly dark as Raveneau talked.

'They need you. You are the key and they don't want you killed. I can get the FBI on the phone. You'll have to show them where you dropped the plywood before you picked it up a second time. They don't care what you got paid. That's not what they're after. Get your deal, then trade.'

'You're lying.'

But there was no conviction in his voice. He was buying in.

'They went through your text and email messages.' Raveneau let that rest a moment in the twilight and then added some bullshit on to it. 'They ran their algorithm and found the pattern.'

'I got two thousand dollars.'

'To drop the plywood and pick it up again?'

After a long pause, Drury said, 'I'm not going to sit in a prison for life. That's what they're telling me I'm going to do. I'm not doing that for two thousand dollars.'

'You were used.'

'Yeah, that guy used me.'

'What guy?'

'I don't even know his fucking name.'

'He offered you the two grand.'

'Yes.'

'OK, we've got to call. You can dial the number if you don't trust me. We've got to get ahead of the local SWAT guys. They'll start moving with dark. They'll only let us sit in here so long. Let's get the Feds on the line. Let's get the deal.'

'Downstairs.'

Drury pushed the gun barrel into his back as they started down. As they reached the bedroom Drury got nervous. He ordered Raveneau down on his belly on the floor again and searched by hand for the phone and gun. The light was gone from the room and Raveneau kept saying, 'Don't turn on a light whatever you do.'

Drury shoved Raveneau's phone at him. 'Find their number. Show it to me.'

Raveneau did that and with the phone to his ear and the gun in his right, Drury called Coe. Coe played his role perfectly, answered crisply, 'FBI.' He spoke loud enough for Raveneau to listen in.

'We know you were used,' Coe said. 'We understand and we want to talk. Hold the phone where I can hear Inspector Raveneau say he's OK.'

Drury held the phone out for Raveneau and as Drury brought the phone back to his ear Coe said loudly, 'We've got a vehicle in the area. We want to pick you up. Are you willing to do that?'

Drury knew it couldn't be that easy, but he couldn't come up with the right questions and Coe kept talking. Maybe Drury didn't know he'd killed a police officer or maybe he fantasized that could be dealt with. Either way, Raveneau could tell Coe was convincing him from the short answers Drury gave. He got the feeling as Drury hung up that he actually believed it was going to happen just as Coe described it.

It at least started that way. Two Fed sedans and a van came down the street. Three FBI agents came to the door though none were standing in front of it when it opened and their guns were drawn when he did come out. Drury laid down his weapon. He accepted their apologies when they told him the wrist restraints were only temporary. As they loaded Drury into the van, the agent in charge turned to Raveneau to thank him.

'You can thank me on the way,' Raveneau answered. 'I'm coming with you.'

TWENTY-NINE

A pair of interrogators worked Drury. They calmed him down. They fed him. They talked about the upcoming Super Bowl and not at all about the patrol officer Drury had murdered. Raveneau was aware from Coe's updates how angry the Oakland police were that the Feds took Drury, and Fox TV took that story national, the federal government running ramshod. By tomorrow Raveneau knew the outrage would grow to a roar unless more information was released.

But it was also clear from Coe that the FBI believed as Raveneau did, that John Drury held critical information. As Raveneau watched through the glass, Drury kept circling back to the same story of the man who hired him at Pete's Corner.

'Where did this Mr Helsing contact you?'

'At the same bar Raveneau followed me to.'

'Why there?'

'It's where we first met.'

'Tell us about that first meeting again.'

'I don't remember. I guess he started a conversation. He bought the drinks. I remember that.' Drury expelled a harsh laugh.

'What were you drinking?'

'What the fuck difference does it make?'

'We want every detail.'

'I don't remember what I was drinking. He won some money gambling or on a lottery ticket or something and said it was good luck to buy someone a drink.'

'Were you sitting at the bar?'

'We were standing.'

'He was standing next to you?'

'That's what I just said.'

'Was he taller or shorter than you?'

Raveneau caught the hesitation. He glanced at Coe. Coe saw it too.

'Shorter.'

'How much shorter?'

'I don't know.'

'An inch, two inches, three inches.'

'Yeah.'

'Yeah, what?'

'Three.'

'Did he buy drinks for anyone else?'

The hesitation again and then, 'There were these guys playing pool. He bought beers for them. That was it that night. We talked and he left. Maybe we shook hands.'

'What did you talk about?'

'I don't remember.'

'Tell us about the second meeting. When was it?'

'Pretty close to Thanksgiving.'

'How close?'

'The day before maybe, it was when he made the offer to pay me if I delivered stuff for him. I got to know him over the next three or four months. When Raveneau came to the bar I freaked because I thought he was a cop and it could be about stuff I did for Helsing.'

'You thought you might get busted by Inspector Raveneau?'

'I knew he was looking around and I wondered if he was a cop. He called me earlier and I took off from my house, so I was kind of freaked anyway.'

The interrogators rolled with it though one of them looked toward the glass.

'Describe his physical features.'

'He has regular features.'

'What are regular features?'

'He's not Arab or anything like that if that's what you're asking.'

'Was he white, black, Hispanic?'

'He's a white guy with nothing special about his face. Sort of like you.'

'What color was his hair?'

'Black with some gray.'

'Show us where the gray was.'

Alongside him, Coe said, 'They want him to describe Helsing and have the artist work from the tape, but I think we'd better get the artist in there now.'

'Not yet, I get what they're doing.'

'Eyes?'

'Dark.'

'Brown, black, what are they?'

Drury smiled. 'Hey, I never exactly looked into his eyes. It happened because I said I needed to make more money and he said he might know a way if I was doing lumber deliveries and it would be a pretty good cash deal for me as long as I figured out a way to add a stop to my regular deliveries without my boss knowing.' Drury turned toward the glass, adding, 'Sounded good to me.'

'You weren't worried about getting fired?'

'I knew how to do it.'

'Tell us about the deliveries and then we'll come back to the description of Helsing. We need more on him.'

'Yeah, we've got a lot of things to talk about before we get to a better description.'

Raveneau glanced at Coe. That was loud and clear from Drury and Raveneau doubted the description he'd given of this Helsing was accurate at all.

'You'd better make your deal with him,' Raveneau said. 'He's just playing your guys in there and they know it.'

Coe folded his arms over his chest. 'We promised Oakland we wouldn't make any deals.'

'You've got to do something to convince him.'

Coe slowly shook his head. He stared through the glass.

'When did you start doing deliveries for Helsing?'

'Right after that, and if you're going to ask me what day, I don't know, end of November, I guess.'

'What did you deliver the first delivery?'

'Some boxes.'

'How many?'

'Half a dozen maybe.'

'How many deliveries have you done altogether?'

'Probably a dozen.'

'Did you keep a record of where?'

'The opposite, I didn't want any record. They went different places. The unit of plywood was the biggest. Most were small enough for me to carry them, boxes and shit. The first ones were test runs. You know, to see if I could make it work and it worked fine because we'd talk and I'd be able to give him my route for the day. It wasn't like his deliveries were urgent. I thought he was just about saving money. It would have cost three times as much to run it through the company.'

'What did you think you were delivering?'

'The wood I knew was plywood obviously. A lot of the other stuff was in boxes or crates. A couple of heavier things went to a machine shop.'

'What was the name of that shop?'

'I don't remember.'

'Where was it?'

'Out toward Vacaville.'

'We'll need you to take us there.'

'That, my man, depends on your offer.'

Outside the glass Raveneau said, 'He doesn't think he's going to be charged with murder.'

'Where did you get paid?'

'At the bar and in cash, and no I don't have some account book I entered it in.'

'Have you been through the photos on his cell phone?'

'We're going through everything. We're in his house. We're in his computer and everything in his life we can find. Eight agents are on this guy tonight.'

One of the interrogators stood up. The other asked, 'Were you paid at the bar at Pete's Corner every time?'

'Yeah, and I know it's a stupid name, but Pete's a good dude.' Drury rubbed his right cheek. 'Look, I'm trying to help here. Am I going to be set-up somewhere in like witness protection or something?'

The interrogator who stood leaned on the table and stared him in the eye.

'Our job in here is to get the information from you. If the information checks out things advance to the next step, but those decisions aren't made by us. Right now, it's not advancing the way we want. I'm not sure about this Helsing, if you know what I mean. The things you're telling are a little hazy at key spots. You keep telling us the same story and it's making me tired. It's making me think we're wasting our time.'

Coe turned. 'Guess they agree with you.'

'You need to go in and sell him.'

'I'll be lying to him.'

In the interview room Drury said, 'I want my deal now.'

'First we need something to make a deal over. We need to be able to find this Helsing without a first name.' There you go, Raveneau thought, give it back to him. 'Did Mr H ever say where he lives or where he's from or what he does for a living?'

'He said he was a broker.'

'What kind of broker?'

Drury shrugged.

'Are you going to tell us a guy like you wouldn't find out who he's dealing with? You're way too smart for that.'

'It wasn't any of my business. He was just saving money hiring me and I needed the cash. He paid up front.'

'A few minutes ago he was paying you afterward at Pete's Corner. So which is it?'

'I'm not fucking giving you this and then getting screwed later. The Coe dude said we'd make a deal.'

Raveneau nudged Coe. 'Go tell him something to get him talking.'

'What would you do with him, right now?'

'Either sell him a car or threaten him. If you sell him a car you'll have to lie to him, but it won't hit him right away and you can take him on that drive early tomorrow before it all blows up. If you take that route you're on his side, so knock down the interrogators, especially her. She's most effective. She's gotten under his skin. Let him name what he wants and agree with him that's fair as long as he comes across with everything you need. Then leave like a car salesman goes back to the dealership manager, which in this case is Bureau headquarters.

'Leave the room to go call Bureau headquarters. Guys like Drury are used to getting screwed by people like auto dealership managers. He expects to get screwed here, too. But he needs to get something in return. He needs a framework he can see his new life in. So it should be prison but not too much and a promise of special privileges while he's there.'

'I'm not doing that.'

'OK, then threaten him. You guys operate outside the boundaries of law anyway. Everyone in the country knows it, so hit him hard. Tell him there's a bunk waiting for him in Guantánamo.'

In the interview room an interrogator, the woman asked him slowly, 'Are you expecting everything that happened today to go away?'

'Coe said he could make things happen.' Drury looked from her to the glass. He spoke to the glass. 'I know the Oakland cop got hurt and you're not talking about him. What about him? Are you going to wait until you're done milking me before you mention him?'

Drury lifted his hands and pretended to make quotation marks in the air as he asked, 'If that's the plan, I should have just shot fucking Raveneau and myself. I'm not sitting in a prison the rest of my life. If you're so worried and you want to know where I took this stuff, you better keep your word. I want to talk to someone who can make decisions. It's not going to happen otherwise.'

In the room the interrogator, the woman said, 'It's just us until you give us something. Then we'll call Special Agent Coe. But no one offered you a deal. You were offered a trade and so far you're not coming across.'

'I'm not talking any more. I'm done.'

'Then so are we.'

They left and Drury sat there for forty-five minutes before Coe went in. Coe sat down across from him and said, 'I've got some bad news. The police officer, the woman you took hostage, those aren't your biggest problems any more. We're close to charging you with aiding terrorists and we may up the charges from there. If we do that, you may never feel sunlight on your face again. You'll never hold a woman again. I can promise you that. You'll never drive again. You'll never go anywhere ever. You won't have a life. You'll have a number and after awhile your name won't really matter to anyone any more, not even you.'

'What are you talking about?'

'The deliveries, the people you're working with. You can't believe the shit we're prepared to charge you with.'

Raveneau saw Drury's face change.

'You got him,' Raveneau said, but there was no one to hear him.

THIRTY

The bar was empty, the lights dimmed for the night when Raveneau and Celeste sat down at a table. In the early evening the wind blew in hard gusts as a storm came in off the ocean. It was raining and outside the street was dark and wet and the sodium street lights threw orange light through sheets of rain on to the oiled wood of the restaurant floor. Raveneau hung his dripping coat on the back of a nearby chair. A bottle of a Rioja sat between them, along with salt cod crostini and a salad of farro, shrimp, and cucumber. She smiled at him and said, 'This is something we can do now. Are you really OK?'

'Yeah, I'm fine, and Drury is with the FBI.'

'He killed an Oakland police officer. He could have killed you.'

'Yeah, he could have.'

'Weren't you scared?'

'Sure.' Raveneau glanced at her. Of course he was scared. 'I didn't know what he was going to do, but I didn't think he wanted to kill himself or me.'

'But you seem so normal now.'

'I'm really not.'

'I hope not.'

He didn't answer that. He poured her wine. He poured himself more wine and lifted his glass, touched hers, took a sip, and then drank more. It was hard not to just talk with her, tell her about the bomb casings and all the rest.

'We had the radio on as we were cleaning up here and they said he was held in connection with the murders at that cabinet shop. How did the FBI get involved?'

'That's about a delivery he was part of. He helped the wrong people and doesn't know where it's going to lead. He screwed up badly. He's like a big truck, an eighteen wheeler that's come over the crest of mountains, started down, and the brakes are fading. He thought he was smart and clever and had control of his life and now it's so out of control he doesn't even realize yet his next fifteen years are in prison, and that's if he gives up what he knows.'

'Which you can't tell me about.'

'That's right, Celeste, I can't tell you what I'd like to.'

'Even though you might have gotten killed today.'

Raveneau picked up one of the little pieces of toast with salt cod on it. He was surprised he had any appetite but he was hungry. He poured more wine and waited.

'We were busy tonight,' she said. 'People are ordering the mixed drinks and that's good. I can tell already we're going to be a place where people come for drinks and crostini. Maybe a few salads will catch on like this one.'

'It'll catch.'

He scooped some of the farro salad and saw she was staring at him.

'You were a hostage at gunpoint and now you're sitting here eating.'

'I'm sitting with you.' He took another bite and another swallow of wine and said, 'We're trying to get from Drury to people who hired him. We may have pushed him too hard.'

'I wish you had called me before you went into that house. Did you think of calling me?'

'Sure.'

'Why didn't you?'

OK, so now they were to it. But even knowing it was coming he didn't have an answer she was going to like.

'There wasn't much time and I needed to get in a frame of mind where I was focused on getting the hostage out and then myself. I think you might have worried and wanted to know why I was taking the risk.'

'I already know why and calling me doesn't mean you have to explain. It means you want to hear my voice before you take a risk like that. It means something could happen. It means what I don't want to ever do again is hear on the radio you're risking your life in a hostage negotiation and not talk to you. I'd rather you called me and said you've got to do it. Then I would know.'

'Next time I'll call you.'

He tried to say that in a light way, but it fell flat.

'You didn't call me for hours after.'

Raveneau nodded. He understood yet it was hard to believe they were having this conversation. Still, it continued a while longer. Then as she got up to get something he brought her chair around the table. He put it alongside his and they sat close to each other. He poured more wine and they watched the rain through the windows and let it be until his phone buzzed.

'Thanks for everything,' Coe said. 'We're touring with Drury at dawn.'

'You won't get much time.'

'I know, and I'll call and let you know if we learn anything. What time do you fly tomorrow?'

'Late morning and I'm back in a couple of days.'

He hung up and felt the fatigue of all the spent adrenaline wash through him, but he didn't want to leave yet. Being with Celeste was when he felt calmest and happiest. He put an arm around her shoulders and held her. For the first time since they started going out he knew he should be living with her. They locked up the bar and left and the rain pounded on the roof as they walked the boardwalk to the deck and inside his place. Late in the night he woke to Celeste shaking him awake. Her voice was soft.

'Ben, Ben, you're having a nightmare.'

Part of it was still with him, but he said, 'I was trying to find a phone to call you.'

'You kept saying hurry. I think you said the word President. What were you dreaming about? You were trying to get some-where. Where were you trying to get to?'

'I don't know.'

She lay back down then rested a cool hand on his forehead.

'You're very hot. You sounded very worried.'

His heart was still pounding but he couldn't remember the dream any more.

THIRTY-ONE

Two days later Raveneau stood along a guard rail on the Kohala Mountain Road on the Big Island and took in the coastline below and the warm sun and the wind with the smell of lava rock and ocean. Beyond the guard rail the grassy slope fell steeply to a highway. Dark lava outcrops dotted the slope as did stands of trees. He used binoculars working his way across the slope, holding the photo in his left hand.

After scanning all of the ranches, and there weren't many, he returned to one and then to a narrow dirt track rising from a stand of trees to a house. He could see the roof of the house but the roof was all that showed in the photo. In the photo with the handwritten note, 'The house, Big Island,' the photograph was taken from closer in. Someone had walked up the steep slope behind the house, he guessed. But still, it looked like the same roofline and the same metal roof.

He lifted the binoculars from the house and studied the coast-line, the long sweep south with its narrow white band of sand. He looked at the coastline in the photo again and now he was almost certain it was the right house. He lowered the binoculars. The blue corrugated metal roof of the house below had faded and rusted. He checked the photo again and though there was no one there to hear him, said, 'That's got to be it.'

Raveneau had already checked for record of a mortgage or deed of trust. There was no record of a Jim Frank owning a house on the Big Island, but maybe Frank had rented or leased. He looked down at the highway and then called up the Big Island map on his phone again. He needed to get to the highway below to get to the house. After studying the map he walked back to the car and was getting ready to pull out when he saw he had missed a call from Coe. He called Coe before pulling away.

'How did the drive go with Drury? I thought I'd have a message from you when I landed.'

'It's why I'm calling. Things strung out through the day, but he showed us a machine shop and a building where he delivered the unit of plywood and then picked it up a week later. The tenant moved out last week and we're looking for him. Tools are gone but it looks like he had what he needed to make the bomb casings. We've got metal filings to compare so we'll know more soon. We've got a description of two men and their vehicles. We'll find them.'

Coe made it sound as if they were following a trail, but to Raveneau it sounded as if they got there too late.

'Any movement with Khan?'

'No, it's ghostly quiet in there. There's a family of rats we see every night but that's it. I've got one more thing for you. I heard back on the Hawaii photos and some confirming information on Jim Frank. He was Navy during the Vietnam War and flew off a carrier, but I don't have the aircraft carrier name in front of me. I'll call or text it to you later. He flew off a carrier and then from one of the forward bases. He had a reputation for taking chances. He got medaled but you probably already have all this.'

He did. His file on Frank doubled every day in the last week, but it was like everything with this case, it still didn't amount to anything.

'What's interesting and why I wanted to catch you this morning is that your expert was right. Two or three of those landscape photos were taken with a very high resolution camera. It either belonged to the US government or a movie maker, a film company. When are you coming back?'

'Tomorrow.'

'Well, have a drink on me somewhere on the island later this afternoon. Thanks again for your help with Drury.' He sounded cautiously upbeat, adding, 'We're farther along than we were a day ago.'

Raveneau got back out of the car after hanging up with Coe. He double-checked the big rock across the highway below he was going to use as a landmark. He checked the house again. It sat on a notch cut into the long-falling slope. Someone must have driven a bulldozer up there and cut a flat pad to build the house on. He wouldn't see much of the roof from the highway below. He would see the trees where the dirt track came up from and figured there were other ranch buildings down there also. He glanced at the coastline once more. None of the resorts in the distance to the south were in the photo.

Now he drove north toward Hawi. When he got there he picked up a text from Celeste, 'Remember the Kona.' She wanted him to pick up samples of a Kona coffee she couldn't find in the Bay Area. Raveneau didn't know when he was going to do that or how before flying out tomorrow.

He texted back after going into a little shop to get a coffee to-go. 'Drinking Kona right now.'

He left Hawi and the road was one lane in either direction and then widened to two. The morning was warming and he could feel the change as he followed an old pickup in the slow lane. He studied the long upslope on his left and as he spotted the landmark rock ahead he slowed even more. Then he was past and knew he'd gone too far. After turning around he pulled over next to a local cop waiting for speeders. Raveneau showed his San Francisco homicide star and explained what he was looking for.

'Look for aluminum gates,' the officer said. 'They open out. You have to close them for cattle and you need to go to the ranch house first. They don't like people they don't know on their property.'

'I'll introduce myself.'

Five minutes later he found the gates.

THIRTY-TWO

T he gates were double-latched, but not locked, the No Trespassing signs impossible to miss. The gates swung across a cattle grate and against a barbed wire fence. Raveneau drove through then closed them again. The road climbed very steeply and he went left at the first fork. It continued the same steep rise before leveling and starting north across the slope and then rising over a lip to an unexpected flat area with a big ranch house and barn set back among a stand of trees.

The house was two-story, deep and long with a porch running down the front and a tall steep roof facing the ocean. A large screened lanai was on the far end and at the north end was the barn. Two vehicles, a yellow jeep open to the air and a brown late model Toyota pickup sat in front of the house. So somebody was home. He parked near the cars then went up the steps to the long porch and knocked on the front door.

After a minute he tried again, and when no one answered walked down the porch to the lanai. Presumptuous maybe, but this was Hawaii, and the people did seem more laidback. He figured it was warm enough that someone might be inside the screened room. But he didn't see anyone.

He crossed to the barn. He opened a door and it was cool and dark inside. When he called hello no one answered and he returned to the house and slid one of his cards in between the front door and jamb. Then he figured he could justify driving the ranch roads looking for the owner so when he got back down to the last fork, instead of continuing down he turned on to a narrow broken asphalt road barely wider than his rental.

It was potholed. It wasn't used much. Grass and plants grew from cracks. It doubled back in a hair pin turn, climbed steeply, and it struck Raveneau that he was yet to see a place to turn the car around. He reached a stand of trees and another fork, one that was a continuation of the road he was on, and the other just a faint track moving into the trees. He studied both and then got out the photo again. This looked like the right spot.

Follow this dirt track up, he thought. He climbed slowly up through the pines and after the car bottomed-out a couple of times he decided to walk from here. The dirt track was steep. He drew deep breaths but was even more confident when he saw the dirt track emerging in a straight line up from the trees. He climbed thinking the only way up here was in a four-wheel drive. Halfway up the last steep pitch he saw the blue rusted roof of the house.

When he reached the flat he caught his breath, and then looked across the ocean at Maui and understood why they built it here. He pulled his phone and took photos of the house and the site. On this end of the house was a palm tree and what had once been a gravel pad big enough for a vehicle to park and turn around. It was hot in the sun along the front of the house and shady as he walked around the back of the house past a palm tree at the corner. A rusted air conditioning unit sat on a concrete pad.

He looked through a dusty window into an empty room, saw sliding doors on the other side, a wood ceiling stained by leaks, flooring warped where water had gotten to it. It was nearly all glass along this face. Light fixtures hung on pendants and the name Eichler came to him, but he couldn't remember whether Eichler was an architect or a builder or both. But it was that style.

Or it was once that style. No one had lived here in a long time, not Jim Frank, not anyone. He continued walking down the side looking in through the sliding doors anywhere he could. He worked his way around to the sun and the front facing the ocean, and rattled a locked sliding door remembering Ryan Candel tapping the blue-painted metal roof in the photo and saying,

'This is my dad's house. I don't know where it is, but that's the house my mom said was his and she called it paradise. She said she could live the rest of her life there. When I was little she used to say, we'll get there someday, and when I got old enough to realize that was never going to happen, I mean, I was

probably thirteen by then, but she was that good in making you believe in stuff. When I finally realized it I yelled at her, don't ever show me that picture again. I can still remember how shocked she was and how she still tried to smile. If I could take something back, it would be that. I don't even know where it came from in me that night. It just kind of exploded out of me. My mom needed to believe. That's how she got by and I ruined that for her.'

Raveneau saw furniture. He saw a stack of papers, yellowed and sitting on a kitchen counter. He returned to the back and debated several minutes before putting some muscle into lifting one of the old sliding doors off its track. He picked it up, lifted it out, and set it carefully against the wall as the house exhaled the stale air from inside.

He didn't step inside yet. He walked back along the side of the house to the parking area and looked down the track to the trees and his car shadowed there. If he discovered a document what was he going to do with it? He didn't have a search warrant. It was breaking and entering no matter how gently he put the sliding door back on its track when he finished.

But then he wasn't going to be here tomorrow and the house had clearly been empty for a long time. The house looked abandoned. He walked back and stepped inside. The living room had one piece of furniture, a side table that was empty except for four or five bamboo place mats. The smallest of three bedrooms held no furniture. The next bedroom had a chair and a nightstand, and a headboard but no other part of the bed. The third bedroom had a dresser with drawers that didn't operate well. Closets were empty. Some pots in the kitchen but no utensils or appliances left other than an oven. He found some papers inside the oven and went through those and learned nothing although he did find a folded yellowed bit of newspaper with the date May 21, 2003.

Still, there was enough here to make a few guesses. If Jim Frank had lived here he was likely the last person to do so. Things were given away but not everything was taken. That's what he was looking at here. Since the last occupant left no one had cared for the building. He continued his search rechecking the kitchen cabinets and drawers, sifting through the papers in the kitchen again, and double-checking the built-in book shelves because a few books remained.

He flipped the pages of the books looking for loose papers and found a book on aerodynamics and commercial aircraft. Because of the subject matter he looked at that one more closely. He looked for underlined sentences, notes, some proof of ownership, and then his eye caught the word *Frank* on the Acknowledgements page. '*Without the help of the legendary Captain James Frank this book would not have been possible. His knowledge, note taking, and generosity in sharing his flying experiences aided in every way. I should also add Frank's squadron at great risk to themselves saved my life and a number of others during a particularly dangerous battle in the War in Vietnam. We've been good friends since.*'

Raveneau had the book in his hand when he stepped outside. He heard movement but before he could turn, 'Freeze. If you move at all, I'll shoot you.'

THIRTY-THREE

'I'm a San Francisco homicide inspector.'

'Bullshit.'

'My inspector's star is in my back pocket. I left a card at the front of the main house. Did you find it?'

'Cops don't trespass and break into houses.'

'I didn't break in and I'm investigating a cold case, the murder of an Alan Krueger in San Francisco in 1989. He knew Jim Frank. I'm looking for Frank or people who knew him.'

'Don't say he killed somebody.'

That sounded very much like a warning and Raveneau didn't show any reaction.

'I don't know what his role was.'

'Keep holding the book. Hold it with both hands and above your head, we're going to walk. My uncle will call the police and you can explain to them.'

'That's fine, but I knocked on the front door of the ranch house when I got here. I checked the barn. I checked the lanai and then I drove around looking for somebody to ask. I've been working from a photo. This is the house in the photo and when I looked through the windows I realized no one had lived here in a long time. The sliding door was loose so I thought I'd take a walk through and then drive back to the ranch house.'

Raveneau lowered the book. He waited a moment to see if the man was going to order him to raise his arm again. When that didn't happen he held the book out. 'There's an acknowledgement in here of Captain Jim Frank by the author.'

'Turn so your back is facing me, hold the book with your arm straight out, and then put your other hand on the pocket with your badge.'

'You're watching too many movies. Look, I'm unarmed. I'm working a cold case like I said.'

Raveneau didn't do what the young man ordered, but he did turn so he could see him reach for his homicide star. As he pulled his star, the man pulled the trigger twice and Raveneau stumbled backwards. He fell into the building and scrambled to his feet. One of the bullets had passed close enough for him to hear the buzz and he was both furious and unsure what would happen next. He quickly crossed the house and went out another sliding door. Behind him, he heard the man ordering him to stop.

But Raveneau didn't stop. He went straight off the steep slope down through the grass toward the trees. He wasn't trying to make it to the car but thought he could make it to one of the bigger trees before the man located him. When he reached the trees he wasn't sure. He lay flat on his belly behind one of the bigger trees. He found his cell.

And then quietly and suddenly the kid was there. He'd made the assumption Raveneau would run to his car and now he was looking around. They weren't far apart.

'I'm going to count to ten and if you're not out here I'm going to start hunting for you and I'm going to assume you aren't who you said you were.'

Raveneau saw him moving around the car looking inside.

'One, two,' and as he turned Raveneau moved in closer, kneeling near a tree and picking up a couple pieces of the lava rock. He heard another vehicle engine and the young man probably heard it as well.

'Three, four, five, six.'

Raveneau threw the rock behind the man and beyond the car. He watched him react, watched him adjust and hold the barrel steady. Looked like he knew how to handle a gun. Now he wheeled and turned to face Raveneau.

'You don't want to shoot me. It's not as much fun as you might think it is.' He held out his phone and used the one name he'd been given before he flew here. 'I just sent a text to an FBI agent named Mike Kawena. He knows I'm here. He's calling the local police so they'll probably show up soon. If anything happens to me he'll come for you.'

'You broke in.'

'You don't shoot people for walking into an abandoned building. You don't have license to do that just because I'm on the property.'

Raveneau heard the other vehicle getting closer but moving very slowly. He saw the man shift, hesitate, and then lower the gun.

'We've had trouble here before.'

Raveneau held up his homicide star and walked with his arm out so he could read more easily.

'My wallet is in the glove compartment.'

Raveneau laid his homicide star on the roof of the car. As he reached in his pocket for his keys the gun rose slightly.

'Either keep that down or put it down. If you don't think that star is real get out your phone and call the San Francisco Police Department or the FBI field office in Honolulu.'

Raveneau took a much harder look at him and asked, 'How close were you trying to get to me with those shots up there?'

The look he got back only made him wonder more. He watched the younger man smile.

'Get your wallet out of the glove compartment.'

Raveneau moved around the car but slowly. The man was older than he had thought, at least thirty-two or three, a mix of Asian and Caucasian, dark-haired, dark-eyed, a light gold tint to his skin. Raveneau reached in the glove box and when he turned the man was four or five steps back and with the gun up again.

'What's the matter with you?'

'Lay your wallet on top of the car.'

Raveneau rested his wallet on the car roof. He stepped away

as ordered. He heard the other vehicle which had stopped, start crawling forward again.

'What's in the trunk?'

'My briefcase.'

'Open the trunk.'

Raveneau hit the button and the lid lifted. He put the briefcase on the ground and watched him go through the contents including the copies of the case files for the Krueger murder. He paused on the crime scene photos but didn't seem to be reading. He put everything back carefully and zipped the leather bag shut. He returned it to the trunk.

'I'm going to check inside your car. I want you to move away while I do it.'

'You've already seen enough.'

'Move over to the trees.'

'I'm done moving around for you. If you want to search the car, go ahead.'

He searched and then abruptly seemed satisfied. He pulled the clip from the gun, removed the chambered bullet, and grasped something under his shirt that turned out to be a microphone.

'We're good. He is who he says he is.'

Raveneau heard a response but couldn't make out the words. The man looked at him and said, 'My uncle wants us to come down to the house.'

'And now that you know who I am, who are you?'

'Matt Frank. I live here.'

Frank wore a blue T-shirt that read *Humphrey Whale Sanctuary*. He lifted his shirt in back and tucked the Glock into his jeans. He stared and said, 'Sorry, we've had a problem with people growing dope on the property.'

'All right, let's start again. I'm San Francisco homicide inspector Ben Raveneau. I'm here for the reason I told you I am. You found my card at the house?'

'Yes.'

'And that wasn't enough?'

'Not for my uncle.'

'Was that him in the jeep down the road?'

'Yes.'

'Why didn't he drive all the way up?'

'He was waiting for the OK from me.'

'And you're miked up? What is this, some sort of paramilitary game?'

'It's not a game. We deal with people growing dope on the property and stealing.'

'Your uncle wanted you to handle it?'

That was right. That was a good guess. Raveneau saw his reaction.

'Where did you get your accent?'

'Kentucky.'

'Your mother was Vietnamese?'

'How do you know that?'

'I recognize your father in your face.'

'Did you know my father?'

'No, but he's why I'm here.'

'He was ashamed of us. He divorced my mother. How do you know about us?'

'You have a half brother in San Francisco. He has a different mother and he has her name, but he's got a lot of your look. His name is Ryan Candel. What's your uncle's name?'

'Tom Casey.'

Raveneau pointed up the slope to the house. 'And your dad, Jim Frank, lived up there?'

'Yes.'

'Where is he now?'

'Follow me.'

They climbed back up the steep dirt track to the house then out past the north end and off the graded flat on to the grassy slope. There Raveneau saw three good-sized black-brown lava rocks stacked on each other, stacked so they would stay that way. He got it. He understood. He took in the dark roughness of the lava, the contrasting lush green of the steep slope, the soft wind off the water.

'Is he buried here?'

'Just his ashes.'

Raveneau stared out at the water for a long moment. Then he said, 'I understand you holding me at gunpoint, but I don't understand you putting those shots so close to me. It makes me wonder about you. I want you to know that.'

'I already know it.'

THIRTY-FOUR

Raveneau bumped back down the broken road in the rental with Matt Frank riding with him. Frank wanted to walk back the way he came but that wasn't OK with Raveneau.

'How did you know to go up to the house?'

'Talk to my uncle about that. He doesn't like people up at the house.'

'That's not what I asked.'

'After Dad died other people came and wanted to go through his things. It was a problem and my Uncle Casey dealt with it and even if it doesn't matter any more he doesn't like people up there.'

'You didn't come up the road, did you?'

Frank smiled but didn't turn his head or say anything.

'What's funny about that?'

'It says you were watching. You knew you were breaking in. There's a trail from the main house. My dad and Uncle Casey used to call it the Drinking Trail because they would meet every night, either my uncle going up or my dad coming down. When we found your card in the door he said go up the trail with a gun. Like I said we didn't know if we could trust the card.'

'You thought someone just printed up a card.'

Now Frank turned but he didn't say anything and then they were at the main house. Thomas Casey greeted him on the porch and Matt Frank disappeared as if his job was done. Casey shook his hand with an odd enthusiasm. At the same time he looked perplexed.

'It's been twenty-two years since AK was killed.'

'Is that what you called him?'

'Yes. His initials, Vietnam, and the gun. Jim Frank, Alan Krueger, and I met when we were in our early twenties and flying for the Navy. We were in Nam together. Do you have a new lead, Inspector?'

'We do.'

'I'd like to hear about it. Was it this new lead that caused you to trespass on my property and break into Jim's house?'

'The door was open and I walked in and took a look around.'

'That's a good story, open door, natural curiosity, and after all you traveled all this way and you left a card to show you were trying to find the property owner.'

'And here you are.'

'But I found you. You didn't find me and the boy might have shot you.'

'He doesn't look like a boy. He must be in his thirties.'

'He is.'

'One of those shots passed pretty close to my head.'

'I bet it did but if you're working on AK's murder you're welcome here for now. I've got a problem with what you did and I'll tell you straight up I may report the trespassing and breaking and entering. But I'll also try to help you with your investigation.' Casey smiled and added, 'I just want to be clear. You look like you're not that far from retirement anyway. Let's go back to the lanai and talk.'

In the lanai he pointed at a table.

'Let's sit here. After having a couple of shots sent your way you must feel like a drink. What about a beer or do you want something harder? Do you like poke? The fish is always fresh here and the poke is a local staple. It's ahi and we've got crackers to put it on. Let me go back and tell Lani, our cook and housekeeper.'

Lani turned out to be a middle-aged Hawaiian woman with a warm smile and an easy way with her employer. Raveneau guessed she lived here and had for a long time. He got the feeling Casey had money but doubted it came from the grass fed cattle business.

As Raveneau tipped the beer he took a longer look at him, angular face, gray-eyed, sharp gaze, blond-brown hair going silver.

'Jim died in 2004 of complications from an old war wound. I can't picture someone else living up there, so I've left the house empty. He was one of a kind from a different time where character and personality were more valued. Americans might be more educated now or more sophisticated or what passes for

sophistication, but they don't have the same moxie. Jim knew
how to live without being afraid of living. Do you know what
I'm saying?'

'I do.'

'If he had an idea he liked he'd act on it.'

Raveneau scooped some of the poke mix on to a cracker. He
took another pull of the beer and moved the conversation back
to Krueger.

'When did you last see him?'

'October 1989. His boyfriend was with him. Do you know
about the boyfriend in San Francisco?'

'I know of a boyfriend and I've talked to him, but he told me
he and Alan broke up in 1986.'

'If his name is Marlin Thames he's lying to you. Marlin and
Alan were here for ten days that October. They were going to
stay longer but they argued so much I asked them to leave early,
and I told the boyfriend never to come back. I didn't like him
or the way he treated AK. I don't give a damn about sexual
preference. Neither did Jim, but Thames was a rude sonofabitch.
I was sorry AK lost his career over being gay. That was a shame
and that visit was the last time I saw Alan.'

'What was Alan Krueger doing for work when you last saw
him?'

'Good question but not one I can answer for you. I can tell
you Jim and I spent a lot of years guessing. AK's comings and
goings were getting a little mysterious by then. I know he worked
for more than one of our government agencies buying counterfeit
US money in Asia. We actually tried to find out and the Secret
Service told us they only use their own agents, but we knew that
wasn't true. We knew from Alan he was doing work for them in
Asia as a contractor. He told us that much. He may have done
contract work for the CIA as well. That's the kind of thing he
would have told Jim, not me. Everyone confessed to Jim.'

'Where did Alan stay when he was in San Francisco?'

'With Thames.'

'Do you have any idea why Thames would lie to me?'

'Maybe he's your killer.' Casey thought a moment on that and
shook his head. 'No, it wasn't him. It was something to do with
the counterfeiters. Or that's what I think.'

'How did Jim Frank come to live here?'

'Oh, you don't want to talk about Thames any more. Well, Jim moved with bold strokes and that didn't always work. We built the house for him here because he was bankrupt. He wasn't good at holding on to money or at staying married. Both of those were weak spots. He was the way he was and I think his wives knew it when they married him. He didn't raise either of his boys. Heck, I did enough to raise Matt that he calls me uncle.'

'Did you teach him how to shoot?'

Casey chuckled.

'He got that on his own. He scared you, didn't he? I'm funding his business right now. I have no idea what happened to the other son. I don't even remember his name.'

'Ryan Candel. He's how I found my way here. From photos his mom had.'

'Had?'

'Allyson died.'

'I'm sorry to hear that. Allyson always made a room a happier place. How did she die?'

'Someone ran a red light.'

'What's the boy like?'

'He's trying to figure out who he is and he's got some issues, one of which is he carries a lot of anger toward his father.'

'Not surprising. Now Matt's mother was Vietnamese. She was married to a colonel for the South Vietnamese and running a bar and a brothel. The Cong killed her husband and she took up with Jim. He personally airlifted her out of Nam, got her pregnant, married her, divorced her, and left her in a relocation camp in Kentucky all in the same year. His attention span wasn't always the longest. Charismatic man, though.'

'Where is she now?'

'The last I heard she was saving Mexicans. She went Baptist in Kentucky and after the boy was old enough signed up with a missionary group that preaches to poor Mexicans in rural areas. Even with the way people are getting shot and beheaded in Mexico I'd bet she's still there. It would take more than a bullet to kill her anyway. Hell, if they beheaded her they'd still have to bury her head a half mile from her body or she'd figure out a way to get it back together. She was tough and had a very sharp tongue. Still does, I'm sure.

'When she decided she was going missionary she contacted Jim and I said send the boy here. She had him on a plane the next day. I'm not making any of this up. Matt still has a little Kentucky twang but he can surf. He's an islander.'

'Are Jim Frank's ashes really up under those rocks?'

'Just ashes and I made sure they burned it all down to nothing, the teeth and every last bone fragment, so that no one could pull any DNA later.'

'Why?'

'Well, let's just say many things were possible with Jim.'

Casey picked up his beer and smiled an odd strained smile. It changed the room.

'There was a judge in San Francisco who lived in the penthouse of an apartment building on Russian Hill. His wife wouldn't let him smoke on the penthouse decks because she didn't like the dope smell drifting inside, so he smoked on the roof deck up with the equipment. He fell off one night. Did Jim know about it? It seemed like he did. Did he have a part in it? How could he but he seemed to know something had happened to the judge other than an accident.'

'Judge Brighton.'

'Is that one of your cold cases? They replaced that judge with an even more liberal judge, so it was all a goddamned waste of time if it was about politics, and God knows he had opinions and he was unusual in what he was willing to do. Jim wasn't a killer but killing didn't weigh on him. We'd take it to the Cong and fry the villagers along with them. None of that ever bothered him as far as I knew. It was just part of the war, yet he was a man with a strict personal code.'

'How was his career as an airline pilot?'

'Whenever they got a new model jet they put him in the seat. Retired him with honors, same as the Navy, but let me go get something and show you.'

He limped out of the room, his leg stiff from sitting, Raveneau guessed. He looked at photos on a wall, in one, Krueger, Casey, and Frank in uniform, Frank somehow standing out in the photo. Then one of Frank and his son here, Frank looking like his health was gone. When Casey returned Raveneau asked, 'What other friends of Alan Krueger are still in the islands?'

'There's an officer up at Bradshaw Air Base named Shay.'

Casey slowly sat down. He slid the bowl with the poke aside and set a small painted metal box with a dragon painted on the lid on the table between them. Then, before sitting he pulled his pant leg up and showed Raveneau a long scar running from his knee.

'This was from flak. It's why I limp and don't play polo any more.' He smiled. 'That last is a joke. You don't need to make a note about looking up polo teams.' He studied Raveneau. 'You just missed Nam, right? But not by much.'

'That's right.'

'Well, Nam was a fucked-up situation if there ever was one, but at least we had a draft so we did it as a country as opposed to the bullshit now. Flying combat missions adrenalized Jim as much as anybody else, but at the same time he enjoyed it. If they hadn't run out of war he probably would have stayed in the military. He was here in Hawaii recovering from wounds when they canceled the war. He celebrated with everyone else but I believe part of him was disappointed. Open the box.'

When Raveneau did he was looking at one, then a second Navy Cross There were stripes that looked like they'd been removed from a uniform.

'Did you save the uniform?'

'No, I had him dressed in it before he was cremated. But that's not to say it was my idea. He got the uniform out, had it cleaned, and then left it hanging with the plastic on it in his closet. I was up there one night for a drink. Just about every night I'd walk up or he'd walk down. It was a regular thing if neither of us had guests. It was always best when it was just the two of us. Near the end it was mostly me going up there. We had a couple of drinks one night and he showed me the uniform hanging in the closet.

'"Dress me in that," he said, and then walked me out to where we spread his ashes. When we were standing there he said, "It'll be before the end of the year." It was two months later in October.

'All the way down he never once complained, or not once that I heard. He died at a place in Waimea, not far from here. He took death as he took life, as a thing to do. He lost a kidney, his spleen, and some his intestines the second time he was hit in Nam. When he started to have trouble, it was the remaining kidney.

'This photo here is us after a bombing run to Da Nang. The woman in the chair there next to Jim had known him for about thirty minutes.'

Jim Frank rested his arm on the back of the woman's chair. The chairs were rattan. His smile lit his face and Raveneau saw both of his sons in him.

'What about the other marriage?'

'Allyson was a great woman. She was the one who understood him and didn't have to change him. He made a big mistake letting her go.'

'Did they see each other after she moved to San Francisco?'

'They did and for several years after the boy was born he'd fly in and stay with her. Here, I've got a photo.'

He led Raveneau to a drawer behind a teak bar in the corner of the lanai.

'The rain blows in here and I can't hang everything I want.'

He slid the drawer open and lifted out a framed photo of Frank and Allyson and Ryan. Frank was in his United Airlines uniform. Ryan Candel looked like he was somewhere between eighteen months and two years. Allyson was beaming.

'That's her. That was her smile.' Casey held the photo out for him to take. 'Would this photo help his son?'

'I think it would.'

'Take it with you.'

'Can I borrow some of these others?'

'Yes.'

Tom Casey walked out with him. He stood alongside Raveneau's car.

'You didn't quite get what you needed, did you? But then you jumped around with your questions.'

'I'm scratching around the edges and I generally know when I'm going to get information that will help the case. Sometimes it's good to get the stories first. Do you have any problem with me calling you?'

'None as long as you're working AK's murder.'

'How often do you leave the island?'

'Not often. Sometimes I tell people I never leave here. That's about the war.' He tapped his palm on the roof of Raveneau's car.

'Jim would have been the first to lift a door off if he wanted to get into a house. He broke a window here once just to get to the whiskey, so I guess it fits you break into his house. You can call me anytime with questions about AK, and if you find his killer I'll fly to San Francisco and buy you the best dinner in town.'

'I'll hold you to that.'

'I hope you do.'

THIRTY-FIVE

'How's Hawaii?' la Rosa asked. 'Where are you?'

Raveneau turned off the highway and on to what was called the Saddle Road. The road crossed the interior of the island connecting the north and south. Along the road was Bradshaw Army Air Field where Raveneau had phoned half an hour before.

'I'm on my way to a military base and I need you to do something for me. After I stop at this air field I'm headed to the airport in Kona, and then on to Bali. I need your help with the lieutenant and the captain. I need to get cleared for Bali for a week.'

'You mean Bali in the South Pacific?'

'Yeah, it turns out Jim Frank rotated through islands and beach areas, possibly as part of a cover. After Bali I'll need a week in a place in Thailand called Phuket. The guy I just interviewed says it is beautiful beach country. I guess that's what the captain liked, beautiful women and beaches. I should have brought more than one swimsuit. You know, you rinse the salt off the suit and you can let one dry while—'

'Guess what, you're way out of touch. You don't know your beaches. No one goes to Phuket any more.'

Raveneau smiled as she realized he was teasing her. It didn't surprise him she knew her beaches.

Up ahead on his left the volcano Mauna Loa towered. In the midday Mauna Loa and the other volcano on the south end were gathering clouds. When he picked up the rental they warned him not to drive the Saddle Road. If he broke down there he'd be on the hook for the towing charges, but the road was much better than they said.

'What I'm not messing with you about is stopping at Bradshaw Army Air Field to try to find an officer who also knew Krueger.'

'Did you find the house?'

'I found the house and learned Jim Frank died in 2004. The house and the surrounding ranch are owned by an old close friend of his named Tom Casey. I just left him, but I can't get a read on him. He raises organic beef. He's got other businesses in the islands and a man living with him who apparently is a second son of Jim Frank's, but through a different marriage. There's more but I'll bring you up to speed when we have better reception.'

'So this Casey owns the property and that's why we couldn't find any record of any property ownership?'

'That's right.'

'And he just let Frank live there?'

'That's what he told me.'

'OK, and what are you hoping to do at the air base?'

'Interview an officer who knew Krueger.'

'Are you still flying home tomorrow?'

'I'm planning to.'

'Things are moving here.'

'What's happened?'

Raveneau listened now as she described Khan and his wife driving through San Francisco last night with two surveillance teams trailing.

'Khan's wife drove and slowly, so they gave her room. Too much as it turned out because two blocks after the Embarcadero Bart Station entrance Khan wasn't in the car any more. He crossed under the bay on Bart, switched trains at the MacArthur Station, went north and got off in El Cerrito. He left El Cerrito without any surveillance and drove away in a car that his daughter borrowed from her boyfriend. They circled the bay and came back into the city via the Golden Gate Bridge.'

'How do we know that?'

'Not sure, bridge video, I think.'

'That doesn't seem likely.'

'I'll find out.'

'OK, so then what happened?'

'He parked five blocks from the cabinet shop and walked in. That's where they picked him up again. Inside, he didn't turn any lights on and examined the unit of larch plywood with a flashlight.'

'So that answers that question.'

'There's more.'

If he knew about the delivery this would make him their prime suspect for the murders.

'He moved the plywood with the forklift, removed the bomb casings, and put them in cardboard boxes before bringing his car up to the loading dock.'

'Did he do all that with just the flashlight?'

'That's what Ortega told me, never turned the lights on. He loaded the boxes into the trunk and this is where it gets bad. By now the surveillance teams were into hyperdrive and when he drove off with the casings the Feds got a helicopter up. He drove southbound on 101 to the airport exit for long term parking. He left the car at long term and rode the shuttle bus to the airport.'

'Bomb casings are still in the car at long term parking?'

'That's right, but not for long. Khan bought a round trip ticket on a United flight to New York, JFK. He paid with a Visa, complained about the price and the extra charge for his luggage, and by then our guys were in the airport. The luggage screened clean but they got him pulled aside and given the extra wand. The decision was made to let him board.'

'Who made it?'

'Someone above Coe. Meanwhile, surveillance was setting up on the vehicle left at long term parking.'

'This was all last night?'

'Yes, and as Khan went to the gate to catch the flight he took a phone call. Short call, but they got it, and it almost certainly came from a man who was already in the parking garage in a van on Level Six where Khan left the car. A man also wheeling luggage and looking like he was just returning from a trip got off the elevator at Level Six then got in a white panel van. He drove slowly down the row where Khan left the car, stopped alongside it, got out, slid the van doors open and transferred the casings to the van. I heard it took eleven seconds to do the transfer. Then he drove south and crossed to 280 southbound.'

'Were our guys there?'

'Yes, but the FBI was calling the shots. The van left 280 and headed toward the coast, and this is what they think happened. Once he was on that road he started making stops every half mile or so. He'd pull over. They figured he was watching for surveillance behind him and one of the teams had to go past. So there was one team behind him, one ahead, and the helicopter in the air. But there was fog and the helicopter could track him but they couldn't tell what he was doing. He was in and out of the fog and still making these stops every half mile or so.'

'And during one of the side of the road stops the bomb casings got unloaded?'

'You got it, that's exactly what they think happened. He stopped just long enough for someone to slide the van door open again, only this time to pull the boxes out. They found two empty cardboard boxes this morning they think held the bomb casings.'

'Where's the van driver now?'

'In a house all the way down in Salinas, but the dumped van is in Santa Cruz. He traded into a pickup in a supermarket parking lot. And the casings are God knows where.'

'Did they get plates on the vehicles that drove the road afterward?'

'Fifty-seven vehicles, they got all of them. They searched four last night. It's a mess, not to mention finger-pointing. I hear Coe is in trouble, but I don't think he was directing the surveillance so I don't get that. But Ben, that's not all. Khan's dead. After the call he took in the airport, he left the airport. Never boarded the plane and got in a cab. Cabbie drove him home and then went into the house with him.'

'Where's Khan's luggage at this point?'

'He's got it with him and the cabbie rolled it up to the door. The cab driver went inside with him. Five minutes later the cab driver leaves. This morning a little after nine o'clock Khan's daughter arrives, unlocks her parents' front door, and finds his body in the front hall and Mom on the stairs. Khan was garroted. His wife's neck was broken.'

'Garroted?'

'Strangled with a wire and a search is on for the cab driver.'

'This was all last night?'

'Yes. How far are you from this air base and do you want me to do anything from here?'

'You could google something for me. My phone is too slow out here. There's a place called the Ka'Ohe Game Management Area. Tell me how far that is from Bradshaw Army Air Base and how many gates the base has. This officer Victor Shay lives in barracks in the back farthest from the road. If you can find out anything about him, text me.'

'I'm looking at Bradshaw right now.'

'If he leaves via the gate nearest his barrack how does he get to the main road?'

'Hold on, OK, hmm, paved road goes back to your Saddle Road about a quarter mile from the base and a dirt one goes straight ahead.'

'Follow the dirt road.'

'OK, recalculating, recalculating, go left at the intersection of Lava Road. Hey, I'm seeing the word lava a lot. Is it sandy and beautiful or is it a rock pile?' She didn't wait for an answer. 'From Lava Road he would take the next left and that would get him to the road you're on. Do you think he'll try to avoid you?'

'I hope not but I'm sure he'll get a heads-up call from Casey, the rancher I just interviewed.'

'Call me afterward.'

'I will.'

THIRTY-SIX

Raveneau waited at the guard gate as the call got made. It was clear Shay was on base, but just as clear he was going to avoid him.

'Sir, he's not on active duty this afternoon.'

'Where does he go when he's off duty?'

'Sir, I can leave a message for him.'

Raveneau left a message and then reasoned there was nothing to lose by continuing down the road to the intersection la Rosa gave him. He pulled away from the guard gate, spotted a road running parallel with the highway and figured it was the Lava Road la Rosa found. Across from the intersection of the road and highway was a paved lot and a ranger station, Mauna Kea State Park. Except for a pickup truck with state park department markings on it, the lot was empty. Raveneau pulled in. He backed the car up so he could see across the highway to Lava Road.

The only real leverage he had as a homicide inspector was if a senior officer ordered Shay to cooperate, and doing this was a little bit ludicrous, but it gave him a chance to think about Khan and the account la Rosa told him. He also had a view of the volcano, Mauna Loa, and he was glad to sit here in the sun and take a break from it all. The mountain was beautiful. He read they had numerous observatories up there because the sky was so clear. He watched clouds move across the mountain and then turned at dust rising on Lava Road.

Not enough dust for a training exercise with tanks, not even enough for a lone Humvee, closer to the amount a lone car would raise. He watched the car approach as he thought about the missing bomb casings. He picked up his phone and called la Rosa.

'I got turned away at the gate and this is a real long shot, but I'm looking at a car coming at me from Lava Road. When it reaches the highway I'm going to follow it and give you the plates. If I lose you I'll text them to you.'

'What kind of vehicle?'

'I can't give you make or model yet. It's too far away, but it looks like a green jeep.' As the jeep turned off Lava Road and toward the highway, he said, 'Lone occupant. Male. Middle-aged, but I have a feeling this base has got a few middle-aged males.'

Raveneau watched the jeep reach the highway and pause long enough to register him across the road in the park lot and looking at him. Then he pulled out and turned left.

'He's going my way,' Raveneau said and then pulled on to the highway behind him. A few minutes later he read off the plates to la Rosa.

'I'll call you back,' she said, and his thoughts turned back to Khan.

When la Rosa called back she said, 'You ought to buy a stack of lottery tickets. That jeep is registered to a Victor William Shay.'

'So he's running away from me. I wonder why he doesn't want to talk to me.'

'I know why. It's because you ask too many questions. What else can I do for you? Do you want me to find you a restaurant to eat at tonight?'

'Sure, look for something.'

'Did Shay pick up on you?'

'Yeah, he did, and he's watching me right now.'

'Hang back and be careful.'

'See what you can find out about his military career. You can tell whoever you talk to we want to question him about an unsolved murder in San Francisco in 1989.'

'Speaking of which, Henry Goya has called a couple of times today.'

'I'll give him a call.'

Shay turned toward the coast when he reached the highway junction. When he reached the coast highway he turned north and Raveneau slid into a line of cars behind him. He almost lost him at the next junction. He went the wrong way then doubled back and found him again in the town of Kawaihae and then only because Shay hadn't hidden his car. He was in a restaurant parking lot and Raveneau drove past reading *Blue Dragon Coastal Cuisine and Musiquarium*. He pulled into a gas station and filled the tank as he debated his next move. He decided to go back to the Blue Dragon and go in.

Inside the Blue Dragon was an open courtyard, and chairs, tables, a stage, and two bars. It was dusk. There were drinkers but he didn't see Shay, but the hostess saw him looking around and came over to help.

'Maybe he's out on the back patio,' she said.

'Where's that?'

She pointed and Raveneau moved to the bar closest to it. He ordered a dark rum and extra ice and paid as he stirred the ice. Then he picked up the drink and walked out on to the back patio.

THIRTY-SEVEN

Tom Casey turned and smiled as if delighted by the coincidence. He glanced at Raveneau's drink.

'Glad to see that you've discovered the best bar on the North Kohala coast. You must be a pretty damn good detective. You know, it's funny, I could have sworn you said you were flying home today.'

Raveneau turned to Shay. 'Before you leave I'd like to talk with you a few minutes.'

'You're a serious guy, Inspector,' Casey said, 'but you may have misunderstood about my friend here. You asked for people who knew AK and I tried to help you. I wasn't providing you a list of suspects.' Casey pulled a chair out. 'Sit with us, ask your questions.'

'I'd rather have that conversation one on one.'

'Suit yourself. We're here to catch up and have some food. You're welcome to join us if you change your mind. What are you going to do otherwise, sit at the bar? Come on, Inspector, you're in Hawaii holding a drink. Sit here in the open air. There's nothing I'd like more than to see you find whoever killed AK and put a bullet in them. If you make real progress that might even keep me from trying to get you fired.'

'I'm going to return a couple of calls but before you leave, Lieutenant, I'd like to talk with you.'

'We may be awhile,' Casey said, and Raveneau moved inside. He took a table in the open courtyard and returned Goya's call. Goya started to tell him about going to visit Govich.

'Ben, the reason he hasn't called you is he's not well. His sister was there. She's been staying with him. She said he had a small stroke about four months ago, and they think he's had another in the past week. She's taking him to his doctor today. He was confused when I brought up the Canadians. He couldn't even remember them. He got frustrated when he couldn't track what I was asking him. You remember I told you we learned they didn't eat at a restaurant they told us they had.'

'It's in the murder files.'

It was in there and it was a dead-end detail unless there was something new to go with it. Barbara Haney explained it as their frustration at being held at the police station and missing a dinner reservation.

'Ed stared off into space as I asked him about that. He hadn't shaved in a couple of days and his sister was hovering over him trying to answer for him. She said he couldn't find his keys yesterday. When you get to my age you hear that one a lot and let me tell you, brother, it doesn't mean good things.'

'I'm sorry for Ed, and let's not bother him any more. It doesn't sound like he's going to be able to help us.'

'I should have gotten a call when he had the first stroke.'

Goya was upset by the changes he'd seen in his former partner and Raveneau didn't question him about Marlin Thames or anything else. He listened and after he was off the phone moved with his drink back to the corner of the bar where he was visible to Shay. He answered emails. He ordered shrimp and shitake egg rolls with dragon dipping sauce and then got a text from Coe.

'Call me,' it read.

Raveneau told the bartender he'd be right back. He walked out the front door and called Coe from out in the parking lot.

'How much do you know?' Coe asked.

'My partner told me the casings got lost. Are they going to pull you?'

'The task force will get restructured, but no, I stay. Would your CIU have stayed with him?'

'They're very good and they know the area.'

'That's what they're saying. It's not pretty here. But I'm calling to see what you've learned if anything about Alan Krueger.'

'I interviewed a Thomas Casey today who was a good friend of Krueger's. Casey thinks Krueger did work for the Secret Service as an independent contractor after he resigned and said he suspected at the time he was also doing work for the CIA. Can you check on that?'

'I can try.'

'Can you get military records on Casey?'

'I get the same records you get.'

'You get them a lot faster and if there's more the Navy will be more likely to give it to you. I've also got questions about a Lieutenant Victor Shay. He's currently stationed at Bradshaw Army Air Base on the Big Island. Right now, he's about thirty yards from me sitting at a patio table drinking with Tom Casey. He went out of his way to avoid me today after Casey called him and told him I was going to try to get in touch with him.'

'Casey gave you Shay's name and then called and warned him to watch out for you?'

'Something like that. He's a piece of work and I get the feeling he's got a lot of money and used to getting his way. Krueger was a regular guest in the 1980s. He broke up his trips back and forth to Hong Kong by stopping here.'

'Give me the officer's name again.'

'Lieutenant Victor Shay and stationed at Bradshaw Army Air Base.' Before hanging up, Raveneau said, 'You're the best I've worked with at the Bureau. You've got to bounce back from this. Don't let it take you down.'

Raveneau returned to the bar. He ate the egg rolls and ordered a beer and another appetizer, ahi won ton. He glanced at the guys. They were going to wait him out, but doing that was making a statement different from what Casey made this morning. Then as he finished the won tons and most of the beer and was ready to confront Shay, Casey came in from the patio.

'I'm on my way to the rest room, why don't you go out and have your one on one with him and I'll take my time coming back. It's painful to watch you lurking in here.'

Raveneau walked out on to the patio.

'What do you do at Bradshaw?'

'Supply chain, sir. That's what Bradshaw is about.'

'When did you and Tom Casey meet?'

'When I was twenty-two and flying jets. Captain Frank introduced me to him. I met Captain Frank on a flight from San Francisco. I was in uniform. He saw my wings and we started talking. He invited me by the ranch.'

'Casey's ranch?'

'Captain Frank's house was there.'

'Did you meet Alan Krueger at Casey's ranch?'

'I don't remember.'

'Did you meet him at a party at Captain Frank's house?'

'I don't know. He had a lot of friends and it was a long time ago.'

'You've got my card.'

'Yes, sir, I've got your card.'

'And you live by a code of conduct in the military, correct?'

'Sir?'

'I'm going to ask once more and if you want to change your answer that's fine. If not, we're clear. You're saying that if you knew Alan Krueger it was only in passing. Is that correct?'

'I knew who he was but I don't think we ever exchanged more than two words.'

Raveneau took a long look at Shay before opening his notebook, talking as he did, explaining, 'I've been working from photographs. Some have people in them that I don't have any idea who they are. With most I have no idea. I'm working my way through putting names to faces, and then figuring out who knew who.

'Alan Krueger was the victim so I've got his face down. Jim Frank, I know him now, and Casey, and Matt Frank. But anyway, I went to my car while you were eating. I had to make a call and I got this photo out at the same time. Here it is, and before today I knew one face but not the other.'

Raveneau slid it across the table then waited.

'Allyson Candel took that. That's you and Krueger holding up your drinks there, isn't it? That's the Krueger you only knew as a passing acquaintance. Was it just a party shot? Or do you want to back up and start this conversation again? I'm giving you the option, but after that I'm going to hold you to the code you are sworn to, and I don't really like to make threats. They don't usually help in investigations. But you're on a military base and harder to get to, so I'm going to tell you today that if I figure out you've lied to me I'll go to your commander. I'll call you out on that code of honor you're sworn to. Do you hear me?'

'I hear you talking.'

'You have a fine night, Lieutenant.'

THIRTY-EIGHT

Raveneau's marriage lasted nearly two decades. He still viewed its failure as his fault and some of the loneliness that came after as deserved. When it ended it took him a long time to learn to live alone. Tell him twenty years ago that living alone is where he would be at this age and he wouldn't have believed you. Post divorce he'd had relationships with several different women, though before Celeste none lasted. He didn't think of himself as remote or cool to the touch, or as someone with blunted emotions, and maybe it was just aging but he was fine coming home to an empty apartment at night. Now that was changing again.

He poured a glass of wine after getting in the door. He walked out in the cold air and the change from the soft warmth of Hawaii was startling. He walked out to the parapet. The city was his front yard. He called Celeste looking out at the night city.

Celeste lived with a boyfriend for nine, almost ten years. When he fell in love with someone else it had devastated her and he knew the story. She told it to him in one form or another many times after they started going out. Then she had been skittish and hopeful and angry all at once. It must have been six months before he heard her really laugh. Her laugh now was the kind that takes you along like a wave coming in.

After they made their plan for tomorrow and talked and he hung up, he made a sandwich and showered. He poured another glass before sitting to read the blog la Rosa forwarded him. La Rosa read Politico, The Daily Beast, Huffington Post, and other politically oriented websites and posts. She kept up with the local scene. What she forwarded was from Owlseye.com, a local blogger gaining a national reputation for his pipeline of inside scandal. That included the police department where several times he'd correctly predicted a shakeup or reorganization; or rather he leaked it after a tip.

In the blog she forwarded the owlseye wrote,

Sources have confirmed Federal agencies and local police are in a frantic search for alleged perpetrators of a planned bomb plot here! Yes, in San Francisco, and my secret source reveals the Feds muffed a critical play. A big shakeup may happen very shortly at the FBI San Francisco Field Office and inside SFPD. More information soon unless I become a target for 'lone wolf' wiretaps, as has happened to the owlseye before. When a federal law enforcement agency gets angry we are all terrorists.

Raveneau thought the tone of it was nauseating, but that didn't matter. That it was finally leaking out didn't surprise him. That someone piped in had contacted this blogger versus more traditional media wasn't even unusual any more.

Very early the next morning he crossed the Bay Bridge and drove south toward SFO and took the long term parking exit. He drove up to the ramp to the upper level and to the space shown on the schematic. He marked the time then clocked the drive south from there to the 92 crossover. He clocked the whole run and tried to picture the surveillance choreography on the winding road leading to Highway 1 and the coast.

Why were Khan and his wife dead? Were the bomb plotters cleaning up behind themselves, systematically removing the links? That was all he could come up with this morning and it wasn't much. And why did they take such a risk to recover the bomb casings? From the way Khan moved around he must have known he was under surveillance. It occurred to him Khan may not have known his employees would be killed.

Raveneau drove out to the coast before turning around. He drove back toward San Francisco still thinking it through. The plotters, even if they didn't know about the video feed inside the cabinet shop, would have to assume that Khan loading boxes outside would be watched and followed. What if Khan had been arrested at SFO? What if he had decided to talk? What then? It could only mean that Khan couldn't connect the dots. He only knew so much. That's why they could go forward. It has to be that, he thought. It's the only thing that explains their actions.

Four bombs when finished, a low tech transfer on a windy road at night and not unsophisticated, more like aware. Maybe we're not seeing these people for what they are. He knew the Feds were here before dawn with dogs working their way up the shoulder of the road, but even now they weren't sure when the casings were transferred. The driver was skilled, the surveillance teams bottle-necked. The driver made eight stops on the road and each time the surveillance assumed he was watching behind for them, but on one of those stops someone stepped out from the trees and unloaded the boxes before he drove on.

As he came down the offramp into San Francisco he called Coe and asked, 'Are these plotters getting inside help from somewhere?'

'How do you come up with that?'

'I'm asking if there's suspicion.'

'There's always suspicion, especially after a big screw-up.'

'Is the shakeup at your field office only about losing the bomb casings or is there another element?'

'We're getting into territory where I can't say much, but I'm going to put you on hold and go talk to my SAC about bringing you in. But first tell me where you're getting this.'

'I don't have anything. You're getting ahead here. I'm just trying to make sense of things. I just drove the route you sent me and I've been thinking it over.'

'Hold on.'

Raveneau stayed on the line a couple of minutes then hung up. Coe had his number. Coe could call him. He did about five minutes later.

'Raveneau, can you come here this morning? We've come to the same conclusion and we'd like to talk more with you. We think we're dealing with people familiar with our methodology.'

'Yeah, that's what I think too.'

'Can you come by this morning?'

'I won't be walking in with anything you don't already know, but, sure, I'll stop by.'

THIRTY-NINE

B ut he didn't go to the FBI Field Office yet. La Rosa called and said Ryan Candel was at the Homicide office and in the family waiting area reading a magazine as if waiting for a dental appointment. The Homicide office had a tiny lobby. It was like walking into a phone booth with an ATM and a door in it. Once you got through the door the family waiting room was on the left. There was a couch, a chair, a coffee table with some magazines. There wasn't a TV but then again it wasn't a place many people wanted to hang-out.

'Tell him I'm ten minutes away and ask him to wait. I'm going to ask him to do something for us.'

Candel probably thought about it and decided he wanted to see that video. Went home, thought about it and decided he needed to know if the shooter was or wasn't his father. When Raveneau walked in he was sitting on the couch texting somebody. He smiled but looked nervous and pale.

'Does being here make you nervous?'

'I don't know but I've got to get outside.'

'How did you get here?'

'Bus.'

'I'll give you a ride. I've got to go downtown anyway. Did you come in to see the video?'

'Yes.'

'It's short. Do you want to watch it first?'

'Not really, but yes.'

'You can watch it on the computer at my desk.'

'OK.'

That's what he did. Candel watched it three times and didn't show any real emotion. Raveneau started it once more and froze the frame on the shooter several times.

'Have you ever seen a snuff film, Ryan?'

'At a party once, but I'm definitely not into anything like that.'

'See the height difference? Your dad was much taller. That's not your dad.'

'You're positive?'

'Yeah, it's been looked at by some film experts.' He waited a beat. 'I just got back from Hawaii and I learned more about your father. I've seen where he lived. He's dead, Ryan. He died in 2004 of kidney failure at a hospital in Honolulu.'

'Probably from drinking.'

'That would more likely be a liver problem. It was more of a long series of complications from being wounded during the Vietnam War. It took some phone calls but I talked to a doctor who remembered him. It seems many people remember him. I found his house and met the man who owns the property. He was a good friend of your dad's. His name is Tom Casey and that friendship goes back to when they were young and pilots in Vietnam. Casey had your dad's remains cremated and his ashes are at a memorial not far from the house. I think you should go there.'

'Why would I want to?'

'Because he's been bigger in your life than you acknowledge and it's time you learn more about him.'

Raveneau popped the CD out and changed the subject.

'Let me show you our file closet here. It'll give you more of an idea about us.'

He was going with his gut here. He wasn't exactly sure why he was doing this. Maybe it was because his own son would have been close to Candel's age. Maybe he understood being young and a little bit unhappy and misguided. He unlocked the door to the closet. On the shelves to the left were cold case files.

'Who was Kevin Collins?'

'He was a boy that went missing and we tried hard to find him. That's why those two big boxes are up there.'

'But it's got to be too late now.'

'Cases get solved. A witness comes forward that can't carry what they know any longer or DNA gives us a connection we didn't have before.'

'What about those? Who is Ramirez?'

'He's better known as the Nightstalker and he's already in prison doing life, but his attorney is working hard on an appeal.

If the attorney is successful we've got five good cases here so he can be charged again.'

Raveneau listed off the five victims. He pulled out the case file of a young woman, Marsha Smith, killed in 1966. He knew Candel didn't really see the effort as worth it so many years after a murder. Yet Raveneau wanted him to see this.

After he shut the door, he said, 'OK, let's go, and I'll drop you off on my way.'

They rode the elevator down and in the car before pulling away from the curb Raveneau reached around back and picked up the photo. It was wrapped in brown paper.

'Tom Casey gave this to me to bring back to you.'

'What is it?'

'Open it.'

Candel unpeeled the brown paper as they waited at a light. He flipped the photo over then rested it on his knees, a studio shot, color, and bigger than 8 x 11, framed in oak, and Raveneau didn't expect the intensity. He didn't make a sound but tears started.

'Mom. She looks beautiful. She looks happy.'

'That's your dad next to her.'

But he wasn't looking at his dad. He was looking at his dad's hand resting on his head and was disbelieving. 'Me?'

'What's the matter? Do you think the kid is too good looking? That's you.'

'That can't be.'

But Candel knew it was and as Raveneau turned left he heard the release and then a sob Candel tried to choke off and couldn't. When he looked over there were tears running down his face. He bowed his head and tears fell on the glass over the photo. Raveneau drove slowly, gave him time before dropping him off.

Candel wiped the tears off his face and said, 'Sorry, I just never . . .'

'So he did know you. You'll have to talk to Tom Casey. He said to tell you that you've got a standing invite at his house.'

Raveneau glanced over. 'He didn't make any offer like that to me. He gave me something else.' Raveneau handed over the box Casey gave him. 'He received two of these. Here's one of them. Casey gave this to me to give you along with the photo.'

Candel took the box from him but didn't open it yet. He cupped it in his left hand.

'Your half brother has the other one. He's on Facebook if you want to contact him that way. He gave me the contact info. I'll give it to you when we stop. Your father married a Vietnamese woman. According to Tom Casey that was to get her out of Vietnam but she was also pregnant by him. Your brother's name is Matt Frank.'

'A brother?'

'Yeah.'

'And he got the last name?'

'He did and he's got mixed feelings like you. That's a story you'll have to get from him. He's older than you by a few years and he's got a specialty coffee business he's trying to take global. He gets to California a couple of times a year so you can meet him here if you don't go to Hawaii first.'

Candel opened the box with the dragon on it. He lifted out the medal.

'Is this for dropping napalm on villagers?'

'War is an often cynical calculation, but this is for exceptional heroism and bravery. They don't hand them out like candy.'

'But another bogus war.'

'I know what you're saying and I've had those feelings. My son died in Iraq. I had to find a way to separate how we got there from how my son did. Go talk to Tom Casey about your dad and figure out what the good things were. It's time to turn the page.'

FORTY

Raveneau didn't have any proof. He didn't have any hard information and the Special Agent in Charge, Coe's SAC, sat listening and then left in what Raveneau read as dismissal. Within ten minutes the other two agents excused themselves and Raveneau said to Coe, 'I don't need this.'

'Everyone is looking for anything.'

'I never said I had anything.'

'I know.'

'All right,' Raveneau said and stood, adding, 'I'm going to go see Drury.'

'Drury was arraigned on murder and kidnapping charges; he's not going to talk to you. He's not going to talk to any of us ever again. We don't have anything he wants and in his view we screwed him.'

'He's right, but we do have something he wants.'

'OK, what's that?'

But Coe wasn't in a mood to listen. His eyes were red from lack of sleep. He was impatient, frustrated, exhausted, under pressure and carrying guilt for the blown surveillance. He expected Raveneau to come in and lay out a theory of the bomb plotters getting information from inside law enforcement at the federal level and Raveneau was nowhere near that.

But he did learn some things. Coe told him before his SAC walked in that the FBI got nothing from Khan's house, his bank and phone records, his emails, his car. 'Zero, zilch,' he said. What Raveneau saw in Coe today was an agent running scared and tired, a guy in his mid thirties, committed to law enforcement and on the climb now wondering if his career arc just flattened out. So Raveneau let it go. He moved the conversation to Drury and held it there.

'Four employees were shot to death in a cabinet shop,' Raveneau said. 'The owner of that shop and his wife are dead. If the same people are cleaning up after themselves it makes sense they would also take out John Drury because Drury can identify the man who hired him. I'd like to point that out to Drury. Why don't you come with me?'

'Right now, if I want to use a bathroom I have to get it cleared.'

Coe sighed. He pressed two fingers against his forehead as if he had a headache.

'I'll let you know if I learn anything,' Raveneau said, and then paused at the door. 'I got a call from Brooks this morning. Is he up to speed on everything?'

'Oh, yeah, he's right in the heart of it. He wants to know why the Secret Service weren't part of the surveillance of Khan. Brooks is loud. Fuck him.'

Raveneau picked up la Rosa and as they drove across the city to knock on the blogger's door, she worried that Raveneau wasn't tuned in enough. He didn't have a Facebook page. He didn't have a Twitter account.

'Isn't Celeste tweeting?'

'Yeah, she thinks it's a good way to get the word out on the bar.'

'So you've seen it. You know what it's about. And you've heard of Andrew Fine, right?' la Rosa asked as they parked. 'Do you read him?'

'I've read him, but I don't read him. He's a good writer but you don't have to read him to know where he stands on everything.'

'Leave that at the door. If anything, we need to flatter this guy. We need him to talk to us. He has a Twitter feed. He's very witty.'

'Do you follow his feed?'

'Yes.'

'Tweet this to him: the police are at the door.'

La Rosa led in the Homicide Detail meetings where they sat around and talked about social networking sites as valuable new tools to reach the public in investigations. All of which Raveneau agreed with, though he didn't think it meant he needed to sign up for Facebook or anything else. But sooner or later, they'd have a serial killer tweeting about kills and taunting them. He didn't doubt that or that tips would come that way, but he had no interest in following the musings of a media celebrity, sports star, or journalist turned blogger.

'I don't know why but I think this could be important,' la Rosa said, and he knew she meant it. She rarely made statements like that, something he admired about her.

Fine either hadn't gone to bed last night or they had just awakened him. He looked puzzled then surprised, and then affected greater surprise and Raveneau guessed he was already in his head writing about the visit. It took him a moment of blinking in the sunlight standing in his doorway, looking a little like an owl he headlined as. But he adjusted fast.

'If you'd called, I would have had coffee ready. My wife is a coffee freak. She's an investment banker and up very early. She buys the best coffee. I was about to make some when you knocked. I usually write late into the night. Why am I getting a surprise visit from two homicide inspectors?'

'We're sorry we woke you up,' la Rosa said.

Raveneau wasn't sorry.

'Any takers on coffee?' Fine asked.

'Sure,' Raveneau said, and remembered he forgot to bring the Kona from Hawaii to work with him to take to Celeste.

Fine showed them the room where he wrote his blog and it wasn't a back closet cubbyhole that he made his start in. It was more like a library with a couple of big-screen TVs and several computers. He pointed at chairs.

'I just about live in this room. Sorry about the crumbs on the table.'

'We have those at our office too,' Raveneau said. 'Don't worry about it.'

'I'll go get the coffee going.'

The chairs were leather, a type la Rosa called man-club style. They were comfortable and Fine's life looked very comfortable, though la Rosa told him Fine paid his dues as a journalist and started the blog in desperation after his newspaper downsized him. Now the blog had strong advertising support. Still, being married to someone in the financial arts couldn't hurt.

He looked at la Rosa. 'Is it what you pictured?'

'Not exactly.'

'Nicer?'

'Very nice.'

The decision to be a cop is a decision to be middle class. It meant you could never be sure about the future. Fire and police pensions were about to get cut, if not this year, next year. California's unfunded pension funds were a five hundred billion dollar time bomb and San Francisco had its own problems. Fine didn't appear to have those problems. He returned carrying a tray with a modern, insulated silver coffee pot and three chipped mugs to keep it casual.

'Sorry to keep you waiting.'

'Sorry we surprised you,' la Rosa said. Raveneau who couldn't think of anything to be sorry about didn't say anything.

'So what can I do for you?'

'We're part of an investigation that you wrote about yesterday,' la Rosa said. 'It's a joint investigation with Federal agencies, but we're very much a part of it.'

'Are you here to ask for my source?'

'We're here to talk with you about your source,' she said. 'As I think you're aware, this is a very significant threat.'

'I don't understand. You're homicide inspectors. It's a terror plot investigation.'

Raveneau believed there was a larger truth in the continuing polarization of politics in the country. Access to information tied into privilege. Fine was among the privileged, yet at the same time Fine obviously prided himself on his empathetic connection to the underprivileged and downtrodden. He wrote his belief in democracy with those threads and Raveneau figured Fine couldn't help but notice right now that before him were two of the middle class. Not lower class but still they were probably pretty good stand-ins this morning. La Rosa's clothes were from Target. His shoes cost less than the slippers on Fine's feet. Fine's desk alone was at least a ten thousand dollar sculpture of glass and steel.

'It's a complex and organized plot,' Raveneau said. 'We followed a lead in a homicide investigation and came into it from a different angle.'

Fine turned to him.

'I understand FBI teams were sent to Pakistan. Is that true?'

'It might be true, but I think they were probably doing just what the plotters wanted.'

'You do?'

Raveneau nodded. Fine held Raveneau's gaze then looked at la Rosa again. Raveneau knew from la Rosa's tutorial that Fine graduated from Stanford, worked in New York then Washington for many years before returning to the Bay Area. He built his blog when competition was still thin and the postings sporadic. He brought a competitor's discipline hardened from years of deadlines.

'Who is most at risk?' Fine asked, and la Rosa was ready. 'We don't know but we do know from the weapons where the real casualties will be.'

That was like soft-pitching him one to hit out of the park. 'On the street?'

'Yes.'

Fine leaned forward and poured himself more coffee. 'Anybody else?'

'I'm good,' Raveneau said and then, 'How much do you know about the bomb threat?'

'If I tell you am I putting my source at risk?'

'No.'

'Not even if the source is inside your department?'

'It's not.'

'That's true, but how could you possibly know that?'

'No one in our department would care about a shakeup at the FBI. But another federal agency might and someone within that agency might have personal ambitions that could jeopardize our chances. I'm not talking about the public being alerted and aware. Frankly, I'm for that.'

'So am I, Inspector.'

'Your source must be too.'

But that wasn't necessarily the case and Fine seemed to acknowledge that.

'There's a point,' la Rosa said, and paused, her lips briefly pursed, 'a point where information can be useful to the plotters.'

'You're not going to try to sell me that old saw, are you?'

'Worse,' Raveneau said. 'We're going to tell you this time it's different.'

'How?'

'There's no proof and you can't print it, but you could ask your source if there's any chance of this. We'd like you to ask and gauge the response.'

'OK.'

'Your source will dismiss the idea but we see a pattern that suggests the plotters are getting help from inside law enforcement. That doesn't mean it is local help.'

'And you say my source will dismiss that?'

'I'm betting he or she will.'

Fine looked down at his coffee and Raveneau got the feeling Fine's source might not be local.

'You are asking me to say something I can't say credibly. I can tell you my source is very bright and if I throw out an idea like this that I can't possibly know about, I'm going to get questions. I may lose my access.'

'Don't lose your access.'

'What's it to you?'

'Just hear us out. We're going to give you something but we can't give you much because we don't know how much the other side knows or doesn't know about the investigation. You'll have to be oblique.'

Fine nodded, barely, but it was a nod.

'Reference the quadruple slaying at Khan's cabinet shop and the subsequent murder of Khan and his wife.'

'The burglar?'

'It wasn't a burglar. That's very vague but can you work with that?'

'Yes.'

'In return we'd like to know what you learn.'

'OK, but is the public going to get warned soon?'

'That will probably come soon in a joint press conference with SFPD and the FBI. It might happen today. It might happen tomorrow, but it will happen because we're not sure where this thing is at.'

'So they're covering their asses.'

Raveneau left that alone and added, 'Your source can't know you were visited by homicide inspectors. That's very important.'

Fine's eyes half closed and he was obviously skeptical. He was quiet then surprised Raveneau, saying, 'That has implications I don't even like to think about.'

'It does and we need to ask one question about your source.'

'I thought we agreed you weren't going to.'

'FBI or Secret Service?'

'Who will know I told you?'

'We'll keep it to ourselves.'

'For how long?'

'For as long as we possibly can.'

'My credibility depends—'

'We'll protect you.'

He looked at la Rosa and back at Raveneau. 'It's an old connection. It's someone I went to school with years ago. He's

moved steadily upward in all that time. He's not in the FBI or
Secret Service, and you'll never touch him. He worked for the
CIA and he's in some offshoot now that doesn't even have a
name.' He looked past Raveneau at the wall behind then said,
'I'll call you.'

FORTY-ONE

'Y ou still get to read,' Brooks said, 'but the situation has
changed. You can sit at my desk and read what was sent
to me, but I'm not going to print anything for you. And
I have to tell you we've had a long-standing good relationship
with SFPD and people here are angry we were bypassed the
night the bomb casings were lost. It wasn't our ineptitude but
it's going to fall on us. The field office here doesn't look very
good right now.'

'I was in Hawaii.'

Brooks was close enough for Raveneau to smell his aftershave.
He was too close and too urgent.

'This wouldn't have happened if we'd been involved or if your
CIU team was on them. The FBI lost them. They added agents.
They brought in people that don't even know the area. They're
arrogant. They are endlessly stupidly fucking arrogant, but it's
going to land here when the White House cancels the President's
visit and after everybody and his brother learns what happened.
Some blogger has already written about them. I'm angry. I'm
very angry.'

Brooks stepped back and looked away. He had a new suit and
a different haircut that left him with a smooth hard clean look.
He wasn't suffering in the shadows. He led Raveneau to his
computer and brought up a PDF file.

'OK, there you go. Now you can read and chase ghosts. You
were in Hawaii working a cold case when the bomb casings got
lost and now you're home focused on this murder that probably
no one will ever solve. But, hey, working it fills the days and
someone has to care for those lost souls. And that's fine. There's

a place for it. But is there a need for it with all the other things going on right now? You have talent at investigating. You've got experience. You know this city. You shouldn't be spending your days on Alan Krueger's murder. He's been dead for a long time and these missing bomb casings are an absolute priority.'

'Slow down, Brooks.'

'No, I'm going to say what I think. That surveillance got botched because we weren't there and SFPD's Criminal Investigation Unit was left sitting in the back seat on a critical, critical surveillance. Of course, ask the FBI and they'll tell you about how they trained this team. They trained this city, that city, these state police, they'll give you their whole big brother academy rap. But you and I know ninety-five percent of FBI agents can't do surveillance. Half of them look alike. Doesn't even matter what color their skin is, they still look like they came from the same factory and when they go anywhere they go in pairs, so pretty soon you've got a car parked down the street with two guys in it who look pretty much the same. What are you going to think when you see that?'

'I'm reading, Brooks.'

'Yeah, yeah, you read, you read, Raveneau, but you know what I'm saying. You know I'm right.'

Raveneau read the usual federal forms. He read the notes on Krueger quitting, two paragraphs devoted to making clear the time, date, and moment Alan Krueger made the decision for 'personal reasons' to 'resign' from the Secret Service. It was recounted in plain language that Krueger did twice while on duty falsely report his whereabouts for which he was reprimanded later after the false representation was exposed. The facts of the reprimand included the name John Pagen, presumably Krueger's supervisor. He went through each page again slowly, this time copying down some of Krueger's background information including the years of his military service.

When he finished he sat in the chair for a few minutes thinking about it. What he read was sanitized. There was really nothing there yet he did get a name, John Pagen. If Pagen was a super-visor then, he was retired now. He might be in the area still.

Raveneau read and took notes, then left quietly. He preferred not to see Brooks on the way out. He would find Pagen. He'd stay focused on this case that mattered the same today as it did when the Canadians found Krueger's body in 1989. From his car he called Secret Service headquarters in Washington, identified himself and said he was working a cold case from 1989 and trying to get in touch with a retired agent named John Pagen. He gave his name and cell number and knew the first call would be to the Homicide Detail to confirm he was who he said he was. If alive, Pagen would have a Fed pension and one way or another Raveneau would find him. He didn't expect to find him that afternoon, but that's what happened. Pagen called him later in the day.

'I retired in 2002,' Pagen said, 'and I've been working harder ever since.' He laughed. 'I inherited my father's ranch outside of Marysville. We grow pistachios and prunes.'

'How do you like it?'

'I love it. Maybe if my career had been something I'd feel differently, but I love growing things and being outside when I want to. I did know Alan. I knew him fairly well and liked him. He was quite talented and bright. He saw the world turning into a global mix long before the rest of us in that office. That's how he ended up working the Asian end. You're wondering what he was working on when he was killed?'

'I am.'

'I'm assuming you know he was there on his own by that point, three or four years.'

'I read his resignation letter this morning.'

'Right, the resignation, that was another thing again. He and another agent had a personal animosity. They couldn't stand each other.'

'I'd like to hear about that.'

'Will talking about it get you closer to who killed him?'

'I don't know.'

'Well, I'll meet you or you can come up here if you want.' Raveneau jotted down directions. 'If you pass Mariani plant number two, you've gone too far. But we can do this over the phone too. You can call me any time.'

'You said you knew Alan fairly well. Did you know any of his friends?'

'Are you asking about the boyfriend?'

'I'm wondering about a Jim Frank and a Tom Casey.'

'I know the names and I know he had a photo on his desk with the three of them in it. The boyfriend I never met and I don't think Alan set foot in our office again after he resigned. I got him his first work in Hong Kong though. We had a lead, Alan spoke the language, and his counterfeiting work was very respected at headquarters.'

'Was that a lead about counterfeit one hundred dollar bills?'

'No, I think it was about twenties. We had a lot of twenties floating around for awhile.'

'He had sixty-one hundred dollar bills on him when he was killed.'

'I remember, and they were brought to our office. They weren't counterfeit.'

'A videotape of the murder was sent to us. Literally, the last few minutes of Alan's life, and I'll show it to you when we meet if you want to watch it. I wouldn't watch it if I were you, but I'm telling you because it's why our Cold Case Unit picked this one up again. I checked the bills out of evidence and the Secret Service took another look and came up with a different conclusion.'

'Is that right?'

'I have to take them at their word.'

'They aren't going to lie to you.'

'Of course not.'

'We made mistakes like everyone else.'

It happened very fast. The hale, good natured sounding man who had answered the phone and seemed more than willing to do what he could to help, now lost spirit and said quietly, 'I'm afraid of where this is going. There was talk at the time, but Alan was killed before the first supernotes were found. That was in the Philippines. It was a banker who picked up on them. If Alan had been alive we might have asked him to go there and work with the agents we sent.'

'You do know where this is going.'

'Alan was carrying supernotes?'

'Yes.'

'I have to think about that. Why don't you give me a few days? Can you do that?'

'I can.'

'And I'll make some calls too. Some of us are still around. Tell you what, I'll call you. If I call Homicide do I ask for the Cold Case Unit?'

'Just ask for me.'

'You'll hear from me soon.'

FORTY-TWO

'Inspector, did I catch you at a bad time? If so, I'm sorry. I don't always think about mainland time.'

'I planned to call you anyway.'

'Then I'm glad I beat you to it.' Casey coughed heavily. As he recovered he said, 'I've caught some damn cold. I apologize how things ended. I read too much into you going out to the air base after leaving here. I figured you'd call him. I didn't mean to focus any suspicion on my friend and he was upset you followed him. He told me you trailed him all the way to the restaurant.'

'I called ahead and he was fine to meet at the base, but not when I got there and I'm like you, I'm getting more ornery as I get older.'

Casey chuckled, coughed because of it.

'That's because I told him you'd gone into Jim's house without permission. I let him know that I wasn't sure about you. But now that I've had some people check up on you I feel better. You've got a reputation for getting the job done. Anyway, as we got to talking I suggested he come into town and told him I'd buy him dinner. Blue Dragon is where we usually meet, so that's what we did. It was a chance to catch up with Victor. Life hasn't been fair or easy for him. He had some bad luck early.

'When you showed up at the Blue Dragon I thought, well, he's flown all the way here and now he's trying to make something happen, trying to connect dots that don't connect. I know that's not what you're doing, and really I'm impressed that San Francisco still cares about what happened to Alan to spend time

and money on trying to solve the murder. So I'm calling to see
what I can do to help. Were those photos any value and did you
give the boy his?'

'I did.'

'Did it mean anything to him?'

'Much more than I would have thought.'

'That means something to me.'

Raveneau thought it might. He wasn't quite sure why Casey
was calling though. But he was fine with talking to him.

'You know Alan's boyfriend had more problems than I
mentioned. Thames did eighteen months in prison in Florida for
ripping off twenty-two cotton tops who thought they were buying
their sunny retirement homes. He owed the IRS about one hundred
and ten thousand as Howard Wright and they were looking for
him. The Marlin Thames social security number he bought in
Los Angeles.'

The first part Raveneau knew about, but not the rest. He
couldn't help but wonder how much Alan Krueger knew.

'One agent there figured him out and went after him, and I
know you and I already talked about that. But I remembered his
last name. It's Pagen and he was probably the best friend AK
had there. If he's still around, he'll remember what happened. I
heard about him for years and met him at the service for Alan.
He's someone you should talk to.'

'I just talked to him.'

'See, there you're ahead of me. Maybe we're on the same
wave length. I'm also calling about someone else I remember
and please don't think worse of me for not remembering this
name until you flew home. There was a young Hawaiian woman
Jim lived with for several years. She was from the other end of
the island down near the volcanoes. Her family is probably still
there. She was half Japanese and around when AK was coming
through on his Hong Kong runs. She was an artist, beautiful
water color artist, very detailed drawings. Beautiful body, too,
graceful, gentle, a bright young woman, and I'm surprised I can't
remember her name. But I will soon and I'll call you. She would
have heard a lot of the conversation in that period of time. She
might remember something that helps you. Are you making any
progress?'

'Some progress and thank you for calling about this woman whose name you can't remember.'

'You're worse than me, you know that.'

'No, I appreciate the call but let's talk more about Victor Shay. What did you mean about his bad luck?'

'He wasn't always a gunnery officer. He was once a young hotshot pilot. He started having vision problems and they found a brain tumor. When they operated it turned out to be benign but the operation caused swelling that they didn't know how to deal with as well as they do now. He was bright and then he wasn't so bright. Still smart enough, but not quite the same. I saw guys get ruined by war but this was sadder in a lot of ways. Eventually he got restored to active duty but the tumor clocked his flying career. That's why he's a forty-five year old with a low rank. That's probably why I jumped you so hard. I'm protective of him.'

He coughed again.

'I'll remember her name and I'll call you.'

'Before you go, let me ask you something.'

'It wouldn't be a complete conversation with you without it ending with a question. Go ahead.'

'When was the last time you were in San Francisco?'

'It's been awhile.'

'What about Matt?'

'He travels with his coffee business. You'll have to ask him.'

'You don't know.'

'I got in trouble for speaking for Shay so I'll let Matt speak for himself. He's got a mind of his own. I guarantee you that. He took that gun of his up there to Jim's house to confront you and I don't like that. I told him not to.'

'Whose idea was wearing the mike?'

'Mine. But that comes from using walkie-talkies around here and because we did have a problem with squatters for a little while. It was a safety thing and maybe you don't believe that, but it's true.'

'It's hard to believe.'

'It probably is but then I don't give a damn whether you believe it or not. My only interest in you is that you solve AK's murder. I'll let you get back to it.'

'Call me when you remember her name.'

Casey didn't hear him. He'd already hung up.

FORTY-THREE

Thomas Casey disturbed la Rosa. His calls were aimed at getting information, not offering it. But of course Raveneau knew that. Since returning from Hawaii Raveneau had taken calls three or four times a day from Casey. She watched his face as he talked to Casey. She saw the notes he wrote. The cryptic quality of those notes was a little bit of a running joke in the office, but the same inspectors came to him for help in solving cases. What he wrote after this conversation with Casey was the word 'prunes.' What did that mean?

She questioned him as they got in the car. 'Is he calling to remind you that you trespassed on his property and went into the house?'

'He lets me know and you should know I've talked with the lieutenant and the captain about going into Jim Frank's house. I also called the Hawaiian police. They thought I was crazy since no complaint was filed. But if it's a crime it's a local crime. They should know about it.'

'What you did isn't breaking and entering. He's working it. He's working you as he tries to make it into something.'

'Of course he is, but we need him. He's the best source on Alan Krueger we're likely to ever have, so if he wants to call fifteen times a day that's fine with me. He likes to talk and he fishes for what I've learned as he eases out more possible leads, so there's some sort of game underway, but he did tell me today about a young woman who lived with Jim Frank during the years Krueger came through. On one of the next calls he'll give me her name.'

'He's dropping bread crumbs for us. It's time to confront him. You're being played and you're going along in part because he's got this leverage over you for trespassing and going into the house.'

That was going to make him angry and she didn't really believe what she had just said, but she sensed he needed a push. He glared at her now.

'So far he's showed you his photo album and talked about what good friends the three of them were, yet he doesn't really know what his good friend AK was doing with the counterfeit money. I don't believe that. I don't believe him. If Captain Frank was ferrying counterfeit money and whatever else in his luggage, then they all knew about Krueger's operations. He gave you Victor Shay's name then warned Shay. He can't remember the name of a woman who lived with his good friend for years in the house up the slope. He remembers. You know he remembers. He's doling out information.'

Raveneau didn't answer.

'He's controlling you and you're going along with it because you're worried about what you did.'

'Do you really believe that?'

'It's what I just said.' After a moment she added, 'No, I don't think that, but I do think you're giving him too much room. He knows more and he should give it to us without the telephone dance.'

'He feels some responsibility for Krueger's death. I don't know why. That's what I'm working towards.'

'I think you need to confront him.'

Raveneau didn't say any more until they got to the Embarcadero and parked. La Rosa thought this was going to be another look at where Krueger was videotaped and shot and where the Canadians crossed and how it all fit together. Raveneau liked to return to where the murders happened. He thought you could pick up a vibe from a place, an idea she entertained but didn't believe in. Maybe if it ever once helped solve a case she would start believing. She didn't see the point in driving here other than to talk away from the office. She rode with him today but she was agitated and less patient.

'Brooks let me read the Secret Service's personnel file on Krueger. He built it up as being something and it didn't turn out to be much of anything. He made the offer, and then dodged me for a week and a half. I read it this morning and got one name out of it, a John Pagen, and it turns out he was the special agent in charge at the time. He's the one who accepted Krueger's resignation and helped him get the outside contracting work. I got a phone number for him and talked to him. I told him the bills Krueger was carrying were supernotes. He was surprised that the Secret Service now identifies them as the first supernotes. When I talked with Casey today he gave me one new name. What do you think that name was?'

'Pagen.'

'That's right, John Pagen, now what do you make of that?'

She didn't know what to make of it and Raveneau gestured in front of them.

'Brooks and I took a drive after the bomb casings were lost. That drive finished here or this was the goal. Brooks believes the President is the target and the bomb casings tie to the counterfeit bills.'

'He's said that several times, hasn't he?'

'He has and he knows this visit will get canceled, but what he's trying to communicate is how worried and powerless he feels to protect the President. The explosive power these bombs could generate scared him to his core. We drove a route the President could take after giving a speech about the new subway system in Union Square. He's supposed to come down here and ride the light rail with the mayor and a senator. That's the part that Brooks worries about.'

Her anger toward him softened a little. 'You believe there's an assassination plot, don't you?'

'I don't know what I believe yet. I can't quite make the cabinet shop murders fit in with a quietly evolving assassination plot. Brooks believes the attempt will come when the President is riding on the light rail car.'

'But if he's not coming it doesn't matter.'

'Between the FBI and the Secret Service there's a belief the plotters are some long range planners. They've showed me a few transcripts, Coe in particular.'

'That doesn't sound like the FBI.'

'Coe is a different cut and a younger generation.'

'So Brooks thinks they'll just move it somewhere else?'

'That's right, and they believe it's referred to as the "first event." Because of Krueger carrying those same series counterfeit bills and Casey's connection to Krueger, they've tapped Casey's phone lines.'

'They can do that?'

'They can do whatever they want. Coe called me this morning and told me that.'

'The Secret Service and FBI really believe there was or is a plot to assassinate the President here?'

'They do and there's worry the plotters have contacts within the Fed law enforcement agencies. There's a reason the Secret Service didn't get invited to the bomb casing bust.'

'How much of this do you believe?'

'I don't know yet. Like all these conspiracy ideas it's grown long legs and if it exists it's probably just a handful of people. Is there a leak from a sympathizer or from someone well-placed? That's hard to say from where we stand. They've brought me in because of the overlap with the counterfeit bills and to make me more cooperative. But they do believe something is in motion. They believed it before those bomb casings but they don't have any way to tie the bomb casings to their previous suspicions. That's where it stands.'

They watched the light rail car approach and the darkness of what Raveneau had described sank in more. She watched the rail car and a tourist taking photos with his phone. The car was light and clattered as it passed by. How do you protect a President from a determined group with weapons like these bombs? You couldn't do it. It was nearly impossible.

FORTY-FOUR

That afternoon Coe showed Raveneau four computer-generated simulations of blast scenarios an Army bomb unit created for the FBI using the dimensions of the missing casings, the probable explosives type, and with close time-proximity detonation sequence. Four San Francisco street scenarios showed, ranging from a near open street configuration along the wider waterfront to a narrow street in Chinatown with buildings on either side capable of partial reflection of the blast waves. The merging waves would generate compression forces the Army calculated would kill in the hundreds and possibly thousands if detonated on crowded streets.

But that was actually good news because the bomb casings were shaped to direct the force of the blast and propel a slug of metal forward. Could they penetrate a Presidential limousine? They weren't sure or if they knew they weren't answering.

When Raveneau returned to the Cold Case office Ortega walked over from the main Homicide office to talk to him. He sat in la Rosa's chair and summarized where the investigation stood with the cabinet shop shootings. Raveneau had heard the rumor and now he got it straight from Ortega.

'The cab driver who killed Khan and his wife was located last night but no arrest is being made yet. He got ID'ed off prints and photo enhancement from video at the airport. His name is Cleg Mathis.'

'Spell that.'

'C-L-E-G, it's as stupid as it sounds. He's six foot four and two hundred thirty pounds according to his driver's license, but he's actually bigger. Black hair, black eyes, a black heart – he's one of those weird ones. He moved here from New Jersey where his business was doing fine but he was getting too much attention. Here, take a look.'

Ortega showed him two photos.

'He was suspected of doing work for the Russian mob and had to leave Jersey. The FBI already has a file on him. He's known as a freak who likes to kill. He gets off on it. The garrote he used on Khan dug several inches into his throat.'

Ortega paused.

'If this is a sophisticated group cleaning up behind itself and severing ties, how does a Mathis fit in? Here, take a look at these.'

The first shot was a photo of a finger lying on a tile floor.

'Khan's finger?'

'You guessed correctly. You win the finger. Do you want to gamble the finger and try for something larger?'

'Khan's head was still attached, wasn't it?'

'Barely, that's how strong Mathis is. The Feds say he lifted

Khan right off his feet and on two previous hits he's a suspect in the same thing happened. After a murder in New Jersey he walked into a restaurant with a bloody shirt on and ordered lunch. No shit, that's in the Fed file. They think he likes the squirming, the struggle, the control, before he starts really sucking that wire in. Now would the bombers you picture have access to someone like Mathis? If they did, would they use him or would they hire someone a little more conventional? The roll-up the carpet behind them theory isn't working for me. I can't see them hiring a guy they must know is going to get arrested.'

'When is he getting picked up?'

'I don't mean they know where he is now. He didn't return to his apartment. But the Feds are looking for him much harder than they look for some people. I think they'll catch up to him. They've got more and more agents involved, but your friend Coe isn't saying much at the task force meetings any more. At yesterday's meeting he didn't say a word.'

Ortega was probably good in the meetings. He was focused. Raveneau asked now about DNA results that as far as he knew they were still waiting for.

'Did you get anything back on the water cooler cups?'

'Just got it yesterday and that's part of why I'm here. One paper cup discarded near the water cooler had DNA that didn't match Khan, Drury, or any of the victims.'

'Did we test the paramedics?'

'You know, we got swabs but good point, I didn't see their names on the excluded. I'll check that.'

A thirsty paramedic may have gotten a drink of water before leaving with the fourth victim. Raveneau doubted that, but it needed to be checked. A cardboard box for empties sat alongside the water cooler. It was full and three or four of the empties had fallen out and were on the floor. Having nothing they had to check everything and the white paper cups, particularly those on top were gathered up. Khan told them there were no visitors the morning of the shooting so Raveneau figured the cups on top were most likely the victims', Khan's, or Drury's.

'In the hits Mathis is suspected of was a gun ever used?' Raveneau asked.

'The Feds say yes, so it could be he came through the cabinet shop and they hired him to take out Khan and his wife as well. You're the one who guessed the shooter took some pleasure in the killing. That fits with Mathis. What do you think?'

'He's big. How did he get in the building?'

Ortega had an answer for that. He'd been thinking about it.

'Whoever the shooter was, Khan let them in early in the morning before the employees arrived. The shooter hid where no one would look and that's how the tight window worked. He knew when Khan was leaving to measure the kitchen job and about the delivery and to listen for the forklift.'

'Where do you hide a six foot four man in the shop?'

'In that locked closet near Khan's office. Khan locked him in there and then unlocked the door before he left. The employees knew they weren't supposed to ever get in that cabinet. Khan told us that on the first interview. I think Mathis sat on the floor of the closet for five or six hours. But think about it, Ben. I want your opinion. I'll check with you later.'

FORTY-FIVE

Raveneau rode with Goya in Goya's old gray Toyota. They drove past Marlin Thames's blue-painted Victorian on Twenty-Second Street, and then to a café in the Noe Valley where they took the lone outdoor table. Inside it was steamy and warm. Outside, the sun was out though probably just for a short while. The street was still wet from the last shower. A strong gust shook droplets from the awning, but it was going to be a lot easier to talk out here than in the crowded steamy interior. Raveneau went back in to get the sandwiches and coffee.

When he returned Goya was sitting at the table looking like a bespectacled Don Quixote and if Goya was having second thoughts about what he was accomplishing, so was Raveneau. But he still felt Goya's presence mattered and Becker figured out a way to pay him something. He had to sign about a dozen waivers first.

'I met Thames,' Raveneau said. 'Anyone would like him. The

real estate deal was thirty some years ago and he settled with the IRS during one of their amnesty deals. He made a mistake and paid for it. He's got his vintage furniture business and a life he likes and I'm sure it's all legit, but in Hawaii Thomas Casey told me that Thames was there with Krueger in 1989. Thames told me they broke up in 1986 and saw little of each other after that. That's too big a gap to be accidental. If Casey is telling the truth then there's a good chance Thames is lying to us.'

'Or maybe he's just mixing up the years.'

'He sounded confident about his dates.'

Goya shrugged. He was still spooked about his old partner's memory loss and underlying that was some worry about his own. Raveneau recounted Casey's story of the visit by Krueger and Thames.

'He told me that was the last time he saw Krueger alive. According to him that was in October 1988 and he sure sounded like he had his dates right.'

'Well, I don't like this Thames. I think he lied to you. When he was Howard Wright he cheated elderly people out of their last years.'

Raveneau nodded. He and Goya had already been over the real estate fraud several times and there wasn't anywhere new to go with it today. He wanted to nudge Goya off it.

'I know, the old people are your people, and he sold them land with alligators on it so you're out for vengeance, but focus on where he lived with Alan Krueger. We want to know where Krueger stayed when he traveled through San Francisco in '89. See if you can figure that out.'

'I'm trying.'

Raveneau took a bite of the sandwich. It was on a baguette and not loaded up with fifty different things. He liked that. Celeste was toying with the idea of small sandwiches at night and discounting them after nine o'clock to draw people in. He ate and as Goya talked about losing his edge Raveneau began to understand that Henry didn't want to go forward. He didn't see himself as being of any value as an investigator, but neither did he want this to end in failure so they left it that he would try to locate the Secret Service agent who ruined Krueger's career. Then they would meet and work out the next step.

When Raveneau got back to the Hall of Justice the Homicide office was emptying out and in the Cold Case Unit he'd missed a redtail hawk that landed on the window sill and stayed for several hours. Ryan Candel was waiting for him.

'Have you been waiting long?'

'Not that long.'

They moved into the kitchen. He got Candel a soda and they sat at the table.

'I connected with Matt on Facebook. We're going to meet up. He's over here with his coffee business pretty regular.'

'How regular?'

'Every month or so. He posted some photos for me. I thought you might want to see them. That's why I came by.'

'OK, let's go back to my computer.'

There were more beach shots. There were shots of his brother as a teenager swimming with turtles and then many the younger Frank took of his dad and his dad's friends. This is where it got interesting.

'One of his interests is photography,' Candel said. 'See, he lists it.'

Another one is guns, Raveneau thought, but that wasn't listed. Candel turned to him.

'You're not on Facebook, right?'

'Me, no.'

'Your partner is. I saw her name.'

'Why don't you friend her?'

'Wouldn't matter, she still wouldn't be able to view these photos. They're limited to me. I asked for any with our dad and everything about Hawaii. There are a couple hundred photos and I'm cool if you just want to take your time. I've got to make some calls on a music gig.'

Raveneau heard him talking but focused on the photos and didn't register any words. The photos were old enough for Matt Frank to have been under ten years old taking these. They probably thought he was cute with his camera. He took a lot of facial shots which was lucky. There must have been more than fifty of Jim Frank in various moods. Most of those were solo shots, but others had people in them. When he saw Shay and Shay looked like he was young and in his twenties, Raveneau leaned back in his chair thinking about it.

He heard Candel on the phone talking in a cool affected voice, a young man still finding himself. He looked back at the computer monitor. Did Matt Frank feed them to Candel knowing that Candel was going to bring them here? Of course, he did.

A half dozen of the photos were of Captain Jim Frank with an arm around Matt Frank. Raveneau saw in the boy's face how much it meant to him to have his dad drape an arm around him. He wondered if he felt that way any more. Several photos were of the memorial with the stacked lava stone and one there with a young woman. It struck him from the way she touched the lava memorial that she had arranged the lava in its sculpture. He realized she must be the half Japanese, half Hawaiian artist Casey talked about. He clicked to the next and she was looking out toward the ocean with tears reflecting in sunlight on her cheeks.

Raveneau got absorbed in another set of photos, several of which were of a younger Thomas Casey. He looked up as Candel tapped him on the shoulder.

'How's it coming, dude?'

'There's a young woman in here. I'd like to know her name.'

'I saw her. She's hot.'

'Ask him her name.'

'That's easy.'

'And see if you can find out when he took most of these.'

'Why don't you sign up and I'll see if he's cool about adding you.'

'Or my partner since she's already signed up.'

'Yeah, maybe, want me to text him?'

'Sure.'

An answer came back within seconds.

'He says that's fine.'

'What's fine, friending la Rosa or do I have to sign up?'

'Oh, yeah, right, hang on.' Raveneau heard the return ping. 'He wants you to sign up.'

'What's the matter with my partner's page?'

'Want me to ask?'

'No, I'll sign up.'

'I'll help you. It won't take long.'

It didn't and then it didn't matter because Matt Frank didn't respond. Raveneau shut his computer down. He knew there was something more Candel needed to say and it came out as they left the Hall.

'Matt said it got weird after you left that day. His uncle is seriously angry about you going into Dad's house. He also ripped him for showing you the memorial. He told Matt he'll be the reason his dad's remains end up in a box in some police storage building. His uncle doesn't think much of the police, dude. And he gets super tweaked when people show up uninvited and blow off the No Trespassing signs on the gate.

'But still, Matt's pretty cool about his uncle. He said he owes him for just about everything. He said Dad acted closer to people he had just met than him, that he liked new people more than he liked people he knew, but Uncle Thomas isn't like that. His uncle is his main investor in the coffee thing.'

'Ask him how his uncle made his money.'

'I already know. They had land, dude, like a whole lot of it.'

'Where?'

'I don't know, but it wasn't in Hawaii. He like sold land here and bought that ranch. He says his uncle has megabucks. But bottom line is Uncle Casey is planning to get even with you.'

'For what?'

'I don't really know. He told Matt to do like a video of what he saw when he went up to our dad's house and you were there. Matt was supposed to FedEx it out today.'

'Did he?'

'Yeah, I think he did.'

'So it's on its way here?'

'Yeah, like FedExing to your boss, whoever that is. He said it would get here tomorrow.'

FORTY-SIX

Late that night a new storm out of the Gulf of Alaska arrived and this one lived up to the hype. When the phone rang at 3:00 a.m. Raveneau automatically reached for it as he had so many years when he was on-call. But it was the alarm company calling for Celeste to tell her the power was out. It was out here too and on the roof the cold rain blew sideways and he didn't see any lights on south of Market Street.

By 5:30 Celeste was anxious to get to the bar, worried about food spoiling with the small walk-in and the refrigerators down. The power was still on where her chef, Bo, lived and she wanted to get crab meat and a few of the more delicate things over to his refrigerator. Raveneau drove with her and loaded the food in the back of his car. It was raining so hard he barely heard his cell ringing when he got in his car.

'Is that rain?' Coe asked.

'It is.'

'Well, that's not good. Drury wants to talk to you. I want to get you on a flight this morning out of SFO. I'll be going with you.'

'Going where?'

'Colorado. He's at ADX Florence.'

'What plane is going to take off in this weather? SFO will be backed up for hours.'

'We'll get out on the corporate side. How are you with turbulence?'

'Oh, I love bouncing around in the air not knowing if the plane is going to come apart. That's my idea of fun.'

It was anything but fun when they crossed over the Sierras. Underneath them, the interstate was closed, not even the snow plow drivers were out. As they crossed into Nevada the plane dropped suddenly and way too long for Raveneau. He heard the engines power-up, and the long fall ended in plane-shuddering turbulence that slammed the jet sideways, and wrenched his gut. He thought anyone who didn't notice these storms were getting more intense wasn't paying attention.

An hour and forty minutes later they were on the ground in a black Suburban eating sandwiches and crossing flat plain covered in snow, rolling toward what Coe jokingly called San Francisco's sister prison because of its nickname 'Alcatraz of the Rockies.' The Unabomber was here. So was the 'Shoe Bomber,' and Timothy McVeigh before his ticket got punched. Ramzi Yousef had a cell, and others.

Drury was in solitary. Raveneau slowly ate the turkey sandwich and thought about that.

'I know what you're thinking,' Coe said. 'You're thinking the FBI has too much money.'

'Why is Drury all the way out here?'

'He's out here because I really don't know where the threat to him might come from. Weren't you the one who said he might be our one link?'

When they turned off Highway 67 Raveneau looked from the guard posts to the snowy mountains beyond. They went through the gate and then it took awhile before Raveneau sat down with Drury.

When he did, Drury was sullen and angry. He was disconnected. His answers came sporadically and he looked away purposefully. Contempt radiated from his eyes. He was nothing like the social animal Raveneau saw at the bar in San Leandro and that wasn't all that long ago.

'Do you know where you are, John?'

'Prison.'

'But do you know where?'

'I don't fucking care where.'

'You're in a supermax in Colorado.'

Drury rattled his shackles and spittle worked its way to the corners of his lips.

'I'm here because I made a deal with scuzzbag liars.'

'You didn't keep up your end.'

'Fuck you, man.'

'I went back to the cabinet shop; I've figured some things I want to talk with you about it.' Raveneau waved his hand slowly at the walls of the room. 'But, I agree, you don't belong here.'

'So get me out now.'

'Your lawyer is working on it. Remember, you wanted to do everything through your lawyer.'

The table was concrete and bolted to the floor. Drury's shackles looped through an iron ring set in the concrete floor. This was a prison that worked on prisoners until they were broken down enough or old enough to get fed into lesser security prisons. Drury had the energy of a young man and was not aware of how systematically and relentlessly his psyche would get destroyed.

'Where are you at on the police officer who was killed?'

'He pushed me. I tripped and fell backwards into him. He fell on to the freeway. It was an accident.'

'Do you think you should do time for the accident?'

'I'm already doing time.'

'Five years, ten years, two years, what do you think?'

'It was an accident. With the woman I got scared the police were going to kill me.'

'They probably were.'

'They definitely were so I didn't have a choice.'

Drury stared and then surprisingly allowed, 'I know I'll do some time.'

'OK, then what's a fair sentence?'

'Fuck your games, man.'

'Give me a number and then we'll talk about how to get you out of here. It's why I flew out from SF this morning.'

'Three years.'

'That might be right.' Raveneau paused. 'But I think it's going to be longer. Here's where you really are, right now. You're where the rule of law doesn't matter, despite what your lawyer tells you. You're being looked at for possible terrorism charges and once they do that they can keep you forever. I mean literally forever. This isn't your parents' United States any more. They can keep you and never charge you. You could go ten years, twenty years, your whole life, just like the guys in Gitmo, and I'm not exaggerating at all. So what you need to do is get yourself back to the place where the rule of law applies, then get sentenced and do your time and get out. You do that by giving up the guys you're protecting.'

'I've already told you everything. I told you everything and then you fucked me.'

'After I last saw you I went back to the cabinet shop and then drove your route from there. When I did, something occurred to me. Do you want to hear it?'

'Not really.'

'Do you want me to leave? Because I don't mind leaving. The FBI asked me to talk to you but I don't need this. I'll leave and I don't think you'll have many visitors for awhile. Whatever your lawyer is feeding you won't happen. Terrorism charges trump everything. But you decide. You've got five seconds. Should I leave?'

When Drury didn't answer immediately, Raveneau ran a hand through his hair, pushed back his chair and stood.

'You're here because of choices you made and I may as well fly home.'

'I'm not getting screwed again.'

'Do you want to talk or not, yes or no?'

'Fuck!'

'Yes or no?'

'Yes.'

Raveneau still stood with his hands on the chair back.

'There's another reason you're in a supermax and that's because they want to keep you alive. Once you don't own that information and it's out there circulating no one will try to kill you. Right now, the trick is to get you first.'

'Bullshit.'

'Other people have died since you got locked up. When I drove your route I included the stop to switch the plywood. I drove everything up to the actual delivery and then I went back to the stop before you picked up the plywood and the one after it. You told the FBI the plywood switchout was a five minute stop. You said you backed up and the forklift driver was "super quick," your words.

'I took the time it was when you called in from your stop before that and added five to ten minutes for the plywood stop and added that to the time difference between when you called in on the stop prior to the plywood and the one after it. I did that and I couldn't make it work. No matter how I added it up there was still a missing fifteen or twenty minutes, so I ran that by some other homicide inspectors and then the Feds and realized there was another stop.'

Drury started to deny that and Raveneau shook his head. He pulled the chair back. He sat down across from Drury.

'This is it, John. This is last chance, and let me tell you something else. When they get tired of waiting for you to break down and talk, they're going to use you as bait. I promise you that's what will happen. Look, you made another stop. But it didn't hit me until later that it wasn't material you were picking up or delivering. It was a person. It was the shooter. Probably you didn't know what was going on when you picked him up, but you sure knew afterwards. You've got to start talking today. It may save you.'

Drury looked away as he said, 'I'm not going to get screwed.'

'Dude, you're already screwed. It's just about how bad and how long now.' Raveneau waited three beats then asked, 'Did you know what he was going to do?'

Drury shook his head.

'Say something.'

'I didn't even know that's where he was getting out.'

'Where was he?'

'He was in the cab with a hoodie hiding his face. He never once turned his head. He told me if I looked at him he'd kill me.'

'So you knew something bad was going to go down.'

'That's all he said to me. He didn't say anything else.'

'But you knew there was a reason.'

'Yeah, but I thought it was something to do with the owner owing them money or something. I didn't know. If anyone asked I was supposed to say he was a new driver I was training.'

'Who said that?'

'The guy who hired me, the one I told you about. I was supposed to meet him that night and get paid but when you called I freaked out and went to the bar instead.'

Raveneau nodded. That was probably why Drury was alive. It probably meant the gunman was dead. They would have broken the link but Drury could still give them the man who hired him.

'And that's why you gave us a bad description, you were scared?'

'Yes.'

'OK, I can understand that. Now give me a better one, first the gunman sitting next to you in the cab. You saw part of his face. You heard his voice. White, black, what?'

'I don't know and I'm not lying, I couldn't tell and I didn't try hard to look.'

'How old?'

'I don't know.'

'How tall?'

'Sort of average.'

'How did you know where to pick him up?'

'I got a text on the phone they gave me.'

'Was he carrying anything?'

'A brown bag with a zipper down the middle and he put it in the back at the very end and said not to touch it. He said he'd get it when the time came.'

'What did you think was in the bag?'

'I didn't know.'

He knew but that didn't matter right now. Probably got very good money to deliver the man with a promise of an even larger payoff once it was over.

'You're going to be asked to work with a sketch artist to come up with an image of what he looks like and you'll have to go back to zero and start over on the man who hired you. No one is going to question that the description may be different this time. That man is very important. With both you need to think about identifying marks, moles, skin aberrations, scars, tats, variance in the eye color. If the man who hired you has hair growing out his ears we want to know about it.

'Now let's go forward again. You're at the cabinet shop. The plywood has been offloaded by Khan's employee. Where is the guy who rode with you and the bag he brought?'

'He's gone to the bathroom.'

'How did that happen?'

'What do you mean?'

'Did he know where the rest room was? Did he get out of the truck and say, hey, I'm going to the rest room? Had he ever been there before? Tell me how it went down.'

Drury didn't want to answer and Raveneau thought about Drury with a gun in his hand, adrenalized, the veins of his neck bulging, his face twisted with anger and fear as Raveneau entered the house in San Leandro. He looked at Drury's scalp, the short hair.

'I didn't know he was going to do what he did. No one said anything to me about any of it.'

'OK, you asked if he could use the bathroom, then what?'

'Then we signed the delivery tags and I told the older guy that worked there – I can't remember his name – that my guy was back in the truck and I needed to hustle.'

'Did he watch you leave?'

'Never does.'

Never did, Raveneau thought, and knew Drury had rehearsed this. Drury and the man who had hired him rehearsed the moves at the cabinet shop. The shooter probably did sit silent and they brought him in with the plywood so there wouldn't be any gap between delivery and taking out the employees. That probably said several things; one being they worried employees would open the unit of plywood and accidentally discover the bomb casings. And they made a cynical calculation that it wouldn't get found during the murder investigation. He stared at Drury. No way was he still supposed to be alive. So they were making mistakes. They were stumbling, but they prepared for stumbles. They were good enough to adjust and send Khan in and get the casings.

'Did you get money upfront and were going to get the balance afterwards?'

'Yeah, the rest after.'

'Do you know how I know you never collected it?'

'How?'

'You're alive. When was he going to give you the final payment?'

'A week later.'

'Where?'

'At Pete's Corner.'

'Is that the only place you met with him?'

'Yes, but after the first time it was in her car in the lot there. She would text me.'

'Not a man.'

'No.'

'OK, but that's over now, right? When I walk out and the FBI walks in, are you going to be ready?'

'Will I know what's going to happen to me?'

'Just answer.'

He nodded instead.

'You help them on this and they'll return you to the real world. You'll still have to deal with everything else you did, but they will return you. This means you're going to do the polygraph tests, everything.'

Raveneau stopped at the door. He turned.

'A woman?'

'She came up to me at the bar at Pete's.'

'She knew who you were.'

'Yeah, she just started talking to me. She said the bartender told her my name. She went home with me, man. Don't try to tell me that was planned too. I know it wasn't.'

'I'm sure you're right.'

They stared at each other, Raveneau wondering if he was lying again but feeling he wasn't. 'It'll be a lot more than just one interview. You heard me when I said lie detector, right?'

'I heard you.'

'So you've got to be patient, and then they'll get you out of here. You only talk to Special Agent Coe about that, OK? He's the one.'

'I know him.'

'I know you do. He's the one. OK, I'm going to get Coe. This is it, man. Don't blow your one last chance.'

FORTY-SEVEN

The FBI flew Raveneau home late that night and the next morning he nursed a coffee in his early morning meeting with Lieutenant Becker. Becker held up an invoice from the film expert, Kelso. He shook it and the paper rattled.

'I don't get this invoice. You went outside. You hired Kelso. I thought the combination of our video unit and the crime lab had this case covered. Why did we need to go to an outside consultant, especially one I thought we all agreed not to use any more? Why him and what about the FBI? I thought they looked at the videotape.'

'They've looked at photos and some old Kodachrome slides. They'll take a look at the videotape when they can but they're backed up with other film analysis.'

'How can Kelso charge this much?'

Kelso probably put in twice as many hours, Raveneau thought. But Kelso would negotiate. Kelso was film-obsessed. He didn't care about anything else. He wore the same oversized T-shirt, shorts, sandals, and faded Giants baseball cap, rain or shine. He was overweight with a Santa Claus beard and a personal hygiene regimen that guaranteed him a private seat on a crowded bus. But he was a trove of information.

'What did he do that we couldn't do here?'

'He validated that the videotape wasn't a fake and that it was a copy made at the time. Without any information from me he came back with dates of 1987 to 1990 for when it was made and a lot more.'

'Get his number down and I don't want to see him in here yelling about getting paid faster. In fact, I don't want to see him at all.'

Now Becker shifted to Raveneau's most recent request and Raveneau had a hard time reading him. Becker had quit the police department abruptly after the murder of his brother last year, but enough people, Raveneau included, wanted him back and he was reinstated after a leave of absence. He was different now though, more introspective, quieter.

'I can't recommend sending you back to Hawaii without more compelling reasons. Write up your request but don't submit it. I told the captain what you told me, so he knows there's a complaint coming. If it arrives as this Candel says it will it won't sit on my desk more than a day before it goes to the captain. That's the deal he and I have, and I'm not forwarding any other requests for travel until that's resolved.'

'Consider la Rosa going on her own.'

'You've been working the case so I don't like that idea, and you don't like it either so don't waste our time here.'

They left it there and Raveneau's cell rang as he left Becker's office.

'Inspector Raveneau, it's Barb Haney. I'm sorry to bother you, but I think you might want to know this. My ex-husband, Larry Benhaime, is in San Francisco at the Four Seasons. He's flying out later this morning and he doesn't know I'm calling you. He's in room 417. I just talked to him. He's planning to stay in his room until a car takes him to the airport. You should catch him before he leaves.'

'What should I ask him?'

When Raveneau interviewed her in Truckee he knew she had something to tell him, and now maybe it was going to come out. The fluttery hesitancy with which Barbara Haney moved from topic to topic and room to room in the big house in the Martis Valley he read first as nervousness, later as something else.

Raveneau was at the Four Seasons within an hour. He asked the desk to call Benhaime and now watched him step out of the elevator. They shook hands and Benhaime looked more curious than surprised.

'Inspector, can we talk over breakfast? I'm starving and I can't come to your police station. I'd miss my flight. What do you say we get some breakfast here and talk?'

Benhaime ordered eggs and toast and coffee, Raveneau coffee. As soon as the waiter walked off with the order Benhaime started talking.

'First thing is we lied to your inspectors, not something we normally did but this was at the request of your government. Barbara and I worked for the RCMP, Royal Canadian Mounted Police in the branch that preceded CAP, the Counterfeit Analysis Program. We weren't newly-weds, but we were soon to be married so as a cover it worked. We had the honeymoon in reverse. For Barbara, that was the last undercover op. She had wanted out for awhile and when we married she quit.'

'Are you still with the Mounties?'

'Hmm, should have done this straightaway this morning.'

He showed a badge. He showed ID.

'Different group now, I'm with the Revenue Service, mostly in Asia, mostly in Hong Kong. Copy the numbers if you like. We were to meet Mr Krueger in front of the Ferry Building and we got there well ahead of time. We had him in sight. We were going to buy some counterfeit bills. He was approaching and then was intercepted by another man and headed off with him. We wondered later if the other man impersonated me.

'We watched a bit and then followed, but far enough back so no one would pick up on us. It's why we found his body. At that point, the best decision was to walk away, but Barbara wouldn't have it. So we phoned it in and all the mess that followed came from that decision.'

'Why didn't you tell the inspectors?'

'Your Secret Service asked us not to. They didn't want to compromise their operation and given that we had already done all we could to help the police it seemed to make sense. But we weren't as good on our feet as we thought and the one inspector in particular suspected we knew more. Don't ask me how he knew, but he did. When he flew to Calgary looking to re-interview us we checked with your people first.'

'The Secret Service?'

'Yes, they were conducting their own investigation into the killing and on hold with their operation until they learned more. They didn't come out and say don't talk with the homicide inspector, but they did strongly imply they wanted us to wait. So we stonewalled him and he all but told us we were lying. He was close to correct but didn't seem to have facts to back it up.'

'Inspector Govich?'

'Yes.'

'Who in the local Secret Service office knew about this?'

'A fellow by the name of John Pagen.'

'What were you going to get out of the meeting with Krueger?'

'A batch of counterfeit one hundred dollar US bills. People Krueger was working with were doing test runs, exchanging hundred dollar bills for Canadian in Vancouver.'

'Test runs?'

'Yes, checking out the bills and the response they got, or more to the point, eh, the response they didn't get. The bills passed easily. They were a remarkable step up. We were working with your Secret Service on this one and looking for the city of origin, looking for where these bills were bubbling out of. We couldn't figure out where they were coming from. First ones showed up in Hong Kong, then the Philippines, and the Yanks said North Korea and pinned it on them, but we were never sure that was true of all the supernotes. Other makes, we thought.'

'What do you think now? Where was the city of origin?'

'I won't say, but I will say we thought the work was too sophisticated for the North Koreans, yet the only people who could have helped them would have been Yanks.'

'The North Koreans have built nuclear weapons and missiles. Why would money be hard?'

'Look at the quality of their money, but there were other reasons. You asked and what I think is someone sold the right printing equipment and taught them how to use it. In other words I think your Secret Service was set-up by another agency in your government who wanted the Koreans for cover. Korean diplomats went out across the world with the counterfeit bills and muddied things up. That allowed those who thought up the scheme to start printing their own money. That money didn't come from any Congressional appropriation. It didn't have any oversight. It was money they could do anything they wanted with.'

Benhaime's eggs arrived and he took time to pepper them before continuing.

'Krueger wasn't direct with your service any more. He was what gets called now non operational cover. He was in-between, feeding information home while making deals with the counterfeiters to get bills out and tested. Dangerous work. They were the very first of a run of extraordinary notes. Krueger was selling for them bills at a strong discount and taking some money and paying the counterfeiter, but we thought he was pocketing some too. He was dealing with criminal elements in Vancouver. We thought he got hit because they figured out he was stepping on the price and ripping them off. Are you with me?'

'What were you going to pay for the counterfeit bills?'

'We were hagglers. Thirty-five cents on the dollar, forty if we had to.'

Raveneau returned to his earlier question. It was a true test since the Secret Service wasn't contacted at the time.

'How many bills were you going to buy in the meeting with Krueger that afternoon?'

'When he called he said he had sixty-one, but was going to keep a bill, so sixty. Sixty bills for twenty-two hundred dollars, but we had planned to knock him down to a straight two thousand when we showed him our cash.'

Raveneau nodded. He didn't reveal it was exactly the right amount. But unless the Secret Service told Benhaime, how would he know? Goya and Govich said they never talked about the money with the Canadians, and Raveneau knew Benhaime's credentials were going to check out.

'Now Barbara wants it all to go away,' Benhaime said, 'and

I'm with her. Enough time has passed. She was quite upset when you came back with more questions after all these years. Didn't expect that.'

'There's a reason.'

'Figured as much.' He picked up his toast. 'It's why we're having breakfast.'

'How much of a look did you get of the man Krueger walked off with?'

'Not much. He was at quite a distance.'

'Have you got a laptop in that briefcase that will play a CD?'

'It will, yes.'

Raveneau pulled the CD from his pocket.

'Change chairs with me so your back is to the wall and no one else will see it.'

'Can I take my eggs?'

'Sure, but it's not very long.'

'I don't want them to get cold.'

It took a minute to change chairs and for Benhaime's laptop to boot up, and to reassure the waiter who came rushing over that nothing was wrong with their seating.

'Just some porn to watch,' Benhaime said, and showed the waiter the CD. He slid it in and the waiter lingered. Benhaime waited for him to leave then started it.

'Tell me when you recognize Krueger.'

'Ah, we're there again. Was this filmed by your Secret Service?'

'I don't know who filmed it. Did they know you were meeting Krueger?'

'They knew we were in San Francisco. They knew we were trying to set up a meeting with Krueger, but Barb and I didn't tell them we had one arranged.' He pointed at the screen. 'There he is. Yes, that's him.'

'Who's with him?'

'I think it's the man who intercepted him, can't be positive but I think it is.' Benhaime leaned over the computer. 'You've got the whole thing.' He watched the rest in silence and when he looked up he looked shocked. 'He was actually quite likeable, even double-dealing. My God, this is hard to watch.'

Raveneau reached over to Benhaime's keyboard. He froze the frame.

'Look at the face of the shooter. Is that who intercepted Krueger?'

'I don't know.'

When Raveneau turned they were eye to eye and not that far apart.

'OK, you don't know, so let me ask you about something you do know. Why did you strip his wallet?'

FORTY-EIGHT

Raveneau left Benhaime in the lobby of the Four Seasons and called Barbara Haney from his cell in his car. He wanted to reach her before Benhaime did.

'That beep is him trying to get through,' she said, and paused, possibly debating asking him to hold then deciding against it.

'You had more communication with him than you told me.'

'Did he tell you that?' She didn't wait for him to answer. 'Yes, I've wanted to end this. He must have told you that I pushed for that. I've wanted that for a long time. Didn't he say that?'

'He did.'

'But yes, Inspector, I did lie. I know that's what you're driving at. But I'm also the one trying to undo this whole thing. You understand that, right?'

'Keep going, Barbara.'

'But I need to know that you believe that.'

'I do believe it.'

'That matters. It's really very, very important.' He got it. He understood she wanted to undo some of what had already happened. 'I've carried this. I've carried this like a weight for more than twenty years.'

Without a pause she said, 'We were waiting for him along the wharf between the Ferry Building and the pier just northwest of it.'

'Alan Krueger?'

'Yes, and he was with another man or he was intercepted by another man, I couldn't tell. But he seemed to know him. I tried to tell who the other man was but they were far enough away and there was glare. I remember the sun off the glass on the building behind us. We didn't really know what to do. In my purse was a small set of binoculars but it was awkward and there wasn't much time to decide what we were going to do. Larry was adamant we meet him alone. We were dealing with Krueger only, so we backed up, we moved away, but it didn't matter. Alan didn't give any sign he was meeting with anyone.'

'Where did you move?'

'We continued down the waterfront in the direction of the bridge and they were coming toward us and then crossed and went among the cars parked under the freeway. There was a lot there. Well, you know that of course. We assumed the man either arrived unanticipated and Krueger continued with him toward our meeting place so we would see he wasn't alone. Or he planned all along to introduce us to him. But our instructions were to meet Krueger alone, so for us the meeting ended when this other man showed up.'

She drew a deep breath. Raveneau heard it. What was coming was still emotional for her.

'So we followed. Larry wanted to know who the other man was but it was more difficult now because their backs were to us as they moved through the cars into more shadowy light. It was a winter afternoon.'

'But it was sunny.'

'Yes, yes, there was light reflecting off the windows while we waited for him, but it didn't last long or there were clouds. I don't know. It just got darker and they moved past the cars and toward two support pillars for the roadway above. We lost sight of them and we waited for them to come back into view, but they didn't. You have to understand our view was blocked by a pillar.'

'The man with him?'

'I don't know where he went. He just sort of melted away and yes, I did hear something. I heard a pop, pop, pop, and thought it was a car backfiring, but now I'm sure it was something else. Oh, that's a lie, that's a lie, I'm doing it again. Oh, God, why can't I just do this, what is the matter with me?'

He heard her gasp. He heard something close to a sob.

'I heard shots. I heard them and when I saw him on the ground I knew that's what they had been, but I told your inspectors I didn't hear anything. Our orders were to be truthful to a point but to disengage.'

'Those were your instructions?'

'Yes, we called in before reporting the murder. It was presumed your Secret Service would be involved in the investigation.'

'Where did he go?'

'The other man?'

'Yes.'

'I wondered if he had a car parked in that lot or someone waiting in a van or something and he stayed low and got to his ride. He must have driven off somehow.'

'How long did you wait?'

'We were cautious. We proceeded toward the pillars and saw him lying there. When we didn't see the other man we moved in. You want to know how long, don't you? It was less than five minutes.'

'Did you see anyone else watching?'

She hesitated and Raveneau knew he was giving her an opening.

'Possibly.'

'Possibly you saw someone else?'

'Yes, and we were watching everyone of course. We assumed the man meeting with Krueger might have backup or accomplices.'

'Backup? Did you think he was with the Secret Service?'

'Until we saw him lying there we thought it possible. There was another man who seemed to be lurking in the car lot. He was taking too long and making too much of a fuss about rearranging things in his car, but he was there before they crossed the street.'

'You were able to make out his face.'

'Somewhat. Not well.'

'You had your binoculars out now.'

Again, she hesitated.

'Yes, but that man left before we passed through the cars. He backed out and left and we went forward and found Krueger. We checked to see if he was alive. No, Larry checked. I didn't check. I saw his skull. I saw he was dead. It was obvious he was dead.'

'Was Larry looking for the counterfeit bills?'

'Yes.'

'Let's talk about the wallet.'

'Yes, I lied to you last time we met. We left the passports but we wanted the rest of the ID, credit cards, driver's licenses, and we wanted the counterfeit money. Larry didn't find the money. It wasn't in the wallet and we thought the man who shot him took it.'

'You knew San Francisco police would investigate.'

'Yes.'

'So why did you strip his wallet?'

'We had our own investigation and we turned the effects over. Your Secret Service got them. We didn't leave the country with any of it, just copies. The actual documents we mailed to your Secret Service office in San Francisco and we confirmed they got them. It was understood they would turn them over to the homicide inspectors.'

'That's not the same.'

'I know it isn't. I knew what we were doing was wrong. We took evidence from the scene.'

'Who did you notify at the Secret Service?'

'Larry made the phone call. I don't know who he spoke to.'

'You didn't ask?'

'By then I didn't want to know. I was very shaken by the killing. You have to understand we were pencil pushers. I came from university in accounting and mathematics. Half of what we were always doing was forensics. We tried to figure out where someone had been and where money had traveled. With Alan Krueger we knew something was up. He had acquired a way of disappearing, so we guessed he was operating under other aliases. Hardly unusual, but we were very interested to know where he stayed in Vancouver and under what name, and what kind of offer he would make us.'

'Who killed Alan Krueger?'

She was quiet a long moment.

'It's all you really want, isn't it? You don't really care about any of the rest of this.'

'Who do you think killed him?'

'Either the criminal elements he was dealing with who didn't like the exchange rate, or your government took him out because he was playing both sides.'

'Our government?'

'Yes.'

'Barbara, I like you. I like it that you were willing to meet with me and talk and that you want to get this off your chest, but it feels to me as if you're still holding back. It feels as if you've colluded on a new version with Larry that's missing some details. If I didn't have the videotape I'd have to look at you as suspects.'

Her voice was much harder as she answered, 'That's already been done and I can't solve the murder for you. I've tried to clear this whole godawful thing. I don't know what else to do. I'm going to say good bye now.'

'Barbara, wait,' but she was gone.

FORTY-NINE

Fox News speculated that a Republican President wouldn't have canceled the trip to San Francisco. Other media focused on the search for the missing explosive devices. Photos of the devices showed. A headline read 'Thousands Could Die.' The White House press secretary stressed that it wasn't the President's decision to cancel the San Francisco trip, it was Secret Service caution. The Secret Service linked the decision to a credible threat that they couldn't elaborate on and so for twenty-four hours the media just winged it.

Raveneau clicked on a video, a three minute in-depth interview with a terrorist expert who appeared to be speaking from a chair in the study of his home. He tied the bomb casing design and pattern of delivery to Al Qaeda. He sounded quite certain but Raveneau had to cut him off to take a call from Becker.

'A package delivered,' Becker said. 'From Hawaii.' Raveneau heard him inhale. 'I'm in my office. Why don't we open it together?'

'See you in a few minutes.'

When Raveneau walked into the office he quietly shut the door behind him. The FedEx box sat center of Becker's desk.

'I have an agreement with Captain Ramirez that I don't hold things like this on my desk after I've opened them. It'll go to him this afternoon.'

'You told me that yesterday. You told me a couple of times.'

'I just don't want there to be any misunderstanding.'

'OK, but you don't have to build a firewall between us. I understand what you have to do.'

Raveneau stared at the box but kept thinking about Barbara Haney and the glibness with which she had lied to him and backtracked. He watched Becker root around in his desk looking for something to cut the packing tape with. And then a text came from Ortega. He read that and laid the phone down. His phone buzzed with other calls but he didn't look at the screen, instead watched Becker lift out an object encased in bubble wrap.

'Has a little weight to it,' Becker said. 'Not much, but something, more than a letter or a CD.'

Didn't look like one either and when Raveneau saw Becker was unsure what to do with it he said, 'Can I take a look?'

Becker handed it to him and as soon as he had it in hand he knew what it was. Raveneau cut away the plastic wrap and Becker said, 'That goes straight to the crime lab.'

Raveneau nodded.

'What type of Glock is that?'

One of the things Raveneau liked about Becker was he didn't pay much attention to guns. Never had and he was notoriously bad out on the range. Raveneau figured it was one of the reasons Becker had such a high solve rate. He always focused on motive, on why things happened.

'This is the model the Austrian engineer Gaston Glock started with. This is a Glock 17. It shoots a nine, a nine by nineteen millimeter parabellum, the NATO standard and one of the design requirements when Glock came up with this gun.'

Raveneau studied it a little longer then folded the bubble wrap back over. He was careful not to touch it. He looked up at Becker and said, 'Alan Krueger was shot with a nine.'

'Did you have any idea this was coming?'

'No.'

Becker picked up the FedEx box and looked it over.

'Did this Thomas Casey send it?'

'Matt Frank sent it for him. That's what Candel told me, but I don't think this is what Casey had in mind to send.'

'You said this Matt Frank travels with his coffee business. He goes to trade shows. He was in Los Angeles not long ago. Isn't that correct?'

'That's what he told us.'

'How about this idea? Matt Frank sent you the videotape from Los Angeles. He FedExed the videotape same as he FedExed this gun.'

'Could be. You should have stayed a homicide inspector.'

'I know, should never have taken the promotion. I'm not cut out to herd cats. But I get the feeling you don't think my idea fits.'

'The kid has anger, a lot of it. He was close to shooting me when he found me at the house. I heard the buzz of one of his shots go past my head and there was a moment there when I could feel him debating. But he was angry before he met me. As soon as he introduced me to Casey, he disappeared. He took off. He may not know it yet, but he doesn't like his uncle much. Uncle Casey calls the shots, writes the checks, and tells him what to do. So by sending this gun instead of the complaint against me he strikes at his Uncle Casey. I'm speculating, but that's how I read it.

'It may be the gun used to kill Krueger, but if it is it'll be a ballistics match only. There won't be any prints, any residue, anything to tie it directly to Casey. It won't be registered to Thomas Casey or anyone we can find. It's probably not registered.'

'You can find that out quickly.'

Raveneau nodded.

'I'll take it to the lab and then I've got to go meet Ortega.'

In his car Raveneau checked to see who the missed calls were from. He figured Ortega followed his text with calls but all three were from Ryan Candel. He didn't call Candel back yet. He called Ortega who said, 'You inspired me, Raveneau. I did another search and found something. We're at the cabinet shop. Come on over.'

FIFTY

'What did you find?'
'Money in a floor safe underneath one of those bolted down saws. This is like a fun house. Everywhere you look here you find something. But like I said, you inspired me.' Ortega turned to him. 'It's the money we found I want you to see.'

Ortega squinted and for whatever the reason looked pained. Bruce Ortega worked his way from uniform officer to sergeant to a stint with Burglary and Robbery to the Homicide Detail by age thirty-four. He came on quietly and Raveneau knew him as a hard worker, knowledgeable about DNA and the more recent forensic advances available to them. He had good instincts and was intuitive about motive. He called himself a steady plodder, but Raveneau didn't think of him that way at all.

This afternoon he was dressed in a charcoal gray sport coat, black pants and black loafers. He once told Raveneau that his wife shopped for him twice a year at Nordstrom's semiannual half-off sales and got her inspiration from watching the remake of the TV series *Hawaii Five-O*. She then toned it down to their budget.

'The safe was underneath the big band saw. I didn't come here looking for anything other than a new idea. Here, let me show you.'

They walked to the tool room where the cutting was done and looked at a saw cut in the concrete surrounding the area where the band saw had sat. Someone pointed it out during the search Raveneau was on, though he couldn't remember who. Ortega ran the edge of his shoe along the saw cut line.

'We cut the bolts holding the saw down and I shoved the saw out of the way with the forklift.'

Raveneau looked into the open safe.

'Where's the money?'

'In Khan's office, the locksmith just left.'

'How much was there?'

'I haven't touched it, but enough for both of us.'

He smiled.

'I want you to look at it before I notify my fearless task force leader. When I do they'll show up here with a dozen agents.'

'You've gone rogue.'

'No, technically you're on my team.' He turned. 'Did you hear they made an arrest this morning?'

'Yeah, I heard a couple of hours ago about Mathis.'

The Bureau had arrested Cleg Mathis, prime suspect in the Khan murders at a McDonald's in St Paul, Minnesota, but headed to Canada with false ID. It happened mid morning Pacific Time. Raveneau was impressed the Bureau had tracked him down.

In Khan's office Raveneau looked in the bag then pulled on latex gloves and lifted out a bundle of bills. It shouldn't surprise him but it did, and as it did, something brushed along the edges of his consciousness again. The blatant aspect was striking. The bills could hardly stick out more but they probably paid Khan with them. In his view it was another mistake, but maybe they had it all so well scripted they were that confident.

'What do you make of these?' Ortega asked.

'They look like the counterfeit bills my guy Krueger was carrying. They're identifiable but not traceable.'

'But you're saying they're the same as what you found on Krueger, right?'

'They look the same to me, but I'm an instant expert. You need to call the Secret Service.'

'Why would you pay anybody with counterfeit notes that look like they were buried in your grandfather's mattress?'

'Maybe they wanted to make it easier for the Feds and us later. Maybe they want the operation rolled up after it's done.'

Raveneau shrugged. He really didn't know what to make of this, but he felt reasonably confident the bills would match.

'How many of these bills got printed?' Ortega asked.

'Good question.'

'They haven't given you any idea?'

'I doubt anyone really knows.'

'And they've been out of circulation all this time?'

Raveneau shrugged, couldn't answer that either. Ortega knew about the buy last July so there was nothing to say about that.

'Is there a big stash over there in Hawaii, Raveneau?'

'There's one somewhere.'

FIFTY-ONE

B ut if there was the connection Larry Benhaime suggested, Raveneau wasn't sure how he was going to prove it. He talked awhile that night with Coe after Ortega called and said the Secret Service had confirmed the bills were counterfeit and in the same series. The next morning ballistics testing matched the Glock 17 to three of the bullets removed from Krueger's body and Raveneau and la Rosa sat down with Becker and the captain.

By late afternoon they were on their way to the airport. They would get to Hawaii tonight, but it was going to be a long one. Their flight routed through Los Angeles and included a two and a half hour layover.

At LAX Raveneau talked again with Coe and learned more details about the Mathis arrest.

'He had the garrote with him and when we showed him everything else we have he caved. He gave us a name and a description of a woman that's close to what Drury gave us, right down to an abdominal scar she told Drury was from a bullet that grazed her. Mathis claims she slept with him same as Drury.'

He sounded puzzled as he continued.

'We still can't figure out who she is. We got a little bit from Interpol, but it may just be chatter. There are rumors of an American woman who fits the description and acts as a go-between. She may have organized the murder of a London banker for Russian clients, but the Russians usually stick with their own. She probably had a role in the kidnapping-torture-murder of two telecom executives in Brazil. Interpol believes she's an independent contractor reached through a website, but they don't have the website link.

'Both Mathis and Drury did describe more or less the same woman. Drury claims she has a Texas accent but looks as if she could be from the Middle East. Mathis told us this afternoon, southern accent and he was sure she was half Lebanese though she didn't tell him that. What that information does for us I don't know. It may not do anything.'

'The similar descriptions are worth something.'

'They are and we've got agents looking hard for her. That said, we should have stayed with Mathis. He was on his way to Canada to get paid fifty thousand dollars for taking out the Khans. We should have followed him but we didn't want him to get over the border. He was carrying a throwaway phone and supposed to get a call from her after reaching a rendezvous point in Toronto. The Mounties are there and we have agents with them watching the area but so far no sign of her. I'll call you if anything changes.'

La Rosa and Raveneau landed late in the night. The plane was quiet before landing then picked up cheerful chatter as it unloaded. Within forty minutes they were headed to their rooms. Before dawn Raveneau made coffee in the room. He talked with Ryan Candel as he waited downstairs outside the lobby for la Rosa. She came off the elevator with a wry smile wearing the lei left on her bed.

'We're here,' she said. 'Let's get some of that coffee you've been talking about.'

'Candel says Matt Frank called him last night and that he was agitated and in his words sort of incoherent. He said it weirded him out and that he alluded to things he's got to get done before he can focus on his business. He said there were problems but didn't say what they were. He asked Candel about me, whether I've questioned him any more and whether his name has come up.'

'Does Ryan know we've got some questions about his new brother?'

'He's getting the picture.' Raveneau paused. 'Matt Frank is supposed to meet us this morning at Hapuna Beach at nine. The beach is north of here. I know where it is. It's not going to take us long to get there.'

'Did Candel say anything else?'

'Not really, and I'd say he was disturbed by the conversation with Frank and having a little trouble with what we're asking him to do. He's conflicted. He's known his half brother for under a week, but part of him wants to protect him.'

They had an hour to kill and made calls sitting in the sun on a bench in a shopping center half a mile from the main highway. La Rosa got her coffee and looked happy with it. Then they drove north toward Hapuna Beach with Raveneau pointing out the rise of North Kohala Road ahead, and farther north around the curve of the island the steep-falling slope where the ranch was.

'Can you see the ranch from here?'

'No.'

'There's so much lava. It's drier than I thought.'

'This is the dry side.'

Raveneau checked the time as they left the highway and drove slowly through a small town along the water before turning into the Hapuna Beach lot. He spotted Frank's gray Toyota pickup and parked nearby. They walked through the entrance past rest rooms and down toward the beach.

'There he is.'

'Where?'

'That guy over there with the green and white shorts carrying the surf board.'

Frank waved and leaned the board against a low concrete retaining wall. He picked up a towel and a can of some drink and came toward them, drinking from the can as he walked. Frank belonged on the beach and he and la Rosa probably looked like a pair of missionaries on a recruiting drive in the third world. He watched Frank closely as he approached, and then the three of them sat down on a concrete bench and Raveneau said, 'A package arrived at our Homicide office.'

'I sent it to you.'

'Then I have to ask you what was in it?'

'A gun, a Glock 17 that came from my uncle's house.'

'Is it his gun?'

'He's had it forever.'

'Why did you send it?'

'Because he used to talk about it like it was a person that went out and did things on its own. He talks some strange shit when he's drunk. He talked about the gun as if it traveled to places, killed bad people, and then came back home. He thought I sent the complaint letter and a video of me telling how you broke in. When he finds out the gun is gone it'll freak him out.'

He stared at Raveneau communicating something else.

'That's the Glock I learned on. Uncle Casey says it belonged to my dad, but it was always sitting in the bar cabinet of the lanai in Uncle Casey's house. Uncle Casey told me he'd give it to me when I became a marksman, but he didn't. He likes owning it. He checks on it regularly, like a habit. If he hasn't already noticed it's missing he's going to real soon and I don't know what he'll do.'

'What do you think he'll do?'

'First he'll ask me where it is.'

'What are you going to tell him?'

'That it's mine and I took it. It was Dad's gun and he promised it to me.'

'Do you know about something in particular the gun was used for?'

Frank tipped the can, swallowed more of the coconut water, and Raveneau knew he wasn't going to answer that directly.

'Was Alan Krueger's name ever mentioned in connection with the gun?'

'What do you mean?'

'Just asking.'

'He was their friend.'

'Did Krueger ever borrow the gun?'

'I don't know. I was pretty young and I knew it got borrowed, but I didn't really know who took it. I guess he could have borrowed it. Other people did. I didn't get it at the time but they would joke and say things like the gun is away on a business trip, shit like that.'

He finished the coconut water and crumpled the middle of the can.

'Our housekeeper cleans it every week or so. It's like a ritual. They used to call it the wipe down. He's going to ask me where it is and get seriously angry.'

'The gun isn't registered to anyone.'

'But that's like the whole trip. They had like this whole story around the gun. It lives in that glass case and then goes out on trips on its own. It goes to do good, that's what they called it, doing good, my dad, Uncle Casey, Shay, Krueger, and some other dudes that I only kind of barely remember. They all knew about it. Maybe it was never registered. Uncle Casey said Dad used to fly with it. As a pilot they didn't usually check his bags. He carried other stuff for their friends.'

'I want to ask you about something else having to do with your dad. Were you there when he died?'

'Uncle Casey found him and woke me up. We walked up there together before he called the police or Dad's doctor. We didn't move him. He'd fallen and hit his head just outside the sliding door in front and it was pretty obvious he was dead.'

He looked away at the ocean remembering it, and Raveneau could see it affected him still. Some closeness there not really recognized in all this.

'That night Uncle Casey and I sat up there in the chairs like Dad did with his friends. We got drunk together and he told me stories about my dad that I'd never heard. In a way it made me feel better and in a way it made me super sad.'

La Rosa spoke softly now, recounting her father's long decline and death, Raveneau taking it in and thinking Frank was down here in shorts and carrying his board so if his uncle showed up he'd look like he was doing what he did every morning. He was afraid of him or very good at acting.

'My dad didn't shoot. He didn't like guns. He said he killed enough in the war and supposedly that's why Uncle Casey kept the gun at his house.'

This was a description of a man different than the one Casey portrayed.

'I wanted to learn to shoot. I wanted to learn when I was little and visited him and he wouldn't let me. That's why my uncle taught me. My dad was pretty messed up by the war.'

'What about your uncle?'

'He says they did what they were told to and what they had to, and that you can't look back.'

'Is it true he doesn't leave the island?'

'No, but that's his thing. He likes the way it sounds, but really it was my dad who wouldn't leave the island any more. My uncle makes a trip or two a year to the mainland. He went with me to a coffee thing in San Francisco a few years ago when I was getting the business started. It's like I said, he just likes to say that. It's sort of a way he wants to be, you know. Since Dad died he's sort of taken on these other things that were like Dad's way.'

Raveneau returned to the gun.

'If he asks where you have it, what are you going to say?'

'That it's in my safe deposit box at the bank. He might say it's OK or he might tell me to move and buy him out of the coffee business tomorrow.'

'What do you think is going to happen?'

'He's going to freak out.'

'Is he home right now?'

'Yes.'

'We're going to go see him. What about you? Where can we find you later?'

'Call me.'

Frank set the empty can on top of the garbage receptacle and then picked up his board.

'I'm going back in the water.'

'We're going to call you later today. We'll want to meet again, Matt.'

'I'm pretty sure we're going to meet.'

He said that and walked away. They watched him, waited until he was out of earshot, and la Rosa said, 'That was weird, especially that at the end.'

He turned to her. 'I told you how he was when he found me up at his dad's house.'

'I was just thinking about that.'

'He was real close up there. He wavered. I felt lucky to get away.'

FIFTY-TWO

Going through the gates reminded la Rosa of the summer she worked on a ranch in Montana before she had any idea what she was going to do with her life. She swung them closed and admired what Casey had here.

But despite the blue sky, soft warmth of the breeze off the ocean and the gentleness of the land, adrenaline kicked in. She felt several hard heartbeats. At home they might have come with backup, even if it was just to ask a patrol unit to park in the street. Raveneau was in touch with an agent in the FBI satellite office in Kona here on the Big Island, but he just wanted to know there was help available if they needed it. He probably hadn't told the Kona office much. His phone rang as she got back in the car.

He looked down at the screen and said, 'That's him. I'm going to answer.'

'Inspector, Tom Casey here. I've got some information for you on the Hawaiian artist I told you about. She's still on the island.'

'That's great, and thanks for making the call.'

'Oh, I'm enjoying our chats.'

'That's good to hear, because we'd like to have one with you this morning. My partner and I are here on the island.' Raveneau glanced over at her, hesitating a moment before saying, 'We're driving up to your house right now. We were hoping to catch you at home.'

'Unannounced.'

'Maybe unannounced, but I'm not much of a believer in coincidence.'

'I'm not either. I'll see you in a few minutes.'

Raveneau put it to her this way, 'Casey wants to know everything about what we're thinking. He's not afraid of us. I think he sees us as civil servants with guns working for a government he doesn't particularly respect. That he's wealthy seems to make him think he knows more than people like you and me. He likes to talk political philosophy while he fishes for information, and in small ways he'll constantly try to control the conversation. You may feel like you're talking to two different people at the same moment. He's bright but troubled and unstable.'

'If he's unstable what are we doing here without backup?'

'We'll be OK.'

But Raveneau asked her to stand to the side and be ready to react. He climbed the steps ahead of her and the door opened just as he reached the porch. Casey thrust out his hand as if greeting an old friend. He smiled down at her and said, 'Elizabeth, nice to meet you finally.'

And la Rosa didn't know why she felt so nervous. It wasn't Raveneau's prepping and it wasn't like her. Her first take was that for a man in his early sixties Thomas Casey looked unusually vigorous and strong. On the porch his gaze was direct and friendly. But then he put on a puzzled expression as he turned back to Raveneau.

'I'll be frank. I'm surprised they let you travel. I thought you'd be disciplined. I sent a letter about the burglary, a very detailed letter and a video of my nephew's account.'

'My lieutenant said something came in from Hawaii. I figured you had sent me a box of macadamia nuts.'

'Did you?'

'Yeah.'

'So you're back and you're smug. Well, that explains a lot of things. Come in, both of you. You've flown a long way with whatever theory you've got. Let's hear it.'

They followed him down a long hallway with a light-colored bamboo floor, Casey walking with a slight limp, his shoe clicking with each step. The limp she hadn't noticed when he greeted them. He must have hid it. He took them to the lanai Raveneau had told her about and moved three wicker chairs over to a low white-painted iron table.

'Sit.' He pointed a finger at Raveneau. 'I know you like beer, but what about you, Elizabeth. What are you drinking?'

'I just had coffee but thank you.'

'What kind of beer, Commander?'

'Whatever you've got.'

'You don't care as long as it has alcohol, right? I once knew that feeling.'

He popped the caps off two Coronas and put the bottles down on the table.

'Now just cut to it,' he said, 'I don't need the roundabout bullshit or have time for it today. You're here because you think you're on to something.'

'Before anything else why don't you give us the name and phone number of the Hawaiian artist,' la Rosa said. She said this quietly. She didn't feel Raveneau's earlier attitude was smug and she read Casey's attitude as bullying. She knew now was the best time to get the phone number from him and she wasn't surprised he resisted.

'I wrote it down on a piece of paper and I don't know what I did with it. It's somewhere in here.'

La Rosa stood. 'I'll help you look for it.'

For a long moment Casey didn't answer. He stared at her then got to his feet and went over to the bar, stood behind it looking down, and la Rosa caught Raveneau's alertness. She registered what it was about and unzipped the small purse she carried her gun in.

'Here it is,' Casey said, and then brought it to her. As she thanked him she pulled her phone from her purse and Casey said, 'Don't call her yet.'

La Rosa smiled at him as the phone rang, saying, 'We don't have much time. We need to set up a meeting with her.'

A woman answered and la Rosa introduced herself and asked if she was speaking to Aolani Ito. She was and la Rosa's first impression was that Ito was unafraid and curious. She asked Ito how long it would take to get there and then agreed on a time.

'So you're going to do lunch,' Casey said, as she hung up. 'Well, it's a long drive. You'll have to hurry. You'll have to cut short whatever you planned here. I think you're getting ahead of yourselves. I think you're making guesses you can't support. You don't really see what's evolving, do you?'

Raveneau was soft spoken, holding the beer bottle but not drinking from it, gesturing slowly with his free hand.

'What's evolving, Tom? What are we missing?'

'Let's get to why you're here first. What have you got?'

'We're here about the Glock you're missing.'

'The Glock the boy protected himself with when you were breaking into Jim's house is a new model and the boy owns it. It's registered to him but you know that by now. I don't have any Glocks registered to me, but you've learned that too by now. Are you asking about the Glock 17 I've kept in that glass case over there and that's gone missing very recently?'

'Yes.'

'Is that what he did, he sent it to you?'

'We have the gun. We've tested it. It's why we're here.'

Casey didn't seem surprised. He must have gotten there on his own already, or maybe it was part of a plan she didn't understand yet.

'Jim Frank bought that gun in Austria when they first came out. He asked me to hold it for him and it has sat in that cabinet there on and off for decades. Sometimes he'd take it back to the house with him or loan it to somebody. The boy will tell you the same thing. The boy learned to shoot with it. It's why he loves Glocks. I'm sure he can remember Jim carrying it back up the trail or loaning it out. Sometime later it would reappear in that case. That was the way it worked. Jim wanted access to it, but he didn't want it in his house.'

'How many years has it been in your possession?' Raveneau asked.

'Since Jim brought it back.'

'When was that?'

'It was—'

La Rosa saw the moment it happened. She watched the change and thought a heart attack was possible. The color drained from Casey's face faster than she had ever seen.

'Don't tell me AK was shot with it. Don't tell me that.'

'He was. We have a ballistics match. Your gun was the murder weapon.'

'The gun went out there and killed AK?'

'What do you mean it went out there?'

'Jim loaned it out.'

'Why would he loan a gun to people?'

'You'd have to ask him.'

'Since we can't interview a dead man I think you had better tell us.'

'Are you suggesting I had something to do with AK's murder? Of course that's what you're suggesting.'

'Who had the gun when he was killed?'

'I don't remember.'

'Then it comes back to you, Tom.'

'No, no, it doesn't come back to me. It was never my gun. I would have killed myself before killing Alan.'

La Rosa had a hard time not believing he was sincere.

'You can see where we're at,' Raveneau said. 'It's the murder weapon. You need to convince us.'

'The gun went out on its own. Someone had a drink with Jim and then it got borrowed. It was only used to do good. But Jim loaned it out so much it got to be a running joke. If someone complained too much about a boss or a wife he'd get the gun and tell them either go take care of it or quit complaining. He didn't like complaining. Other people borrowed it to learn to shoot and that's what I mean when I say used for good. Like the boy learning to shoot so he'll be ready when the time comes.'

'When what time comes?'

'Change is always coming, Ben. One event can trigger a historical convulsion. The Archduke Ferdinand and his wife were shot in their car on a side street in Sarajevo early on a summer afternoon on the twenty-eighth of June in 1914 by a young man with a Browning .32 exactly the same as the one in the case behind you.'

He pointed. He wanted Raveneau to turn to look and she looked but Raveneau didn't. Raveneau took a drink of beer.

'You have to understand, anything he had Jim would loan out. It wasn't about guns and as I said earlier he didn't like to be around guns. I have to remember. I have to think back. I just can't get my head around what you're saying, that he was killed with the Glock. Are you sure about the ballistics test?'

'We are and we may be taking you back with us.'

Casey reacted immediately to that. The look of pain left his eyes. A bright hardness replaced it.

'Oh, I can guarantee that you won't be doing that.'

'Then you need to convince us.'

'That's what I'm thinking about right now. I'm considering a way to irrevocably convince you.'

La Rosa felt a prickle along her spine and as Raveneau continued to meet Casey's gaze, she asked, 'Are you in some way threatening us, Mr Casey?'

Casey turned to her.

'The idea of you speculating I murdered Alan or assisted in any manner is repulsive. It fills me with disgust for the type of bureaucracy that produces your type. I couldn't possibly explain that to you because you wouldn't understand, but no, I'm not threatening you. I'm considering what to do. I'm debating what action to take. Do you understand that?'

Raveneau stepped back in. 'We don't have your breadth, Tom, and we're forced to work with facts, so our range is more limited. According to you, the gun other than being loaned out occasionally has been here in a glass case since the day Jim Frank returned from Austria with it. You can help us by giving us the names of those it was loaned out to, starting with who had it in January 1989.'

'We both know the boy sent you the gun. He's angry at me.' Casey waved at the other guns on display in the room. 'Keeping it in the glass case was about salt and corrosion. It was an original Glock, one of the first. I'm trying to remember at what date Jim gave me the gun to hold for him. There were times when his temper got the better of him and he didn't want it in his house. But he wanted it where he could come get it if he needed it. So we picked that case there, and frankly I can't remember if that was before or after January 11, 1989. I think now it was after. It may have been the spring of that year. Let's just say it was.'

'That's different than what you said a few minutes ago.'

'There's also another thing to consider. This house is never locked. We had an intruder a few years ago, a dope grower that the boy shot and killed, but even with that I haven't started locking the doors. I'll never lock the doors here.'

He nodded at Raveneau.

'Your first instinct was right, Ben. Shooting that grower gave him a taste of a thing he craved. The power of life is what I would call it. Killing affirms one's power. The boy craved that feeling. I could read it in his eyes years before we had the problem with the dope grower. I have no doubt you were right in sensing he was close to shooting you. I heard the conversation through the mike. You did the right thing to try to get away.'

He shook his head and looked down at the table.

'I can't get my head around this, but Jim may have been working with AK on an investigation, helping with the contract work Krueger was doing. He sometimes played a part as AK sold or bought counterfeit bills. He backed him up. He delivered money or carried it when he flew. The Secret Service may or may not have known that. They probably knew all about that.

You should tell them the gun is a match, confront them with it. Demand to know what they know.'

'We'll be back this afternoon looking for names.'

Casey leaned forward. He looked at Raveneau and then her.

'A month ago I sat here holding the gun to my head. I had a very large decision to make and it was necessary to consider all alternatives. My prints should be all over the gun from that night, but they aren't because my housekeeper cleans and oils the weapons in this house. That keeps the salt from corroding them.'

He pointed at the screening keeping insects out of the lanai that was otherwise open to the air.

'Most don't realize they choose the mark they make on history. The first time I burned a village that wasn't on the target list I didn't feel a thing for any of the gooks. If they weren't helping the Cong, they would be soon. It was that simple and that's what I told the captain. He didn't mind either. He used me for certain missions after that. He knew before I did. You can see it in a man's eyes before he knows inside.

'Now, there is something I'm remembering now. Four or five months before he was killed, Alan decided Jim was pocketing some of the bills he was ferrying. He got very angry about it. Words got exchanged and Jim didn't like to be threatened. I can tell you that.'

La Rosa re-entered the conversation.

'Why did you consider killing yourself?'

'A man should only exist as long as he has the will and the stomach to do what needs to be done. Waiting has sapped me. I'm like a hunter succumbing to cold.'

'What is it you're waiting for?'

'For the right moment and now it's arriving. Most of us pass without making a difference. I'll use the example of Inspector Benjamin Tomlinson Raveneau. His career isn't over but it's winding down. He's had a good solve record on the San Francisco Homicide Detail and for many years was the best among his peers. But has he made any real difference? I have to say no. He'll retire. He'll get a pension. He'll do some private work perhaps and he may even go on living in that apartment up on the roof. That's a little isolated and his girlfriend, I'm told, is more nervous about it, particularly at night, but who wouldn't be?

'Maybe they'll marry and settle in closer to her new bar if it catches on, but it's a difficult city to compete in and chances are her bar will just limp along. The inspector will see a fine goodbye party with the police force, but will the police force or the city be any different for his having been there? I don't think so and though they'll use him sporadically after he retires, his utility will decline. His purpose in life will vanish and with it his reason for being. That night I went to that threshold. You have to act to make a difference.'

La Rosa wasn't going to let this pass, but Raveneau caught her eye. Raveneau didn't care if Casey had hired private investigators to look into his life. His look said let that part be, so she asked, 'Have you ever killed anyone other than in war?'

'I'm going to ask you to leave now. We're both out of time. I need to think about my plans and you need to drive to make it to your lunch.'

'We can call and tell her we're running late. We'd like to know more about you.'

He turned to Raveneau.

'A thing can be justified if you have a higher object and you achieve it, but focus has to stay on the goal, the result. I know you understand that. You flew over here because you have the murder weapon and the sense you're closing in. But even if it's true that's the gun used to kill Alan, and I suppose it's likely true, you still don't know what you can do with it, do you? Or are you just hoping things will evolve? I've passed the point where I can wait for that evolution.'

'Tell us about the argument between Jim Frank and Alan Krueger,' Raveneau said.

'Jim was able to walk on and off a flight without any risk of his luggage being checked. He sometimes smuggled money or weapons for AK. He may have stolen counterfeit bills he was carrying from here to the mainland. He was very short of money. He had a fairly large land deal go bad here and lost everything. Ask his ex-wives how much alimony they ever saw. Alan accused him, they argued, and that was the last I saw of Alan, but, of course, I'm not saying Jim had anything to do with killing him.'

He smiled at la Rosa.

'When you get back I'll tell you what it feels like to napalm a village and watch some of them try to run while their skin is melting. The kids didn't get far, but some of those women would get twenty or thirty yards, like a torch moving in the twilight. When I put a gun to my head I think about them, but I don't feel guilty. I just think about them as part of a balance sheet, an expense. The meaning of our lives is capital we spend and you cannot make a mark on history without inflicting some pain on some people.'

'What are you focused on now?' Raveneau asked.

'That's already in motion.'

'Are you going to tell us about that?' la Rosa asked. 'We'd really like to know.'

'I'm sure you would.'

FIFTY-THREE

'What was that about?' la Rosa asked. 'Was he threatening us?'

'I don't know.'

'Has he talked this way before?'

'Not quite like this, but he can move quickly from threatening to get me fired to asking what I want to drink.'

'You ought to call Coe and ask for help finding out more about him. He knew Krueger. Krueger is tied into the counterfeit notes and the counterfeit money ties into the Secret Service/FBI investigation. The Feds will help us on this, don't you think?'

'They will and I'll call him when we get down to the beach.'

'Why are we going back there?'

'Before we make the drive to Ito's gallery, I want to see if Matt Frank is still at Hapuna.'

When they didn't spot Frank's pickup in the beach lot, Raveneau said, 'Let's pick up the can he was drinking from. I saw him put it down on top of a garbage can. But we need something to put it in.'

'I've got a plastic bag in my purse and I'll go get the can while you call Coe. I know where to look for it.'

Coe picked up on the first ring and asked, 'Have you met with him?'

'We left his house fifteen minutes ago. We're on our way to interview a woman on the other end of the island and then we want to meet with him again. He's nervous and agitated.'

'You checked in with our satellite office?'

'Yeah, they said call if we need backup. We'll give them a call but what can you do to help us find out more about Casey?'

'I'll do what I can. I'll call you.'

The can was still there. La Rosa had it with her as she walked back. By the time she reached the car he was off the phone. They drove south skirting Hilo and then the long grade on the road up to Volcanoes National Park. The gallery was set back among trees. They parked in a gravel lot across from an outdoor garden where it looked like pieces of sculpture were for sale. Inside the gallery were paintings and photographs. Many depicted scenes from the park up the road.

Raveneau spotted a woman in the back with a customer and couldn't be certain it was her, but it looked like it was. She became aware of them but she was still in conversation with her customer. As they waited, Raveneau studied a black and white photograph of a small group of men at the edge of Kilauea Crater taken perhaps a hundred years ago. The starkness of the crater and the small figures of the men at the edge of it said something he couldn't quite put a name to.

Then from behind him a voice said, 'I like that photograph very much myself. In a scene that is so stark you realize what is fragile. Are you looking for a particular artist?'

'We have an appointment with Aolani Ito.'

'That's me.'

It turned out Ito knew Thomas Casey as an islander whose family through a corporation had wrested control of a large block of ranchland and an even larger former sugar plantation in the interior. She believed Casey to be very wealthy and heard the money came from timber, coal, and land long before Casey was born.

'I didn't like him,' she said. 'He thought Jim wanted me there because I was pretty and young and it was all about sexual pleasure. He thought I was there to get away from my family and have a place to live for free and play at being an artist. He came on to me once and his way of doing that was to remind me that the land and the house and Jim being there was because of his generosity. But he inherited it all. He got Captain Jim into the land deal where he lost all his money.'

'What about politics?' la Rosa asked.

'I didn't listen to that. When they drank the things they said were all crazy. They would talk about killing like you would talk about picking fruit, as if it was normal to make plans and then kill your enemies. Even Captain Jim was that way but I didn't listen too closely to any of that.'

Raveneau had divided the photos in half. One stack was face down. He showed her a photo of Krueger.

'Do you recognize this man?'

'Of course, that's Alan. He and Captain Jim were good friends until they had an argument and I don't really know what it was about, but it was Alan who was angry first. He was a gentle man. He was funny and kind and sort of sad. He was a government agent of some sort and there were other men that came with him sometimes. They also worked for the government. There were two of them. One in particular who came around more and several times on his own. He was careful not to talk too much around me. But he was nice.'

'Would you look through the photos and tell me who you recognize?'

'Sure.'

Raveneau handed her the partial stack printed from Matt Frank's Facebook photos. She had barely looked through ten before she said, 'These are from little Matt. He was so cute with the camera around his neck all the time. He saw a professional photographer and copied the movements. He was very serious and made everybody laugh, but look at these. He was good.'

She touched another photo.

'I remember this man. He did things for them. He wanted to be like them and they told him stories. He was in the Air Force, I think, but something happened to his eyes and he couldn't fly any more.'

'Do you remember his name?'

'I'm embarrassed I don't. He came around to the parties. He was like a hanger-on. When they ran out of beer or rum they would send him to town.'

She slowly shuffled through the stack and Raveneau saw the younger woman in the hollows of her cheeks. Her eyes were lined, her features less distinct now, but she was still beautiful.

'Are you looking for the two younger men you talked about?'

'I am, but I'm not seeing them. One of them was careful not to let Matt photograph him. The other one didn't seem to care but I don't see him either.'

'But they both came with Krueger?'

'That's what I remember, but I don't know if it's right. I associate them with Alan. They were sort of detached though and one came by more than the other, and then the other didn't come by at all any more. They weren't from the island.'

'What were their names?'

'Hmmm . . . I'm terrible at names.'

'Was Alan called AK?'

'Only by Jim, it was a joke about a gun. It was some joke between them that went back to the war in Vietnam. They were all in that together. Thomas was the serious one. He was the most damaged by whatever he did in the war. Jim had done things too he regretted and tried different ways to make them go away.'

'The younger men in these photos weren't in the Vietnam War.'

She looked up at him, dark eyes studying him. 'You're very interested in them,' she said. 'Why?'

'I'm fishing. I'm looking for connections.'

'Where is Matt now?'

'He lives with Casey on the ranch and calls him Uncle Casey.'

'So he didn't get away. I'm sorry to hear that.'

'He's talking about moving. He's got a business he's working on.'

'Will you give him my card and ask him to call me?'

'Yes.'

She handed Raveneau a card and went slowly through all of the photos again, this time keeping many of her thoughts to herself. When she laid the photos down Raveneau told her about the videotape.

'Would you be willing to watch it?'

'How long is it?'

'A couple of minutes but very graphic.'

La Rosa touched his arm and Raveneau handed her the car keys. Ito was talking again as la Rosa returned with the laptop.

'Everybody, except me, called him Captain or Captain Frank. He was meant to be in a uniform, but also to be barefoot. He was not afraid to be who he was. I learned a lot from him. People said, he is your father's age. He's too old for you, but for me it was lucky I met him. He taught me how to live without fear.'

Ito turned quiet as la Rosa booted up the laptop.

'Will I be able to forget this video later?'

'I don't think so.'

'Then I want to sit quiet for a few minutes.'

Raveneau and la Rosa didn't talk. Raveneau opened the tray and laid the CD in. He turned to her and she nodded. Then with something close to happiness in recognizing an old friend she said, 'That looks like Alan but it's not a very good video.'

'No, it's not good quality, but watch the man with him and I can freeze the screen at any point.'

As Krueger was shot she bowed her head, gasped, and wept. She didn't watch the rest and then was quiet and didn't say anything for several minutes. La Rosa started to fold down the computer screen to shutdown the laptop. Raveneau quietly reached and stopped her. He could tell. He knew. When Ito spoke again it was without looking up.

'I have to watch again.'

'You see something?'

'I think so, in how he walks.'

Both the shooter and Krueger continued toward the pylons and as she leaned toward the screen and studied the man she said, 'His last name was Gray or something like that. Colin was his first name, Colin Gray, only I'm not sure that Gray is right. He was one of the two younger men who I think came first with Krueger.'

'Is he the one who came around more or less?'

'More, and you should ask the one who was in the Air Force who was also my age and whose name I can't remember. He knew him, too.'

'Shay.'

'Yes, that's right, Shay. So you really are a detective.'

She tried to smile but was too shaken.

'How sure are you, Aolani?'

She reached and rested her hand over his. He felt the warmth of her palm as she said, 'It's the walk.' She stared at the screen. 'I am sure. That's him.'

FIFTY-FOUR

C oe called as they rose out of Hilo on the Saddle Road. Raveneau put him on speaker phone. The reception wasn't great, but they could hear.

'We've got an agent along the highway outside the property. He'll move in when you do. How long before you get there?'

'At least three hours. We've got another stop to make.'

'Where's that?'

'Bradshaw Air Base.'

'Does he know you're coming?'

'His commander does and we've got something else. Elizabeth will tell you. She just got off the phone with the state police here.'

'OK.'

'Matt Frank shot and killed an intruder last year, a man who entered Casey's house through an unlocked door at night. He was unarmed. Frank claimed the man started to attack him and he shot him in self defense. One bullet went through his palm and into his jaw. The state police believe he had his hands up, but the shooting was ruled self defense.'

'Self defense is what you'll get if you come into my house in the middle of the night,' Coe said, showing a different side.

'Point is,' Raveneau said, 'we don't know about him. The agents should be aware. I'm pretty sure he debated taking a shot at me the first time I was here.'

'I'll get the word to them. Call when you leave the air base.'

'You got it.'

As Raveneau ended the call he said, 'I'm thinking there's something wrong with this whole Glock story.'

'Ballistics matched.'

'Right, but did Casey know the gun was coming to us?'

'Why would he want us to have the gun?'

'I don't know why; I can't think of a reason why.'

After a quiet, la Rosa asked, 'What are we going to do with the coconut water can?'

'Overnight it home and ask the Feds to expedite DNA.'

'That's pushing it.'

'I know.'

After a pause she changed the subject and asked, 'Is that Bradshaw Air Base coming up on the left?'

'Yeah, and this is the little park on the right where I was when he drove out.'

As they turned in at the gate at Bradshaw Army Air Field Raveneau did as the lieutenant colonel running the base instructed him. He showed his ID and gave his name, nothing more, and the guard didn't ask any questions. He said, 'Welcome to Camp Pohakuloa,' and then directed them to the old Quonset where Shay was sequestered.

'Where's the air field?' la Rosa asked, and Raveneau pointed out the airstrip.

'That's it?'

'They're not about flying here. They test artillery and do live fire exercises. That Lava Road you found for me is on the other side of the base outside the fence. It's for tanks. He's in this Quonset hut right up here, third one down. The lieutenant colonel said he'd be here. We're about ten minutes late. I'm going to apologize and then show the lieutenant colonel the photo enhancement comparison the FBI did.'

When they got out of the car the air smelled of dust and the sulphureous pungent smell Raveneau associated with lava rock. Inside the Quonset hut it was cooler and dark. Somewhere further down and outside the building an air conditioning compressor hummed and vibrated. Shay was in a room alone. He sat at a chair at a table waiting with his hands resting on his thighs. He looked anxious and confused.

'Are those the photos?' the lieutenant colonel asked.

Raveneau handed them to him and watched him read the FBI notes and then look at the profile comparisons. When he looked up he said, 'He was arrested yesterday shortly after we talked. He's had no communication with anyone since but seven phone calls this morning.'

Raveneau was ready for that and handed the lieutenant colonel a piece of paper with the cell numbers as well as business and landline numbers for Tom Casey and Matt Frank. The lieutenant colonel compared that to his list of seven and nodded. He handed both lists back to Raveneau and Raveneau saw that the photo enhancements which were by no means definitive and the phone numbers matching the cells of Tom Casey and Matt Frank had swayed him.

'We don't know how he will react,' Raveneau said, 'but maybe you can tell us more about him. What's he like? What do facts mean to him?'

'They mean everything to him, so do statistics and probability. That's why he runs the gunnery range.'

'Do you know anything about his politics?'

'I can't say that I do.'

When they entered the room Raveneau carried the photo enhancements with the FBI stamp prominently displayed as planned. His guess was Shay as a career soldier was predisposed to respect law enforcement. He hoped that was so. He knew they would only get one chance and that the photos themselves carried probability numbers that a competent defense lawyer would tear in half.

The lieutenant colonel also entered the room with him but remained standing. He wanted to be there and Raveneau seconded the idea as a reinforcement of authority. But his real hope lay with shock and he was glad to see the computer and monitor arranged so they faced Shay.

'I think you know why we're here,' Raveneau said. 'We'd like to start by showing you a videotape that arrived at our Homicide office two weeks ago. What we're going to show you is a digitized version. It's short and self-explanatory. It was shot in San Francisco January 11, 1989, the day of the killing of Alan Krueger.'

Shay watched him as if from behind a scrim, his eyes flat and opaque as la Rosa slid in the CD and adjusted the monitor. The lieutenant colonel moved closer but kept his eyes on Shay. He saw him flinch and glanced at the screen long enough to know the flinch occurred as Krueger was shot.

As the video finished he asked Shay, 'Would you like to see it again?'

'I don't need to.'

It was the first time he had spoken. Raveneau heard defeat in his tone and guessed he could probably question him with just the video but stayed with the plan of building on logic.

'We sent the video to an FBI lab that specializes among other things in photo enhancement techniques. The results arrived yesterday and we booked a flight immediately. You may or may not be familiar with enhancement software, but generally speaking a computer program makes thousands of comparisons.' He let a beat pass. 'The computer says it's you.'

Because that claim was false Raveneau worried the lieutenant colonel would react and give it away, but Shay's eyes stayed on the computer monitor. The best the FBI techs could do was put the odds at thirty-five percent that Shay was the shooter. Meaning he almost certainly wasn't and Raveneau agreed.

Shay now stared down at the table. 'I was a stupid kid and they led me into helping. I didn't shoot him.'

'The FBI says you did.'

'They're wrong.'

'We're here to take you back. We're prepared to charge you with murder. We have the gun used and you know the gun.' Raveneau took a flyer. He took a chance here. 'Your fingerprints were found on the gun.'

'I've used it before, but they couldn't still be there.'

'Why not?'

Shay just shook his head.

'You used it to murder Alan Krueger.'

'No, that's not true. I might have picked it up last time I was at the house, but I didn't kill him. If that's the gun—'

'You know it's the gun.'

'No sir, I don't know that. It would surprise me.'

'You just admitted you did.'

'No, I wasn't saying that but the gun got borrowed by people.'

'You borrowed it. We know that.'

'Other people, friends of the captain used it.'

'It was used to kill Alan Krueger. It was used to kill other people. It's over. We have a ballistics match and we have you in the video. Now we want to know who else it was used on.'

'I didn't kill Alan Krueger.'

'Is the video wrong?'

'That's not me.'

'Oh, the FBI specialists are wrong. It's not you then who is it?'

'Other people borrowed the gun.'

'What do you mean borrowed?'

'There were missions. They took the gun and brought it back.'

'What missions did you go on?'

Shay didn't answer. He stared down at the table and Raveneau's voice softened. He spoke slowly.

'The FBI has the most sophisticated program in the world that enhances and compares facial profiles. We have the fact that you lied to me about knowing Alan Krueger. I have even more photos now and we just came from an interview with Aolani Ito who says you were there often and that you didn't like Alan Krueger. Tell me why we shouldn't charge you right now.'

'I carried the gun over and brought it back, that's all. I didn't know what it was for. It was unregistered and I was carrying it as a favor because it was easy for me on a military transport. I took it to the mainland on one ride and brought it back months later on another trip. They were always moving stuff. Captain Frank carried something every trip.'

'What did he carry?'

'You name it. Mangoes, coffee, fish, he didn't like to deal with the California agriculture laws and he liked to bring presents to his friends.'

'You're admitting you transported illegally the gun used to kill Alan Krueger, but you're still claiming you didn't kill him. Then who did? Who did you give the gun to?'

Shay closed his eyes. He said, 'To one of the guys Krueger brought to Jim's house.'

'What's his name?'

'I don't know. I didn't see him. I just know he knew Krueger and Jim. I left the gun for him.'

'Where?'

'In San Francisco where he told me to in this mail drop at a business.'

'You're trying to tell us this man you can't identify shot Alan Krueger and not you.'

Shay looked up suddenly.

'He must have set me up. He left the gun for me to pick up again and I brought it back to Hawaii.'

'You went on a mission with it. Tell us who else you killed.'

'I didn't kill Krueger.'

'Who did you kill?'

'I was just stupid and young. I wanted them to like me. I did a lot of errands for them and they used me, but I never shot anybody.'

Raveneau looked at la Rosa. He was inclined to believe him.

FIFTY-FIVE

Without being asked, the lieutenant colonel said he would keep Shay confined to base and order him not to speak to Thomas Casey or Matt Frank.

'Will that be enough?'

Raveneau didn't know but he and la Rosa were glad to get the cooperation and he thanked him several times. After they left, Raveneau gave Coe the heads-up call he wanted and they began the long descent from the high plain.

'I keep getting the feeling there's more here,' la Rosa said, 'like the FBI has a different interest in Casey and they aren't telling us. Is that possible? Would Coe do that?'

'I think he's telling us what he can, but you may be right.'

'Look.'

La Rosa touched his arm and pointed at the gray pickup truck rounding a curve ahead in the opposite lane and accelerating toward them.

'Yeah, that's Matt Frank.'

Frank didn't recognize them until he was alongside them. He braked hard and made a tire-screeching U-turn.

'Coming after us,' la Rosa said. 'He's gaining fast.'

'I see him.'

'I don't like this.' She opened her purse and took out her gun. 'How's our car?'

'Not great. Let's see what he does. We're about fifteen miles from Waikoloa Village and there's nothing in between and that's just a shopping center. I don't know if we'll get any backup out of any of the nearest towns but see what you can do in case this escalates into something.'

Raveneau checked his rear view mirror again. He saw Frank's face, the mirrored sunglasses. Frank's jaw was set. Frank closed to within ten yards and Raveneau was gradually speeding up.

'What's in the water over here?' la Rosa asked. 'What happened between when we met him this morning and now?'

'Uncle Casey talked to him and Frank hasn't been straight with us, though we haven't exactly been straight with him either. Either way, I'm starting to get the picture. Hang on, it's about to get a little rough.'

Raveneau didn't want Frank to think they were running from him or had any fear, and in truth, Raveneau wouldn't run either way. But he didn't doubt Frank was armed. Behind them, Frank swept over the line into the opposite lane and sliced the curve. He was right on their bumper now. Raveneau listened as la Rosa got through to somebody, and then lowered the phone abruptly, saying, 'He's got a gun out.'

They squealed through the next curve and when he didn't see any oncoming traffic Raveneau straddled the middle of the road blocking Frank from passing. And that's what Frank wanted to do. The passenger window was down. Frank was right-handed. Unless he could pass in the opposite lane he was going to be shooting with his left hand, but that's what he did now. It took him several rounds before he put two through their rear window and now a bullet slapped into the dash to the right of Raveneau and la Rosa started firing.

La Rosa started at Homicide with something to prove and made more of the required range days shooting practice than any other inspector. She was also the best shot with or without the practice regardless of the claims of Deming and a couple of the other inspectors once they had a couple of drinks in them. No one could shoot with her.

'Hold a straight line,' she yelled and as he did, she got off four quick shots. Frank backed off. He backed off and then he slowed and his truck started to drift left. It straightened and then veered left again, though now he wasn't traveling more than twenty miles an hour. He went off the embankment even slower than that as if he didn't have quite enough strength to hold the brake pedal down.

The truck hung in the air before tipping forward, landing with a metal wrenching tear then tumbling end over end down the steep lava-strewn slope. They heard more than they saw, but Raveneau saw the end. He saw the truck come to rest on its side, the passenger door gone, roof crushed. There was a silence and then a *whoosh* as the gas tank ignited. Raveneau skidded and slid as he ran down. Heat washed up the slope as the cab interior burned. Ammunition started cooking off and Raveneau backed away. There was nothing he could do. So much ammo was popping it sounded like popcorn.

From above he watched the truck burn. He couldn't think of a way to have gotten Frank out, yet felt as if he should have. He turned to look at la Rosa sitting in the car, passenger door open with her shoes on the pavement, stunned as she stared down the slope. He knew he needed to get her out of the car and talk to her before the locals arrived. But he pulled out his phone instead and called Coe.

'He came after you?'

'Elizabeth returned fire and must have hit him. He went off a steep embankment. His truck is down the slope burning with him inside. You better check on Casey. Is an agent still on the road in front of his house?'

'I'll call you back.'

'We're headed to his house when we leave here, but we're going to be here awhile.'

Two cars pulled over and people spilled out to check out where the column of black smoke was coming from. A man hustled over.

'What happened? Did you call for help?'

Raveneau nodded and far in the distance were sirens. He

stepped away. He got Elizabeth out of the car and walked with her fifty yards down the road away from the smoke into the sunlight and warm breeze blowing upslope. He talked with her. He called Becker before the locals showed and a detective about an hour later. The detective wanted la Rosa's statement without Raveneau listening in. He asked for her gun. As Raveneau waited he took a call from Coe.

'We're having trouble reaching our agent out of the Kona office.'

'I thought he was getting backup hours ago.'

'They got delayed.'

'Casey will have an escape hatch. He's not going to wait. I think he sent Frank after us. It's why he gave us Ito's name. He knew we'd come back on the Saddle Road.'

'Our agents are going to go ahead and search the house.'

'I figured you would. We'll see you there.'

FIFTY-SIX

Casey's ranch house was fully lit when Raveneau and la Rosa arrived and there was nowhere to park near the house or in the clearing in front of the barn. Raveneau backed up to the fork leading to Jim Frank's house. He parked their car between the trees and they walked the broken asphalt road back down to the ranch house.

The FBI special agent in charge of the search was out of Oahu and had flown over in the late afternoon. His name was Carl Norris. He sat out on the porch with them and directed his questions at Raveneau as la Rosa listened. Special Agent Han and his vehicle were missing. So was Casey. Raveneau listened then said, 'We got rough directions today from a woman we interviewed to a large former sugar plantation that Casey owns. It may be under a corporate name and he may be there.'

'We're pretty sure he's off the island.'

'How do you know that?'

'It's an ongoing investigation.'

'How long has that been going on?'

'I can't say.'

'All right, well, the plantation still needs to be checked.' Raveneau glanced at la Rosa, adding, 'We'll go there.'

'I want agents to go with you.'

'We want to see what you've found first. What's in the boxes your agents are carrying out?'

'Desktop computers, other documents, we'll go through in the field office. We appreciate everything you've done, but we've got enough agents inside. If you want to drive roads and look for his vehicle we'd appreciate any effort you make.'

Raveneau walked down the steps and moved away from the floodlights into darkness to call Coe.

'I know what I'm looking for, they don't.'

'Put Norris on.'

'Do you know him?'

'Not really, but I know what he's working on.'

'OK, hold on.'

Raveneau walked back and handed Norris his phone. After listening to Coe for a few moments Norris walked out of earshot. When he returned he handed the phone to Raveneau and said, 'You can go in and you can watch, but we don't need help with the search. It makes more sense for you to lead our agents to this sugar plantation you talked about.'

'Show us what you've found.'

'Most of it's packed up. We're almost done.'

Raveneau went inside anyway. They were in the lanai when agents opened a locked waterproof cabinet in an out building near the barn. In it he'd found two laptops and four handguns.

'What do you think?' la Rosa asked quietly.

'Let's go see what they found in the cabinet and then try to find the sugar plantation.'

He talked to Coe again as they waited outside the building where the laptops were found.

'We're going to move on,' he told Coe. 'We'll help look for the missing special agent, but there are a couple more things we should talk about first. We interviewed a woman today who ID'ed Krueger's killer from photos Matt Frank sent his half brother via Facebook. This woman lived with Jim Frank from 1987 to 1991. She saw this

man a half dozen times. He was young. His connection was Alan
Krueger. She gave me a name for him, but also said she's bad with
names. The name she gave me was Colin Gray. She's sure of the
first name but hazy about the Gray. She thought he was working
with Krueger and that he worked for the government. Can you do
anything with that?'

'That's sketchy.'

'You aren't hearing me. This is who shot Alan Krueger and
she thinks he was working for our government. Casey pointed
us toward her. If he hadn't given us her name we wouldn't have
driven to the other end of the island.'

'He sent you that direction so he could ambush you with Matt
Frank.'

'That's what I think too but I don't think that became a plan
until after we met with him this morning. What's going on with
the FBI? Why is the FBI looking at Casey?'

'Ben, I can't keep up with this. You're jumping around and
I'm exhausted.'

'OK, set that aside, and listen to this. Andrew Fine the blogger
who broke the bomb story has a source in Washington, someone
he's known since college. I keep asking myself why it's in the
source's interest to feed Fine the bomb casing story.'

'Fine probably lied about his source. It's more likely someone
local.'

'I don't think he lied to us, but I think we need to know his
source. We fly home tomorrow. I'll go back to Fine but I might
ask your help if I get more from him.'

'I don't know what you're seeing, but I can't follow you right
now.'

'Talk to you later.'

Raveneau and la Rosa followed the laptops back to the main
house and hovered as an agent powered them up and got stuck
for lack of a password. He asked Norris if he could try to get
in.

'Why don't you just give us what you think the password might
be?'

'Let me try.'

The agents hovered over him and Raveneau remembered
Casey preaching simplicity. Casey told him he used computers

but sparingly. He believed they had weakened the character of the American people, dampening their independence and self-reliance.

He typed in several passwords that didn't work and as the agents gradually lost interest he signaled la Rosa. She started talking, asking questions of both agents, touching one on the sleeve as Raveneau pulled a sixteen gig memory stick from his pocket and slid it into the computer in front of him. He typed *Jericho* into the password box. The screen changed and he angled the computer away from the agent and found his way to the files. He copied. He pulled the memory stick. He moved to the next computer as la Rosa recounted the directions to the sugar plantation.

Raveneau slipped the memory stick back into his pocket. It didn't feel right to do that, but he knew it was their last chance. He stood then interrupted the conversation, saying, 'I got in.'

'What do you mean you got in?'

'Write this down. The password is Jericho.'

Raveneau knew later they wouldn't be given any access at all. If there was information on the computers that pertained to their murder investigation they'd be informed and given sanitized copies. They might even be asked to submit a request for information, but that was the tension the country faced with terrorist threats. We give up our freedoms in the name of national security or we keep the society more open. Raveneau had heard the argument both ways and stood with those who said it was better to protect the freedoms. He saw in the eyes of the agent who took possession of the laptops again the confident authority that was becoming habit.

They drove about ten miles and were back behind Hawi searching in the dark with their headlights. It took forty minutes and a lot of backtracking to find the long graveled road running in to a large white-painted house with a metal roof. Moments later the headlights caught the unmarked sedan.

The agent with them shined a flashlight inside. Blood splatter. He followed the blood then moved the light abruptly to the back seat. Empty.

Raveneau asked the FBI agent if he'd ever been part of a homicide investigation and the agent said, 'Just one.' Raveneau

took charge. He and la Rosa looked at the blood smeared on the
passenger seat and on the door and then worked the area around
the car with the light, looking at the drag marks.

'I'm going to pop the trunk,' Raveneau said and located the
trunk release before leaning in through the open driver's window.
He knew what they were going to find and he and la Rosa stayed
with Han's body as the FBI agent called it in.

FIFTY-SEVEN

R aveneau texted Fine then called him and called again when
he didn't answer.

'This is why I don't trust the police,' Fine said as he
finally picked up.

'Just hear me out. I'm in Hawaii on the north end of the Big
Island and I don't have much time.'

'This is when I work. I'm trying to write tomorrow's blog.'

'What are you writing about?'

'The President.'

'Did you get a new hot tip?'

'Inspector, what is it you need?'

'I need you to call me on a cell phone that's not yours. Use
your wife's phone and make the call from outside your house.'

'Have you been drinking?'

'No, I'm serious.'

'OK, then give me your phone number. Your call came in as
restricted so I don't have it.'

Raveneau read off the number then hung up. Except for a dog
wandering past the town of Hawi was still and dark. La Rosa
was at the plantation house with the FBI. He drove here for better
phone reception and it still wasn't very good. When Fine called
back he said he was outside in the garden and it was cold.

'Is your blog tomorrow a hot tip on the President's travel
plans?'

'It is and how did you know?'

'Tell me what you know.'

'The trip is back on minus the San Francisco stop. He'll attend a fund-raiser in Hollywood and the day after tomorrow visit a new solar plant being built in the Mojave Desert. That plant will be the biggest in the world when it's finished. It'll double the energy we get from solar.'

'Is this coming from your Washington source?'

'This isn't the deal we struck.'

'All right, tell me this,' and Raveneau knew he would, 'how much ahead of the cable networks are you?'

'At least six hours.'

'What does it do for the Owlseye to beat them?'

'It keeps the White House from controlling the timing and spin.'

'Leaves the White House off balance?'

'It's a democracy.'

Raveneau turned that a moment. Leaked travel plans wouldn't affect the Secret Service. Might annoy them but wouldn't affect their planning. He was about to brush past it and lay out the chain of events for Fine, and then it hit him.

'You're ahead of the cable networks by six hours?'

'That's a guess, but what's up? I can't stay on the phone and I'm freezing my ass out here.'

'I think you're in significant danger, but I need to walk through this with you. I'm trying to connect dots and it's not easy. The twenty-two year old murder we told you about, we now know who killed our victim.'

'I want to do a piece on Alan Krueger. If there was agency cover-up I want it.'

'I hear you and we'll help you, but you've got to listen to me and nothing I'm going to tell you now can go in your blog. I'm taking you completely into confidence. Are you with me on that?'

'Yeah, OK, go ahead. Why am I in danger?'

'There's no Pakistan link with the bomb casings. They probably chose Khan because he was Pakistani in origin and they knew how the groupthink would run. Khan didn't know what was going to happen. They got to him with money. That's one piece.

'The second piece is the real conspirators may be a fragmented group of like-thinking individuals who communicate rarely and operate with signals. The architects of that group want to reshape America. I won't get into their politics but I will tell you the FBI tapped into them.'

'Wiretapping?'

'Of course, but it started with a bank fraud case. From that they learned about this well-meaning group intending what they called a trigger event on a Presidential visit to a California city. When they learned this they also learned that some members of the group are in our military and inside government agencies.'

'You know, I worked in Washington a long time. I didn't tell you that one of the many reasons I was glad to leave there is the constant swirl of the cesspool of conspiracy theories. I can't stand them.'

Yet you traffic in gossip, Raveneau thought, but said, 'I don't think this group is quite as big or with the reach imagined, but I've read transcripts and heard tapes and have other reasons now to believe they're serious and exist, and have existed for some time. There's a link to counterfeit money that I'm not sure I could explain if I wanted to right now. I will tell you that FBI and Secret Service are working on this together.'

'They wouldn't know how to work together. They'd need a task force for that.'

'Point is, both agencies are worried.'

Before making the call Raveneau had decided to take a chance with Fine. He pushed forward.

'You know about the quadruple murder at the cabinet shop, finding the bomb casings and the subsequent focus on Khan.'

'I know the FBI screwed up and lost them.'

'But you probably don't know the extent of the finger pointing about law enforcement leaks. No, that's not right. Leak isn't the correct word. It's when everyone became aware the other side understands how the FBI surveillance teams work.'

'This is the type of conspiracy talk I moved west to escape.'

'Right now, I'm sitting in a rented car in a little town on the north end of the Big Island in Hawaii. My partner is here but she's not with me because she's on a former sugar plantation inland a few miles from here where a few hours ago we found the body of an FBI agent murdered today. Earlier in the afternoon we were ambushed and shot at and my partner then shot dead the assailant who happens to be the quasi-adopted son of someone suspected as being at least peripherally part of this conspiracy. Are you following me?'

'Yes.'

'Then you see why I'm coming around to believing there's something behind this conspiracy theory, so you may too. I think the young man who shot at us today will turn out to be the shooter at the cabinet shop but that killing them was not part of the original plan. It was a contingency plan that he acted on by himself.'

'What's his name?'

'We'll get there but not yet, not tonight. When the time comes I'll talk to you first if you're still alive.'

'Why do you keep saying that?'

'Because I think you're in real danger. I don't have any proof but I think it's likely you're in position to put things together. You got that first scoop on the bomb casings and now you've got this one on the President's travel plans and—'

'Look, I'm just a few hours ahead of everyone else.'

'I started thinking that your old friend isn't giving you information just to help you with your blog or in trade for something in the future. I think he's getting something back from you at the same time he's giving you something.'

'I could take a lot of offense to that.'

'You could but don't take it yet because it's only speculation and it's just one idea. Here's another. You're being used as a conduit to get information out. Your source is using you. Your source is involved.'

'That's absurd. You have no idea what you're saying.'

'My killer in the 1989 murder was probably right around twenty-six or seven at the time. He's dark-haired, medium build, and was experienced with guns when he shot Alan Krueger. People who knew him then believed he worked for our government out of DC. He may have been tied to an investigative unit. He may have worked with our victim on a counterfeit one hundred dollar bill investigation and not just any bills, but the first super-notes. To be that young and working on something like that he must have been tagged as gifted and capable. Today, with a combination of photos and the videotape of the killing we told you about, we got an ID on him.'

'Who ID'ed him?'

'A woman whose name I can't give you yet. She ID'ed him and then struggled with his last name. She was confident about the first name, but not about the last. But I don't want to give away too much information yet, and you probably don't either, so let's do this in steps. I'm going to give you initials and you tell me if they mean anything to you. If they do, then I'm probably right.'

'Go ahead.'

'C.G.'

Raveneau heard him breathing. He waited. He looked out at the night, the empty road below and knew he'd hit home. The delay was too long.

'Why should I believe any of this?'

'You don't have to. I can hang up right now. Do you want me to do that?'

'No, don't hang up. I just don't see how it's possible.'

'I'm not sure what I believe either, but pieces are coming together and two more people died today. One of them tried to kill my partner and me.'

Fine now sounded as if he was struggling for breath as he said, 'Greiston. Colin Greiston. He's on his way out. He gets into SFO sometime in the next few days. He's going to try to make time to see me.'

'You don't want to make that meeting. I'm going to call the FBI and an agent named Mark Coe. He's the only one you should talk to at this point. Do you have anything you can write with or do you want me to text his cell number to your wife's phone?'

'I've got something to write with.'

Raveneau gave him Coe's number and listened as he recited it back. Then he told Fine, 'I'm going to call him now and you should call in ten minutes, but use your wife's phone. Just to be safe don't use your computer or any of your phones. Tell me again when Greiston said he would come through.'

'Day after tomorrow.'

'Do you have friends you can stay with?'

'What?'

'If I were you I'd go somewhere he won't look for you.'

FIFTY-EIGHT

The bomb casings were real. Jericho worked as a password on Casey's laptops and Coe revealed last night the FBI was aware of a Hawaiian link. They got that through an IP address, though not one linked yet to Casey. After his conversation with Coe late last night it was clear the Feds would help hunt for Colin Greiston. He expected to hear more this morning. He hoped Coe would call early and say they had taken him into custody in Washington. But from what Fine said it was just as likely Greiston was on the move and Casey was still missing. Casey was Jericho and losing him was big. Casey could easily have alerted everyone he was in contact with. No doubt they had a plan for shutting everything down.

But in the dawn Raveneau sat in front of a computer looking at a satellite image of the east Mojave Desert. He pulled up articles on the solar thermal plants being built there and thought about the President's impending west coast trip. When completed, these solar thermal projects would double US solar capacity and become the largest solar installations in the world. He looked at photos of the dry lakebed in the Ivanpah Valley where the plant would be built, and at renderings of what it would look like when finished. He drank more coffee. He mulled over the conversation with Fine last night and then his phone rang.

He hoped it was Coe. He hoped Coe would say they found Casey and arrested Greiston and he and la Rosa could fly home knowing the plot was foiled and Krueger's killer was on his way to justice. It was la Rosa asking if he'd heard anything yet.

'Nothing yet.'

'A lot of this may go down when we're sitting in an airplane.'

'It could.'

'Let's hope they find Greiston first.'

Raveneau hoped that as well, but he doubted they would. He kept talking with la Rosa and walked out on the small balcony deck. Clouds wrapping Mauna Loa turned pink then crimson in the sunrise. They were leaving for Kona Airport within the hour, their routing a reverse of the flight over, back through Los Angeles and then north.

'I just don't get it,' she said. 'I don't get Casey. I don't get the philosophy. He's got money. He's got that beautiful ranch. He's living in friggin' Hawaii. What more does he need. Why would someone like him join a conspiracy?'

'He's a true believer.'

'Meaning what?'

'Meaning he's sure he's right so things won't go wrong, or if they do he still did the right thing.'

'That still doesn't answer it for me.'

Raveneau walked back in and before closing his laptop and packing, he googled the drive from LAX to the Mojave Desert. The President was vulnerable in the Mojave. The Mojave visit was the type of nightmare scenario Brooks talked about. He didn't say anything to la Rosa about that until the airport. Then he worried aloud and quietly, sitting with her, talking, sketching the scenario that kept him awake all night. He felt a cold fear that it wasn't over yet.

On the plane he finally dozed off, but woke with the same worries. Men make history, Casey had told him. History is not something that just happens. It's not some implacable river. History is created by people with will. Change is driven by need and desire. That was Casey the first time they met. Raveneau listened to the plane's engines. He kept eyes closed. He turned it all again in his head. When they touched down at LAX and he powered up his phone he stared waiting for the voice mail alert, and there were messages but none from the FBI. As they walked off the plane Raveneau said quietly, 'We need to go there. The President's Mojave visit is like a perfect storm.'

'It's too big for us, Ben. It's not our job. It's beyond us.'

'The best thing would be to fly on to Vegas, but I think we pick up a rental and drive from here.'

La Rosa sighed. She understood how he got there. She didn't need him to go through it again. He should call Coe or Brooks if he was so certain and Raveneau kept repeating, the President's visit is tomorrow. An hour later they were on their way to the

Mojave Desert, Raveneau talking as he drove, la Rosa working from a map on her phone.

'Why aren't you in some conference call with Coe and Brooks if you're so certain?'

'Let's talk it through first. Let's get a look at the solar plant and the land. We can fly home from Vegas tomorrow morning if it looks like I'm way off base.'

'What's Greiston doing while we're out here? We could be there when he gets off a plane in San Francisco.'

'He won't be there. He won't do what he told Fine and by now Casey has alerted whatever network they have. They've either rolled it up or are thinking they have a short window of time.'

She didn't answer and he continued. 'They took a real risk to liberate those bomb casings. These are people willing to take a chance and they don't have much time. This solar installation is just starting construction. Its main roads might not even be paved and road building is restricted because of desert tortoises they're trying to save.'

'You're an overnight expert.'

'I bet after we've been there five minutes we'll be able to point to the road the President will drive down and no matter what security they have it is open desert. It's too big to police and protect in such a short amount of time. Look, the plotters took the risk to recover those bomb casings even though they knew Obama's visit to San Francisco was going to get canceled if they were successful. To me that says they started looking for another opportunity. I think they have a team in place in California or close enough so they can adjust to a new location that's within reach. This Mojave visit fits perfectly.'

'Ben, it is a fine theory, and that's theory with a capital T, but it's just you and me and a rented car. I'm going to say it again, if you're that sure, call Coe and Brooks.'

'Let's look at it first. We'll be there before dark.'

Raveneau wasn't even sure which airport was closest to the project, probably Vegas, but maybe the President would helicopter from there. Maybe there was a landing pad near the construction of the solar thermal plant. But at some point the President was on the ground in a vehicle. It might be a short tour but he'd do a tour and shake some hands. The solar thermal project covered five square miles. Its main roadways would be simple and practical. Where possible the roads would be flat and straight.

'Here's my problem,' she said, 'and this is something you do occasionally. You get caught up in an idea and you rush off. Tomorrow we may be waving to Obama as he flies over or we may talk our way in, but it makes more sense to organize by phone. Lay out your theory for Brooks. He's already paranoid. He'll get the Secret Service stoked up. Lay it out for Coe. They've got a thousand agents on this conspiracy by now and they've got a field office in Vegas. How much of a drive is it from Las Vegas to this solar site?'

'About an hour.'

'There you go. It's in their backyard.'

She answered email on her phone and looked out the window as they crossed the desert. They didn't get there before dark and couldn't see anything and drove on. They crossed the state line, ate at Buffalo Bill's Resort and Casino and then looked for a motel.

Raveneau said, 'I'll wake you very early.'

La Rosa closed the door to her motel room without answering. He opened his. There was a bed, worn carpet, a small bathroom with a faucet that leaked and whose hard water left brown-red stains in the dirty bowl. He showered. He thought it through again and picked up his phone and called Coe.

'You're home,' Coe said.

'No, we're near the eastern edge of the Mojave Desert close to where the President will visit tomorrow. I think there's a real problem here. Let me tell you why.'

FIFTY-NINE

Before dawn Raveneau knocked softly on la Rosa's door, but not before he had another conversation with Coe. 'Your name has made it all the way to the White House, Raveneau. But it turns out a San Francisco homicide inspector's speculation isn't enough reason for the White House to cancel. They want evidence. They see a perception issue after already having canceled San Francisco. But on the upside our analysts here don't think you are crazy at all and we're going to get help from the Air Force. I asked for something quiet with lookdown capacity that will fly until the President has come and gone. It went up very early this morning from Edwards Air Force Base and it'll float around up there until after the President has come and gone.'

'What time is he due here?'

'Noon, and you're right, this is a road that runs through the project and up over a mountain to the town of Ivanpah. There's a camp near the base of the mountain that biologists use. Two from the Wildlife Heritage Foundation are there right now.'

'Yeah, we saw the road last night but that was about all we could see. Who else outside the contractor is working in the area?'

'There may be others, but looking at satellite photos the project looks like it's surrounded by desert.'

'How do you know about these biologists?'

'Oh, there was a dispute we kept track of over whether these solar thermal plants should get built or not and some threats made online by unrelated splinter groups who were opposed to the plant. The two biologists have been out there for the last eight days so they were out there before the White House changed travel plans. I got that from the site superintendent a few minutes ago. I can text you the names of the biologists. Desert tortoises got relocated ahead of the build and they're monitoring them.'

'OK, do that and if you have the site superintendent's name send that too. We'll go see him first.'

'He's there right now.'

'Are there agents coming here from the Las Vegas field office?'

'Yes.'

'Too many of us on the project will be a dead giveaway.'

'They're going to work the periphery and the Secret Service will have a problem with you being too active.'

'We'll check out the biologists this morning. Give the Vegas agents my cell number. There's a golf course nearby there with

a bar and a place to eat. We can use that as a spot to meet if
there's a reason or a need. What about Casey or Colin Greiston?'

'No leads on Casey but he left some writings that suggest he
would not let himself be taken prisoner. You can interpret that
however you want. Greiston is cleared at some high levels and
we're being asked to prove our interest in him, but I didn't want
to do anything until I talked with you. Basically, he'll get told
we want to interview him. Do you want him to get advance
notice?'

'Not yet.'

'Two more things about the biologists, first thing is you need
a four-wheel drive to get to their camp. The second thing is
they're due to leave this morning ahead of the road closure today.
Everything gets shutdown for the President's visit. He's flying
into Las Vegas and they'll helicopter him to an airport in Jean
and drive from there. Do you know where Jean is?'

'Yeah, we're close to it right now. It's just off the highway.
We went by there last night.'

Raveneau was in his new Hawaiian shirt and the one light
jacket he took to Hawaii, but it was much colder here. La Rosa
wore a T-shirt she bought at Buffalo Bill's Resort and Casino.
In their rental they looked like tourists, holding paper cups of
coffee against the cold as they drove toward the Ivanpah dry
lake bed and the first sunlight touching high on the gray desert
mountains ahead. When they left the highway they could
already see the construction site. A few minutes later they
knocked on the door of a construction trailer with lights on
inside.

The superintendent was friendly and excited about the
Presidential visit. Because of his earlier conversation with Coe,
he knew who they were. He was hazy on why they were here
but printed them a map, sketched some additional dirt roads, and
answered all the questions he could about the biologists and
where the President would tour.

Raveneau showed him the enhanced photo of Greiston made
from the video.

'Have you seen anyone who looks at all like this?'

'No, I don't think so.'

'We'll show it to the biologists. They've been out there awhile.

Maybe they've seen somebody. How do you communicate with them?'

'Radio when they are at their camp on the mountain. Otherwise cell phones work fine.'

The superintendent tried to reach them now by radio but didn't have any luck before leaving for what he said was a quick meeting at the tower. Work was underway at the base of the four hundred fifty foot tower. When the three sites of the project were finished mirrors would focus sunlight on the tower and superheat water to drive a turbine to produce electricity.

Raveneau and la Rosa went back to their car and were glad to get the heater on. The morning was cold and windy. Coe called after they drove the roads on the superintendent's map.

'We're getting some feedback from the air,' Coe said. 'We've got a vehicle coming off the mountain and moving your way. That's probably the two biologists trying to get out of there before the President arrives. Can you see them? They started driving a few minutes ago and they're on the southeastern face. That's the road I told you about that runs through the project and then on over a mountain to Ivanpah.'

'We're on the road right now.'

It took Raveneau several minutes then he caught a reflection in sunlight. But there was no need to hold the binoculars and track them all the way down. There was only this road. He lowered the binoculars, looked at the gray-green of the mountain and knew they were most likely just what they claimed to be. That got reinforced even more as they made several stops when they came off the mountain and started down the sloping plain.

'Stopping to look at tortoise burrows,' Coe said, and they had him on speaker phone now. Raveneau's phone sat up on the dash, its volume turned up. 'That's what they do. It's why they're there. The superintendent told me they usually check in with him on their way out though sometimes they just phone and let him know they're gone. Basically, if his truck is there they stop and let him know they're leaving.'

'OK, got it, and we'll see them as they come out.'

Raveneau was less sure of his theory this morning and it agitated him. The solar thermal plant had three sites and none were very far along yet, so the President's visit would be largely symbolic.

Considering how far along the project wasn't, it was probably a short visit.

'Is that the tortoise fencing?' la Rosa asked, and pointed at silver mesh attached to the fencing alongside the road and no more than knee high.

'Looks like it.'

Raveneau gauged the distance to the mountains. If the biologists weren't making stops they'd be out by now. He turned back toward the dry lakebed and highway as la Rosa said, 'They must be moving the visit up.'

Three black Suburbans were just arriving. They drove toward the superintendent's office and la Rosa was guessing they were Secret Service vehicles. Raveneau picked up his phone to check the time before calling Coe.

'Have you heard anything about the visit getting moved up? I'm asking because it looks like the Secret Service has arrived.'

'No one has said anything to me. I'll make a call and let you know.'

'Thanks. How clearly are the Air Force guys seeing the biologists?'

'They told me the one getting out checking the burrows needs a shave. Is that clear enough?'

'Plenty.'

Another ten minutes went past and Raveneau's mind was racing. The biologists still weren't in view but were moving faster and should drive past soon. As they waited la Rosa said, 'When they go past maybe we should follow and if they leave the project we can head to Vegas and catch a flight home from there.'

'Here they come.'

Raveneau saw sunglasses and hats and a tinted windshield that made it hard to read features. He read *Heritage Wildlife Institute* on the driver's door. There was similar white lettering on the back. They drove straight through. They didn't slow. They didn't stop at any burrows or ostensible burrows anywhere on the project site, nor did they stop at the superintendent's office even though his pickup was there.

Maybe they saw the big black Suburbans and decided to get

out while there was still time. Could be they were picturing getting breakfast somewhere with a clean table and a waitress rather than their campsite.

Raveneau turned to la Rosa. 'Let's get the superintendent to call these biologists. Their cell phones will work now.'

La Rosa didn't follow him up the metal stairs of the construction trailer and Raveneau was inside when four helicopters in a line veered from the mountain and swept overhead. He saw their shadows sweep across the road. The biologists didn't answer their cell phones. The superintendent tried and so did Raveneau as he looked out the window at the helicopters. Could be the White House decided to do the tour by air, but the superintendent said no, the President was still coming. The Secret Service had confirmed that a few minutes ago.

Raveneau nodded, then asked, 'Can I borrow your truck?'

'Why?'

'I need to go up to the biologists' camp.'

'It's a company truck, I'm not supposed to ever loan it out.'

'Bend the rules, these are special circumstances and I don't have a four-wheel drive. It won't take fifteen minutes to get there and I can't get in an accident. There's no one to run into.'

'They already left.'

'Yeah, we saw the Heritage Wildlife vehicle go by.'

'Then why go up there?'

'I'll get the truck back to you in forty minutes.'

Raveneau held his hand out and the superintendent reluctantly handed him the keys.

SIXTY

After la Rosa climbed into the cab Raveneau engaged the truck's four-wheel drive, then lowered the window to talk with two Secret Service agents who were suddenly interested.

'Where are you headed?'

'To a camp the tortoise biologists use up on the mountain. It's

fifteen to twenty minutes up that road.' He pointed at the dirt
road rising into the scrub. 'Want to come with us?'

'The road may be closed when you come back down. If it is,
you'll have to wait until after the visit.'

'How much time have we got?'

'Not long.'

Raveneau handed his phone to la Rosa after they pulled away,
saying, 'We're hoping Coe calls before we're out of cell range.
I'm driving. It'll be easier for you to talk to him.'

But Coe didn't call and the road was hard and fairly smooth
so they made good time. Or at least they did until hitting a patch
of sand before the mountains. On the mountain the road got
rockier and narrowed.

'We're looking for two faded orange tents. The superintendent
told me it's about a half mile up and behind a rock outcrop that
blocks the sun, but also makes it possible to drive past it without
noticing. He said at the half mile mark start watching.'

'And we're doing this because the biologists didn't answer
their cell phones?'

'We're doing it to be certain. They don't always answer their
phones. They didn't stop and check in with the superintendent
before leaving.'

'But now they're out on the highway and the FBI is following
them, right?'

'That's what Coe said.'

'You don't think that's happening?'

'It's probably happening.'

'They can get pulled over and asked for ID.'

'They'll have ID no matter what and we're almost here.'

But they weren't. It was closer to a mile and they were midway
up the mountain before they spotted the tents.

'Remind me never to loan you my car,' la Rosa said, as they
got there.

'If we don't find anything we'll drive back much more slowly.
We'll enjoy the morning. We'll go get coffee at the golf course
and fly home.'

It was desert beautiful this morning, the winter sky blue and
clear, a line of dry brown mountains etched at the horizon. The
Ivanpah lakebed below was white, almost silvered in this light.

They started at the first tent and didn't have to go any farther. Raveneau didn't even unzip the mosquito netting flies were trying to get through. Bright morning sunlight hitting the tent fabric illuminated the interior and he and la Rosa looked in at dark dried blood on the floor of the tent. He saw multiple bullet holes on the tent floor and realized they were shot from where he was standing leaning over looking in.

It took them a few minutes to get their heads around it, and then Raveneau guessed they were shot while they slept and then dragged and buried somewhere around here.

'But we can't look for them. It's why they weren't answering their phones. It's why the two men didn't stop. The superintendent wouldn't have recognized them and realized something was up. And I really screwed up. I should have asked the superintendent for a radio. We've got to get back into cell range fast.'

La Rosa kept trying her cell phone and Raveneau drove very hard. He slid through the dry switchbacks ignoring la Rosa's frightened gasps. He hoped someone would see dust rising and put it together. He hoped they were in time. By now the President was on the ground and in a car. By now he was close. He fishtailed through the bad sand and then pushed the truck as they dropped down the alluvial plain toward the solar sites and the highway.

La Rosa got a ring, but the call dropped. She tried again and as she got through Raveneau slowed so she could hear Coe.

'We found dried blood and bullet holes. Inspector Raveneau and I believe something very violent happened and firearms were involved. The biologists may have been murdered. Someone needs to stop the Wildlife Heritage vehicle and stop the President's tour right now.'

Raveneau spotted vehicles and knew the tour was already underway. He turned to la Rosa. 'Describe this truck to Coe. He needs to tell the Secret Service not to shoot us.'

But now he doubted there would even be time for that. They were almost back to the project and as the agents had warned, the road was blocked. And he could see the President's entourage below and starting to turn up this direction. There wasn't going to be time to explain anything to anyone. They skidded to a stop where the road was blocked and the two agents had their guns out as Raveneau yelled at them.

'Stop the President's car! Get him out of here now! There may be bombs buried in the roadbed. We're going around you to block them from coming up.'

He didn't wait for their answer and gunned the truck. One of the Secret Service agents swung his gun and got ready to shoot. Raveneau registered that out of the corner of his eye but didn't stop. They slid around the nose of the Suburban and bounced hard through a drainage ditch and back on to the road. Now he drove as hard as he could straight at the vehicles coming up the road. As soon as they started to react he hit the brakes hard. He turned the truck sideways and yelled at la Rosa, 'Run toward them.'

They ran toward the vehicles and then there was a flash of light and a roar and more light as the view in front of him bent and wavered. He felt a slamming blow on his back and was off his feet tumbling forward. One moment he was looking at the vehicles and a Secret Service agent ordering them to stop, and then he was looking at a blue sky and couldn't hear anything. He looked for la Rosa and saw her sitting, bleeding from her right cheek. He tried to speak to her and his voice was faraway as he got to his feet calling to her.

He looked up at a column of black smoke and the billowing cloud of dust. The superintendent's truck was sheared in half, part of it burning in the sage, the cab pointing nose up at the sky. The black Suburban up the road was lying on its side and all but one of the vehicles below had turned around and were driving hard away.

Raveneau focused on walking to la Rosa. He got his balance back though his ears rang with a high-pitched whine. He helped la Rosa to her feet and then someone helped them. She's OK, he thought, and ran a hand over the knot on his head. Blood ran from his elbow and he knew his right shoulder had road rash and his shirt was wet and torn. La Rosa could barely put weight on her right knee. He put an arm around her to help support her and someone restrained him, saying, 'We've got her. We're getting an ambulance. You need to sit.'

But Raveneau didn't sit. He walked up and looked at the craters the bombs left. He saw where they joined. When he walked back down he found his phone and the battery lying on the road. He put it back together and it rang almost immediately. Raveneau had to turn the sound all the way up to hear Coe.

'They told me you're both fine. Are you?'

'Oh, never better. Elizabeth's knee is a little sore and we've cleaned up the blood. The blast threw us forward, but we were far enough away.'

'We've got one man and we're looking for the other.'

'I thought agents followed them back to Primm.'

'They did and what I'm hearing is one went out the back door of a restaurant and left in another vehicle. This isn't confirmed, but a man was seen out on a fairway of the golf course which might be close enough. They're saying the bomb detonation was probably by a radio or cell signal. It may have had a built in delay of thirty to sixty seconds, or maybe when he realized what you were doing he went ahead and blew them anyway to minimize evidence.'

'And the other man is in Primm?'

'Yes. Can you get there and get a look at him?'

'I'm on my way.'

SIXTY-ONE

La Rosa's knee was bad enough to where she couldn't come with him. She was already on her way to a Vegas hospital when Raveneau got in the rental car and drove to Primm. He spotted the Heritage Wildlife vehicle first, and then the FBI car with a man sitting alone in the back. They were parked out in a big lot and he counted eight Fed cars. The man claimed to be Mark Davis, a Heritage Wildlife employee, but Raveneau knew Davis's body would be found up on the mountain. His and that of the other biologist buried just deep enough to avoid attracting vultures or coyotes.

He talked with the Las Vegas FBI agents and then walked up to the car with two agents. The man sat in the back seat, his wrists held by constraints. The agents were clearly ready to take him on into Las Vegas to start questioning him. They were tolerant but anxious to get on with it, but if Raveneau recognized him he was going to get wanted time with him first.

After the car doors were unlocked, Raveneau got in the back seat with the man. He knew immediately but didn't say anything until he'd eased down on to the seat. He left the door open. His back would be very stiff in an hour. But he was OK sitting without moving on the seat. The breeze was warmer now and the sun on him felt good. The ringing in his ears was mostly gone.

'That was quite an explosion,' Raveneau said.

'I wasn't there. We broke camp about forty-five minutes before. I don't know why I'm being detained.'

'What's the hurry, Colin? Where would you go? Where would you hide?'

With that Greiston turned his head. He didn't say anything but he was waiting and attentive.

'You can let the Mark Davis alias go now. We went up to the camp. We saw what happened. When they find the bodies there, you'll be charged with those murders too. But that's not the one I'm here about. It's an old one and I've got something I want to show you. I've got some questions and then the FBI is going to take you on into Vegas.'

Raveneau had the lone one hundred dollar bill he'd kept in the same clear plastic wrap the Secret Service used. With his hands behind him Greiston couldn't hold the bill, so Raveneau held it for him. He held it up in front of him for several long seconds.

'Who are you?'

'Ben Raveneau, a homicide inspector from San Francisco. I work cold cases. I've got a couple of questions. Are you OK with that?'

'What would you know to ask?'

'My first question is do you think Thomas Casey is still alive?'

For several minutes, maybe longer, Greiston didn't answer and that was fine. Raveneau was glad just to sit in the sun and be. All of his back hurt but particularly lower back. The road rash on his elbow hurt. It was deep and would take awhile to heal.

Blood had soaked through the gauze he got before driving here. He rested that arm on his thigh, careful not to let the raw part get any pressure. It was a close call.

He turned and looked at Greiston. He knew the FBI was sure Casey didn't leave the Big Island on a plane and now doubted their boat theory. Coe told him they thought he was hiding somewhere on the island.

'He could kill himself,' Greiston said, and added, 'I hope he does. He has a grandiose image of himself. He sees himself as a founder on par with Thomas Jefferson. You met him, what do you think?'

'He was very conflicted when I last saw him.'

'He is how you got here.'

'No, he isn't. How much money did he contribute over the years?'

'What does it matter to you?'

In the front seat the two agents stirred and Raveneau got it. This conversation should be videotaped. If Greiston was going to talk this easily they needed to get him in as soon as possible.

'What was Jim Frank's role?'

'Captain Frank? Wow, what time machine did you walk out of?'

'Was he ever a part of it?'

'No.'

'Alan Krueger?'

'He wasn't either but Casey said too much to him after we started using his counterfeit money. Casey thought he could bring him in. But Krueger didn't want anything to do with it and we couldn't risk him talking to anyone.'

'So you killed him.'

'Nice try, Inspector, but I've never harmed anybody. Neither is my association with Casey or others illegal.'

'Casey kept the Glock in a glass case in his lanai. We tested it and the ballistics matched. Why would he keep it in a glass case?'

When Greiston didn't answer, Raveneau said, 'My theory is he never got over providing you the gun you killed Alan Krueger with. He kept supplying money to the organization you were slowly building, but he never forgave himself for betraying his friend. What do you think of that idea?'

'I think you can go fuck yourself. I didn't kill Alan Krueger or anyone.'

Raveneau let long minutes go by. He closed his eyes and felt the desert breeze across his face. The venom in Greiston's voice affected him. He couldn't say why but it affected him in a peculiar way today. Maybe because Greiston, despite acknowledging he was caught, still acted as if somehow he was on the right side. When Raveneau spoke again his voice was harder.

'In January we were FedExed a videotape of the shooting. I opened it and took it down to our Criminal Investigation Unit. You and Krueger are in the video, in fact, you and Krueger are the video, shooter and victim. It starts before you crossed the lot under the old Embarcadero Freeway. It's how we tracked you down. We're going to charge you with the murder of Alan Krueger.'

'I guarantee that you don't want to do that.'

Raveneau waited a few more minutes, then eased himself out of the car. He nodded to the other FBI agents as he approached them.

'It's him.'

And that was how it ended, or almost. Garner in Utah, and an Army general in Kentucky were arrested and charged, as was an officer inside the Pentagon. Coe told Raveneau a week later that the general held out for three days before cutting a deal and was talking. Several more arrests were made but the group was much smaller than Coe had believed. Still, they were recruiting and Coe believed they had raised tens of millions of dollars, much of which he didn't think they would ever be able to trace.

'It started in Hawaii long ago,' Coe said, 'and they did use a large stash of counterfeit supernotes they knew where to look for after killing Krueger. Greiston double-crossed Krueger and when Krueger figured it out he killed him. Greiston has laid all the blame he can on Casey.'

'And Casey is dead.'

'Very dead. His body was found by a K-9 unit after a helicopter spotted his car out on a remote dirt track part way up a flank of Mauna Loa. Dogs found him. In Hawaii they're saying he put a gun in his mouth and shot himself. A handgun was found nearby. The bullet exited the top of his skull.'

'How sure are they that is how it happened?'

'I don't know. They do things a little differently in Hawaii.

But to go on, Greiston claimed the initial plan was to finance operations for years with the counterfeit money. What scares me is how much money they've raised in the last five years and how recruitment has picked up.'

'To what end?'

'To save America, and each one we've interviewed has got the same rap, the great Republic in danger from within. They see what they're doing as noble, if you can believe that.'

Raveneau could.

'Ben, thanks for everything you did and I should tell you I hear you and la Rosa are also going to get a call from someone else soon.'

La Rosa and Raveneau were at their desks when the President called to thank them. But the call he was really waiting for came about a month later. That was after he'd gone to visit Pagen, though Pagen wasn't expecting him. He found him at a breakfast spot in Marysville in the foothills of the Sierras. The dry month of January gave way to heavy snow and the mountain peaks off to his right were bright white and floating in the sky in the early sun. The orchards he drove past were sodden. In Marysville sunlight through a window fell on a plate of food and the craggy face of a man sitting alone at a booth. He offered his hand after Raveneau introduced himself.

'I thought you had forgotten about me, Inspector.'

'Far from it.' Raveneau slid into the booth across from him. 'I just needed to learn more first.'

'Have breakfast with me.'

'No thanks, I drank coffee on the drive here. I just want to ask a few questions. Here's the one that I wonder most about. You were the one Alan Krueger was closest to. Why didn't you protect him?'

'I don't know what you're saying. I did everything I could.'

'You and the Canadians thought he was working both sides. You thought he was making himself rich, but he wasn't. You told Greiston about the planned meeting along the wharf with the Canadians. You're the only way Greiston could have known to be there.'

'Greiston told me he never made the meeting.'

'He not only made the meeting, he shot Alan Krueger.'

'Greiston did? Your homicide inspectors concluded he was robbed and killed.'

'You let him down and he was forced to resign. When he went out on his own he kept on being the same guy he always was, but you made him into someone different. He was as true as when he worked under you. You gave him to Greiston. You let it happen because you thought he was double-dealing.'

'That's all bullshit.'

'I can't prove it, but you and I know it's not. I'm sure you've worried since Greiston's arrest and I'm sure the FBI has talked with you and everyone else that had any dealings with those supernotes and Greiston. I'm sure you've told your story, but I just wanted to let you know that I know what you did. I'll see you later.'

Raveneau left him staring at his eggs. A few days later he got another call when he was sitting with Celeste at a table after the bar had closed. March moonlight was bright and clear through the windows along the street. On the phone screen he saw Barbara Haney's name.

'We took the video to record who he was meeting with. It was spur of the moment. He was supposed to meet us and then suddenly there was this other man so I recorded it. We wanted to figure out later who the other man was.'

'I thought so.'

'One night toward the end of last year I was alone here and thinking about what I had done with my life, and where I had failed. I FedExed the videotape from Los Angeles the following weekend. I guess in a way I was trying to make up for what you really can't.'

'I understand that.'

'I know you do, and you take care, Inspector. We'll meet again someday.'

They both knew they never would, but it was as good a way as any to say good bye.